"No offense taken," h̶ That wasn't quite true *overwhelming quaintness* of his home town. **"So you're not from Iowa?"**

"First, Iowa *has* cities. I grew up in Des Moines, but I lived in Chicago for five years, and it was never boring." She smiled, and more of the distrust faded from her eyes, which were more golden than green now. "I like the energy and the diversity—there's always something interesting going on."

"You haven't seen the Cape in season yet," he pointed out, still feeling defensive. "The population explodes, and there's a festival or fair somewhere every weekend. The farmers' markets open up—the whole place really starts buzzing after Memorial Day."

She didn't look convinced. "For what...three or four months? And then what happens? The sidewalks roll back up again and everyone hibernates?"

He spread his hands wide in defeat. "I get it. Small towns. Simple pleasures. Not your thing. So when do you head back to Chicago?"

What kind of job could she have where she could take weeks away from it? There was a quick pinch of pain in her expression.

"Chicago's my past, not my future."

There was definitely a story behind *that* sentence.

"Where's your future, then?"

She gave a quick laugh. "Anywhere but here, Sam. Anywhere but here."

Dear Reader,

Welcome to the first book of a brand-new series! Winsome Cove is a fictional town on Cape Cod in Massachusetts. Like many small towns on Cape Cod, Winsome Cove has tourists and summer residents as well as a core of fiercely independent locals. I had fun getting to know all the new characters and their stories.

In this book, unemployed chef Lexi Bellamy is only in Winsome Cove for the summer, to help her newly divorced mom take on the motel she inherited—the Sassy Mermaid Motor Lodge. Lexi hopes to convince Mom to sell the place and go back home to Iowa. But Phyllis is enjoying her rebirth as a single woman—pink hair and all—and she has no intention of leaving.

Marina owner Sam Knight despises change, and the Bellamy women bring nothing *but* change to his town. He thinks love is a fool's game, because everything ends. Lexi is just as skeptical about trusting again after being burned by an ex. But they can't seem to keep their hands off each other. These two cautious hearts find their destiny in Winsome Cove. Lexi has two siblings who might just do the same in books to come!

Thank you to my Harlequin editor, Gail Chasan, and my agent, Jill Marsal. Thank you to my readers for following me to a brand-new setting in my twentieth (!) book. And hugs and kisses to my loving husband (and Boston guy), Himself, who helped me with lots of Cape Cod and boating details.

Jo McNally

A CAPE COD SUMMER

JO McNALLY

HARLEQUIN

SPECIAL
EDITION

HARLEQUIN®
SPECIAL EDITION™

Recycling programs for this product may not exist in your area.

ISBN-13: 978-1-335-59464-8

A Cape Cod Summer

Copyright © 2024 by Jo McNally

For questions and comments about the quality of this book, please contact us at CustomerService@Harlequin.com.

TM and ® are trademarks of Harlequin Enterprises ULC.

Harlequin Enterprises ULC
22 Adelaide St. West, 41st Floor
Toronto, Ontario M5H 4E3, Canada
www.Harlequin.com

Printed in Lithuania

MIX
Paper | Supporting responsible forestry
FSC® C021394

Award-winning romance author **Jo McNally** lives in her beloved upstate New York with her very own romance hero husband. When she's not writing or reading romance novels, she loves to travel and explore new places and experiences. She's a big fan of leisurely lunches with her besties. Her favorite room at home is the sunroom, where she enjoys both morning coffee and evening cocktails with her husband while listening to an eclectic (and often Irish) playlist.

Books by Jo McNally

Harlequin Special Edition

Winsome Cove

A Cape Cod Summer

Gallant Lake Stories

A Man You Can Trust
It Started at Christmas...
Her Homecoming Wish
Changing His Plans
Her Mountainside Haven
Second-Chance Summer
Expecting His Holiday Surprise

The Fortunes of Texas: The Wedding Gift

A Soldier's Dare

Visit the Author Profile page
at Harlequin.com for more titles.

This first book in my new Winsome Cove series is dedicated to two of my favorite Cape Cod experts and, more importantly, our longtime and wonderful friends.

To Dan and Dee with love and gratitude.

Chapter One

The Sassy Mermaid Motor Lodge didn't look too terribly bad at night. Thanks to traffic delays, Mom's insistence that they stop at what felt like every other exit to "see what looked interesting" and Lexi getting lost on the dark, winding side roads of Cape Cod, she and her mother didn't arrive at their motel until two in the morning.

Not just the place where they were staying. It was *literally* their motel. Or at least…*Mom's* motel. Phyllis Bellamy had inherited the Sassy Mermaid Motor Lodge from an uncle no one had spoken to in decades. And their first time seeing it was right now. In the dark.

There were a few cars in the parking lot of the long, low, two-story motel, so the place was at least pulling in *some* money. That would make it easier to sell, which would happen just as soon as Lexi could convince her mother to dump this place. But despite the No Vacancy sign being lit, it was definitely not full. The lawyers said the motel had thirty rooms, and there were only ten cars parked there. The reception office was located near the center of the building, but it was dark, too.

"Thank goodness I have the keys, right?" Mom shook the giant ring of keys the attorneys had sent her. Each was carefully labeled—apartment, office, laundry, pool, storage one, storage two, etc. Lexi parked in front of the office and stared into the darkened room beyond the plate glass.

"It feels creepy to just let ourselves in like this."

"Don't be silly." Mom hopped out of the car. "It's *my* motel, so we're not trespassing. Oh, wow—I can smell the ocean!"

Lexi got out and stretched. It had been a long three days since they'd left Des Moines, and she'd driven most of it. Not because Mom hadn't offered to drive, but because her mother was quite possibly the world's worst driver. Lexi's life might be a flaming hot mess right now, but she still wanted to keep *living* it awhile longer.

She took a deep breath as she stretched, and realized what Mom was talking about. The rich, salty aroma of the ocean was heavy in the breeze. She could hear the surf splashing against rocks coming from somewhere out there in the night. For all her doubts about this journey, Lexi was looking forward to spending a little time near the ocean. But right now, exhaustion was catching up with her—she was hitting the proverbial wall, barely able to stay on her feet.

"Let's get inside and hope that mystery uncle of yours left you some comfortable beds."

"Right. Let me find the key here…" Mom flipped through the keys, her bright pink hair falling over her face. It had been a little like watching a butterfly leaving its cocoon to watch her mother transform over the past year. From a meek housewife to a fearlessly liberated woman, and all because her husband—Lexi's father—had left her for a woman younger than two of his children.

Meanwhile, Lexi had followed the opposite path since her own life imploded. She'd gone from being confident and successful to nursing her emotional wounds and avoiding everyone she used to know or work with. Maybe Mom's year of living dangerously would rub off on *her*, now that they'd escaped Des Moines and Chicago. Never mind that neither of them had ever been to Massachusetts before and knew nothing about running a motel. Details, details. With any luck, she'd convince Mom to sell by the end of the summer. That was all the time that Lexi could give to this project. It was mid-April now, so they should be able to get this place on the market and sold by August.

"Okay, sweetie, I got it open." Mom waved her hand to get Lexi's attention. "I feel like this should be a more momentous entrance, but we don't want to wake up our guests by popping champagne in the middle of the night." She pushed the door open and a tiny bell rang above it. They both froze, but they didn't hear any movement inside. Whoever was watching the office had obviously gone home for the night. The lights from the parking lot cast a soft light through the windows into the office. There was nothing surprising—an ice machine, a reception counter, a coffee counter and a few chairs scattered around. All in shades of brown and gold. There was a door in back with a sign that said Private.

Mom giggled, whispering for some reason. "This is so exciting! My very own motel and a brand-new life on the *ocean*. I've seen the ocean exactly once in my life, and your father bitched the entire weekend we spent in Virginia Beach. It was too hot, it was too sandy, there was nothing to do, blah, blah, blah." She pushed the back door open. "This must be the residence. Where's the light switch? Oh, there it is." She hit the switch and the room lit up.

"Jesus," Lexi muttered, "turn them back off."

The sign out front said the Sassy Mermaid had been open since 1948. From the looks of things, this room hadn't been updated once since then. It was wood, layered on wood, layered on wood—parquet wood floors, paneled walls and a plywood-coffered ceiling. There was a well-worn braided rug of brown, gold and orange in front of a brown plaid sofa to the right. Over the sofa was a giant oil painting of a tri-masted schooner speeding across an angry sea. On the left wall was a kitchenette with a small sink, an apartment-size refrigerator and a hot plate. Along the back wall was a twin-size day bed with a rusted white iron frame. Beyond the kitchenette was a staircase that was partially enclosed, showing only the bottom four steps. If this was the so-called living quarters the lawyers emailed her mom about, there was no way the two of them could stay here.

Lexi walked across the room to check out the two doors in the back. The first was a small bathroom with one of those old metal shower stalls that belonged in a camp or cabin somewhere. Spots of rust looked like brown snow-flakes on the sides. The other door led to a weird combination of hallway and storage closet, with painted plywood shelves narrowing the space even more. The shelves were packed to the ceiling with cleaning supplies and boxes of who-knew-what. There was a door marked Exit at the back.

"Do you really think Uncle Tim *lived* in here?" Mom was moving papers around on a small desk in the corner. "The lawyers said—"

"Clearly the lawyers had no clue what they were talking about," Lexi said. "We'll figure it out in the morning, but for now, why don't you take the bed and I'll sleep on the sofa. I'm exhausted—" There was a sound behind her. A footstep on the stairs. *We aren't alone!* She spun toward the narrow, carpeted staircase…

"If you're here looking for drug money, you're going to be very disappointed." A rough male voice spoke coldly, but calmly, with a heavy New England accent. She could see bare feet and legs coming down the stairs—long legs, with one calf sporting a large, ornate tattoo of a ship's anchor. The intruder took another step and Lexi backed up as he spoke again. "If you don't get your dumb *ahsses* out of here, you're going to find yourselves sitting in the back seat of a police *cah*…with fresh bruises." Another step. He was wearing blue boxer briefs, and nothing else.

But Lexi didn't spend much time thinking about the man's physique. Not when he was uttering threats with a dangerous growl. And carrying an iron fireplace poker. She put herself between him and her mother. She was the daughter of one large, angry man and had almost been the wife of another. She didn't intimidate easily. Not anymore.

She didn't see his face until he stepped onto the bottom landing. He was tall, with dark hair and startling blue eyes. Those eyes were cold as steel right now, his square jaw tight. He'd started to raise the fire poker, but he stopped when he got a look at them.

"Who the hell are you?" he asked.

"I think—" Mom was using her full *Mom* voice, low and cold, which had always sent her three children scurrying "—*we* should be asking that question, young man." The guy was at least mid-thirties, maybe even forties. From his tan and the weathered lines on his face, she'd guess he spent a lot of time outdoors. Mom continued. "I *own* this motel, so why don't you tell us who *you* are and what you're doing here. Or maybe we should call the police to sort this out?"

The man's jaw dropped. "*You're* Curly's niece?"

"If by Curly, you mean Timothy Neely, then yes, I am."

He set down the poker in the corner and stepped into the room, apparently forgetting he was in his underwear. "Damn. I didn't think you'd be here until the weekend. Uh…

I'm Sam Knight. The estate lawyers—" he pronounced it *law-yahs* "—have been paying my cousin and I to keep the old place open for, well…you, I guess. Phyllis, right?" He started to step forward as if to shake her hand, then looked down. Color rose in his cheeks. "Oh…son of—excuse me." He stepped into the bathroom just long enough to grab a brightly colored beach towel, which he wrapped around his waist.

Now that he wasn't clutching a weapon in his hand, Lexi tried to shift herself out of fight mode and join the conversation.

"And you *live* here?" That came out as more of an accusation than a question, but she was so damn tired, not to mention being extremely wary of this rough-looking guy making himself at home on her mother's property. Although he didn't look quite as tough now that he was wearing a green beach-towel skirt covered with pink dolphins and yellow starfish.

"No," he answered, having the grace to look a little guilty. "But someone has to take the overnight shift. Tonight was my turn." He glanced up toward the top of the stairs. "I had no idea you'd be here tonight, or I wouldn't have stayed upstairs."

Mom let out a loud sigh of relief. "You mean this isn't the living quarters?"

"For the owners? Hell, no." He glanced around the room with a look that mirrored their first impression. "This is basically just an extension of the office. The bed's there for someone to use if they're covering the office overnight. The upstairs is a full two-bedroom apartment. Do you have luggage to bring in? I can take it up for you."

"But weren't *you* covering the office overnight?" Lexi sounded contrary. She knew it from the warning look on

Mom's face. There was just something about this guy that set her on edge. Or maybe it was the fourteen hours of driving she'd done that day.

His gaze settled fully on her for the first time. He did one of those annoying head-to-toe appraisals, and she bristled. Sam raised one eyebrow, and she could swear she saw a glint of amusement in his eye. "And you are...?"

"Oh, this is my daughter, Lexi," Mom answered for her. She was a thirty-six-year-old woman and didn't need her mother speaking for her. But right now, exhaustion was pressing down on her more every minute.

"The only bags we need tonight are there by the door." Lexi nodded at the two small-wheeled suitcases. "I really need to get some sleep before I start dealing with—" she gestured in his general direction "—this."

Her tone made it sound like he was the bellhop. She really didn't care at this point. She wanted a bed and she wanted it now. She just prayed the upstairs was a hell of a lot nicer than this time capsule from the forties. She brushed past him, being sure to keep her eyes away from the towel around his waist, and headed up the stairs. He scrambled to turn on the light switch on the wall behind her.

"I thought I was sneaking up on a robbery, so I left the lights off."

Mom followed Lexi as he grabbed the bags. "Do you have a lot of robberies here?" Her voice made the question sound naively innocent, as if she was asking how often it rained on Cape Cod.

"At the motel? No. But every small town has its share of bored teenagers looking for mischief. Once tourist season starts, that number goes up substantially." He called up to Lexi. "There's a double light switch at the top of the stairs on the right."

She flipped the switches and looked around with relief. The apartment was, most importantly, clean, and second, *not* brown. The floor plan was open, and it had a nice living area with textured laminate floors the color of driftwood. The decor was a blend of midcentury modern and coastal, with a large blue sofa facing a wall of windows with a sliding glass door. There was a small white brick fireplace in the corner. The beadboard ceiling was vaulted, giving a sense of space. Behind her was a bright kitchen—not huge, but efficient. The counters, including the long peninsula, were blue and white tiles in a checkerboard pattern. A little busy for her taste, but it was cute. A hallway led past the kitchen, presumably to where the bedrooms were. The layout reminded her of the shotgun houses she'd seen in New Orleans—long and narrow. But livable for the short time they'd be here.

Her mom and Sam stepped up into the living room, and he swept his arm around, giving a bullet-point tour as he pointed. "The sliding door leads out to a big deck above the motel office. Obviously, that's the kitchen back there. Bathroom over there with a shower. Two bedrooms share a full bath down the hall. They don't have the view this space does, but they're pretty good sized. The apartment gets wider as it goes back. There's an outside entrance back there with stairs down to a private parking area behind the motel."

Now that he mentioned it, she could see the apartment was pie-shaped, narrowest at the window wall. It certainly wasn't as traditional and ornate as the house she'd grown up in, but it was bright and inviting. This would be her home for a few months, until she could convince Mom that neither of them belonged in Winsome Cove.

That was the deal she'd made with Max and Jennifer.

All three Bellamy siblings agreed someone needed to keep an eye on Mom until she came to her senses. Going a *little* wild after the divorce was one thing. But insisting she was going to move to Cape Cod to run a motel she'd just inherited was a lot more dramatic than dying her hair hot pink, or trading her Talbots wardrobe for one from Forever 21.

Phyllis Bellamy had been the quintessential stay-at-home soccer mom and socialite housewife throughout her forty-year marriage to Bob Bellamy. She'd kept the house spotless. She'd joined Dad at the country club every Friday for dinner. She'd hosted bridge club and run fundraisers for all the most socially acceptable charities. She'd attended the United Methodist Church every Sunday, always sitting in the same center pew. But she'd never once run any kind of business. When she'd insisted she wasn't going to sell the motel until she'd "checked it out," they figured they had to protect her.

Lexi had been first up, since she was unemployed and had already been living with Mom for a few months after losing her job, her Chicago apartment *and* her reputation. Max and Jennifer had promised they'd each take a turn here in New England if she couldn't get Mom to sell right away.

"Point me to the smaller bedroom." Right now, she just wanted to sleep. "And please tell me the bed is made." She took the handle of her suitcase and turned toward the hallway.

"Uh, yeah… I gotta get my stuff out of there first." He moved ahead of her. "That's the room I was using tonight. Like I said, we didn't expect you for a few more days…"

She waved her hand. She didn't care. "Are the sheets clean?"

"Well…they were fresh tonight but I'll change them—"

"Don't bother." What a weird welcome to Cape Cod—a

towel-clad hottie threatening her with a fireplace poker before offering to make her bed.

Sam turned on the light in the bedroom and dashed around, grabbing a T-shirt off the dresser and yanking it over his head. He gripped khaki shorts in one hand while he picked up a small duffel bag. "I'll, uh…give you a better tour of the place tomorrow."

"Yup. Whatever. Good night." She crawled into the bed and fell onto the pillow. "And goodbye."

Chapter Two

Sam Knight watched the sun come up over the Atlantic, a mug of lukewarm tea in his hand. He hadn't wanted to wake anyone with Curly's old coffeemaker, so he'd dropped a tea bag into the hot water from the tap. He was on the deck over the motel office, outside the apartment where he'd spent the night on the sofa at Phyllis Bellamy's insistence. After her daughter had rightfully kicked him out of the room he'd been using, he'd planned to go downstairs to sleep, but Phyllis stopped him.

"It smells musty down there. Sleep on the sofa and when morning comes, I'll make us all breakfast—I have pancake mix and some other kitchen basics in the car—and you can start to show me what I've gotten myself into." Her brown eyes were warm and her voice was sincere. He wasn't sure what her prickly daughter, Lexi, would think of the idea. Then again, Curly had left the place to Phyllis, not her. She'd probably just helped her mom drive here and would be heading home again soon.

Having his night interrupted by their arrival kept him from getting any good sleep after that. That was a pity, since his nights at the motel were usually when he slept best. There were no ghosts here. He took a sip of his tea, but it wasn't hot enough to keep the damp morning chill at bay. This was probably going to be his last morning enjoying this peaceful view, which was one of his favorites in Winsome Cove.

Phyllis was…interesting. No one in town had any idea what to expect from some Midwestern stranger, but he had a hunch no one had imagined an energetic older woman with bright pink hair, ripped skinny jeans and leopard-print ankle boots. The lady seemed to be a character and a half. He liked characters.

Her daughter was also interesting, but in a way that made him want to keep his distance. She was sharp. Gutsy, too— she'd stepped right between him and her mother when he'd threatened them. She didn't seem pretentious, since she'd crawled into the bed that he'd just exited a while earlier. That was… Hell, it was kind of a turn-on.

The ocean was quiet this morning, with the waves coming in like ripples in gray-blue silk. A few streets behind the motel was the cove itself. The town of Winsome Cove had built up around the quiet harbor, which protected lobster boats as well as pleasure craft. The harbor view was pretty, but this ocean view was what people wanted to see. And the motel was one of the few places in town where they could enjoy it.

He could hear a few seals barking below on the rocks. The town was learning to embrace the seal population, which had grown rapidly over the past few decades. Tourists loved them. Curly had even built an overlook above the rocks so people could enjoy watching them safely. A few more seals barked. He couldn't see them from here, but they sounded like the large gray seals, which now lived here year-round. The much smaller harbor seals would be leaving soon—they were on the Cape from September through May, then headed north for the warmer months.

The locals were having a harder time embracing the

great white sharks that had started hanging out here in the summer to feast on those now-plentiful seals. The overlook was often used these days by volunteer monitors to watch for sharks getting too close to swimmers on the beach below.

Some blowhard from Boston had tried to convince Sam to run "shark tours" from the marina, but he'd wanted it to include chumming to draw the sharks close. Not only was that illegal in most areas, but Sam didn't believe in interfering with nature just to make a buck. He was also worried it would bring *more* sharks to the area. It was hard enough finding the balance between getting tourists on the beaches, while also keeping them out of danger. The Boston guy had pointed out if Sam wouldn't do it, he'd find someone else. Probably true, but hopefully that *someone* would be in a different town. A different beach. Not *his* town and *his* beach.

He knew every inch of this town, and close to every rock and pebble of sand. His parents and grandparents had instilled a love for Winsome he couldn't shake, no matter how much tragedy he'd experienced here. Some days he felt chained to the marina, the house and this long, narrow peninsula known as Cape Cod. But at times like this, with the orange globe of the sun coming up over the satin sea, burning the fog into wisps, he knew this was where he belonged.

"Pretty fancy view for a dodgy old motor lodge." Lexi Bellamy's voice was morning-rough, as if she'd just rolled out of bed with no coffee. He hadn't even heard the door slide open behind him.

He didn't look back at her. "Old, maybe, but not dodgy. Just…tired. Curly ran out of energy, money and interest over the last ten years or so."

She walked past him, wearing gray jeans and a yellow sweater. She rested her forearms on the railing, clutching a bright blue water bottle. Playing his game, she didn't look back, talking instead to the ocean.

"Why do you keep calling him *Curly*?"

"You never met your uncle?"

She scoffed. "He was my *great* uncle, and I didn't even know he existed until Mom told us he'd left her a motel in his will."

Interesting. Curly had never mentioned Lexi or her mom, either.

"Well—" he smiled at the memory "—the guy had a head full of curls. I guess his hair was bright red in his youth, but I remember it with a lot more gray. He wore it shaggy and wild. He looked like an aging rock star."

She turned, leaning back against the railing. "You slept out here last night?"

"No, but I have in the past. It was a little cool for that last night. Your mom offered me the sofa."

She slapped a hand to her face, covering her eyes and shaking her head. "And that's why one of us had to come with her—a total stranger sleeping on the couch…" The words were spoken low, and had an edge of annoyance to them.

"I'm sorry?"

She straightened, taking a drink of her water. "Never mind. Just know that my mom has three kids who will *not* let her get bamboozled by anyone in this sleepy little town." Her eyes moved down his body. "Nice to see you were able to ditch the towel kilt for something more appropriate."

Okay. Maybe it hadn't been just the long day of driving that had her sounding so sharp last night. Maybe snark was her native language. He wasn't sure what color her eyes were. Her mom's were brown, but Lexi's were more on the golden-green side, but not quite green. Her hair was past her shoulders and was a blend of colors—not just brown, but not exactly red. She was average height and slender, without a lot of curves. But her body looked strong and athletic.

He looked down at his khaki shorts and sweatshirt, then shrugged. "Like I said, I wasn't expecting company last night. Sorry for putting on a show."

"The fireplace poker was a nice touch—it balanced the near-nakedness with some machismo." She paused. "So... you know this old place pretty well?"

"The Mermaid? I practically grew up here. My home is only a few streets toward town, and this is the easiest path for the locals to get to the beach. Got my first part-time job here." At least the first one that wasn't with the family business. "It's prime real estate now."

"I'll bet. We tried to talk Mom into just selling, but she's on a personal quest to try new things, so she insisted she had to come here to try running it."

Sell the Mermaid? That had been everyone's fear when they heard Curly left it to some distant relative in Iowa. This property meant something to the year-round residents of Winsome. Sure, there were other access points to the beaches, but so many of them were getting tangled up as so-called "private beaches." As if the ocean could be owned. Curly had not only continued the tradition of allowing locals to use the property to access the beach, but he'd also built events around it, so it felt like a party.

Lexi glanced back to the water, where the swells were gradually picking up in pace and size with an onshore breeze rising. "I'm surprised this land was never converted into some mansion for someone. Like that one next door."

She lifted her chin toward Andrew Malcolm's home— a contemporary monstrosity built five years ago after the

Malcolms tore down three older, more humble, houses on the beach and built their "compound," as they called it. Andrew's wife had died suddenly last year, so Sam couldn't feel too angry about that house anymore. But houses like it were popping up all along the coast of the Cape, as older houses with actual character and history gave way to sharp lines and lots of glass. Change was inevitable—no one knew that quite as well as Sam did. But as Cape Cod turned into an extension of the Boston suburbs, he was afraid it would lose the cozy community feeling that made it unique.

"You know how stubborn your uncle…" He looked up. "Well, I guess you *don't* know. You really didn't know he existed?"

The breeze blew her hair across her face. She caught the stray strands with one hand and tucked them behind her ear. "After we heard about the will, Mom said her uncle had some big argument with my grandfather about the family business when she was just a girl, and the family lost touch. But I guess he remembered he *had* a family, since he specified she get this place." She looked up at the outside of the motel, with the fading white stain on the cedar shakes, and squinted. "Not sure if it was meant as a nice gesture or a punishment passed through the generations."

Sam huffed out a soft laugh. "I promise, it's not that bad. Just needs some love." He looked out at the view. "And some good marketing. It's a hidden gem—*too* hidden."

"Why didn't the old man just sell it?"

"Curly loved this place. He wasn't born on the Cape, but he managed to become a local, anyway. One of his big things was that people should have access to the coast. He hated the idea of private beaches. Technically, the motel has a private stretch of beach, but Curly never enforced it. Anyone in town—hell, anyone who *wanted* to—could use the stairs he built, leading down to the beach. He knew if the motel was ever torn down for a residence, this whole stretch of coastline could be inaccessible."

"So instead of making millions for himself, he decided to be the Robin Hood of motel owners?"

She was mocking, but he didn't laugh. "Pretty much, yeah. He was proud of this old place, even though he had a hard time keeping it up over the last few years. And that pride of his kept him from accepting help from anyone."

She didn't respond. Instead, she walked to one side of the deck and leaned over to look at the shorter stretch of rooms to the north, each with a brightly colored door and a picture window facing the parking lot, but with only partial ocean views. At each end and in the middle were stairs from the second floor to the ground with simple iron railings. On the longer, southern stretch, closer to the water, there was a large swimming pool and patio area. All the rooms had ocean views. She walked over and looked down at the pool.

"It has potential, between the view and the pool. How are the rooms? Please tell me they don't look like that studio apartment behind the office." Sam winced, and she rolled her eyes again. "Oh, God, they *are* like that, aren't they? Dark and gloomy and old-fashioned?"

"Not all of them. Curly painted some of the rooms on the town side—the short section over there." He pointed. The town side of the motel only had twelve rooms, while the ocean side had eighteen. "And Curly was eighty-eight when he passed, so his taste wasn't always, you know…hip."

Lexi gave a small laugh—the first he'd heard from her. Unfortunately, it was at his expense. "If you think *hip* is the current slang," she said, "you probably shouldn't criticize my great uncle. But I get what you're saying. If there's one thing Mom loves to do, it's brighten a place up."

"I got that impression. She's…interesting."

"You have no idea." She looked past him to the apartment. "Speak of the devil, there she is in the kitchen."

"She said something last night about breakfast pancakes."

Lexi shook her head as she started past him. "Let me guess—out of a box mix. She's killing me. Let me go help…" She stopped abruptly, looking down. "Oh…the cupboards and fridge are bare, aren't they?"

"Mostly, yeah. My cousin and I keep a few things here for ourselves, though. Milk, eggs, cereal, junk food."

One of her eyebrows rose. "Um…cereal *is* junk food. I guess we're stuck with pancakes from a mix. Let me see if I can at least scrounge up something to use as a topping. Please tell me there's decent coffee. And a good grocery store nearby?"

"There's coffee. I consider it decent, but I don't know if a foodie like you will think so."

"You think I'm a foodie because I think sugar flakes are gross?"

"Well, either that or a health nut, but health nuts don't usually crave coffee."

Lexi smirked and headed for the door again.

"I'm not big on labels, but I do enjoy good food and good coffee."

"Well, you'll find both on Cape Cod while you're visiting."

The door slid open behind him.

"Who said I'm just visiting?"

The door slid closed again before her words registered. Maybe the daughter *wasn't* just her mom's driver. Maybe she was going to hang around for a while with all her *not*-Midwest-nice opinions. He sat up and watched through the door as she took over the breakfast preparations in the kitchen.

Wouldn't that be just great?

Chapter Three

"Mom, I *love* you. You *know* that." Lexi set down her pink Sassy Mermaid coffee mug—the one with the fewest cracks and only one chip on the handle. She'd learned over the past few days here that Great Uncle Tim hadn't been much for the finer things in life. His kitchen supplies were utilitarian, but that was about it. "I'm all for this rebirth you've had since Dad, well…"

"Fell in love with one of the skirts he was always chasing?" Mom said, finishing Lexi's sentence. "Moved into a condo with some chickie younger than you and left me in a four-bedroom Colonial in the suburbs I'd never wanted in the first place? Is that what you were trying to say?"

"Um…yeah. Something like that, but I would have said it with less bitterness."

Mom gave a huff. "Like you've handled *your* betrayal without any residual anger?"

"Oh. Well. That was…" She was going to say it was different. But just because Karl was a business partner as well as her fiancé when he destroyed her life didn't make her anger that much different from any other jilted woman. Screwed over was screwed over. And it was something she and her mom had in common. "Okay. Point taken. But we're not talking about *me* this morning. We're talking about you and this disaster of a motel."

She looked out the big windows of the apartment to the ocean, which was angry and gray today. It had been raining off and on all morning. A drizzly, dreary Monday. The only thing different from a dreary day here and a dreary day back in Des Moines was the vastly improved view.

"It's not a disaster. It's just been…neglected a bit. We can fix it up together."

Lexi sat back, holding up one hand to deflect that idea from landing.

"Together? Mom, I'm not staying. I mean… I *am* staying for a while, but only until I figure out my next move. And my next move is *not* going to be cleaning rooms at the Sassy Mermaid Motor Lodge. And *your* next move should be putting this place on the market and cashing out."

There. She'd said it. The original plan was to gently nudge Mom in that direction, but now that they'd seen the place—they'd had a detailed tour over the weekend with Sam Knight—it seemed silly to waste time being subtle. The motel was a money pit. Great Uncle Tim hadn't paid his property taxes in two years. The utility bills were in a stack on the old man's desk, and the most recent threatened to terminate service.

"Cash out? Are you saying I should *sell*?" Mom seemed genuinely shocked. Had she not been paying attention? "Some new buyer might come in and just tear all this down."

"If they were smart, that's exactly what they'd do."

"Alexa Marie Bellamy! What is wrong with you? This place has *history.* And it's a family legacy from a branch of the family I didn't even know. I want to embrace that, not dump it after being here for four days." Her mom got up from the tiled kitchen peninsula where they'd been sitting and walked to the windows, waving her arm at the view. "Look at that! This is a million-dollar view."

"Wouldn't you rather have the actual million dollars?"

"No, I wouldn't." Mom's voice was firm. "Your dad may not have been a millionaire, but we lived a nice life in Des Moines, filled with cocktail parties and country-club dinners. And what did that get me? Nothing. A sham of a marriage, and when I got dumped, guess who got to keep all those country-club pals? Your father, that's who. The women treated me as if a cheating husband asking for a divorce might be contagious. I was a living, breathing reminder that it could happen to them at any moment."

Lexi joined her mom at the windows. The past year had been tough on the whole family, but she knew the pain was far worse for Phyllis Bellamy. She'd lost not only her husband, but also her place in the community. It was logical that she was acting out, like a child who'd been hurt. Maybe this motel thing wasn't quite as cut-and-dried as Lexi had thought. Maybe she *was* going to have to be more gentle about convincing her mom to sell. She put her arm around Mom's shoulders and kept her voice low and kind.

"I'm sorry all of that happened, Mom. And I'm sorry if I sounded like I was pushing you. But I'm a little overwhelmed at how much work the motel needs. I'm worried about the debts you've inherited at this stage of your life…" She gave her mom's shoulders a squeeze. "I'm worried about you taking on too much."

Mom reached up and patted Lexi's hand on her shoulder. "I know, honey. But you don't need to worry about the debts. The Iowa house will cover the taxes and the other bills."

"The *Iowa* house? *Our* house? You're getting a mortgage on it?" Mom had originally said she might rent out the family home while she was here. It never occurred to Lexi that she'd get a mortgage on the place, which would eat up any income from renting.

"No, someone *else* is getting a mortgage on it. I told my friend Monica—you remember, she has a real-estate office—to test the market, and she had *four* offers in no time. I'm going to call her today and tell her to take the highest bid. That money will help me get the motel back on its feet and give me something to live on while we update things around here."

Lexi's mouth opened and closed a few times, and she was sure she looked like a guppy gasping for air. Mom was selling the home Lexi and her siblings grew up in. Which meant she had no intention of returning to Iowa. If Mom poured that money into this motel, she could end up losing it all.

But the land was still worth a fortune. As long as her mom didn't get too deeply into debt, she might come out okay once she came to her senses. Which would hopefully be sooner, rather than later.

"Breathe, Alexa. I know what I'm doing."

"*Do* you, Mom?" Lexi stepped back, trying to absorb the impact of this latest bombshell. "Because it feels like you're making huge life decisions on a whim. This is your *home* you're talking about selling. *Our* home. All those holidays. All those memories… I mean…we grew up there." She scrubbed her hands down her face. This was beginning to feel like a bad dream. "You want to throw that away after a few days in a crappy old motel you think you have to save? Make it make sense!"

Mom took Lexi's hands in hers and stared straight into her eyes. Calm. Strong. Steady. And determined. Lexi knew that look. It meant Phyllis Bellamy's mind was made up.

"I hate to break this to you, dear, but I have no interest in living in a big, empty house filled with *your* happy memories. The truth is I have memories there that are *not* very happy. And your memories don't have to go away with the house." She smiled at Lexi, her eyes bright. Was she... was she *crying*? "You're all adults now. Hell, *you* moved to Chicago five years ago. You're building your own lives." Mom wiped her cheek and took a breath. "This crappy old motel is *mine*. Yes, it was unexpected, but I wanted a new life and I got one dropped right in my lap! I have to at least give it a chance, to see if this is where I'm meant to be." She paused, a glint of steely defiance returning to her expression. "Do you think I don't know you, Max and Jenny are trying to chaperone me? What are you three afraid of—that I'll spend your inheritance?"

"More like you'll spend your *retirement*. There's no big conspiracy or anything..." Not that Lexi would admit to, anyway. "We were worried about you coming out here alone, and I was unencumbered by a job, so... I'm here for a few months. To make sure you're okay." She gestured out the window at the motel, which looked even more sad in the rain. The doors to the rooms were painted in different colors—olive green, turquoise and orange. "Come on, Mom. How long are you going to be able to scrub bathtubs and fix backed-up toilets in this old place? This is not a good retirement plan. Wouldn't you rather be free to travel and relax?"

"I know my own mind, Lexi. I'm where I want to be. And frankly, it's my decision to make. Not yours."

She was right. Her decisions might *affect* her children, but they were her choices to make. The work here would overwhelm her mother eventually, and she'd see the logic of cashing out and moving on, even if she didn't want to go back to her Des Moines cul-de-sac.

In the meantime, Lexi wasn't escaping the Sassy Mermaid anytime soon.

"You really think they'll sell the Mermaid?" Sam's cousin, Devlin, grimaced as he sat in the brown plaid easy chair. "Jesus, I think I just got poked by a spring in the cushion." His voice dropped to a mutter. "You gotta get some furniture from the current century in this damn place."

Sam ignored the suggestion. He'd heard it before, of course. Nothing much had changed in this house since losing his parents and grandparents. And that was just the way he liked it. He handed Devlin a tumbler of Irish whiskey and sat in the matching chair on the opposite side of the fireplace, then took a sip from his own glass.

"If the daughter has anything to do with it, there'll be a For Sale sign there within the month. But Phyllis seems to have a mind of her own, so maybe not." He sagged back in the chair. "Too soon to tell."

"It's the mom who has the pink hair, right? Dad saw her yesterday on Wharf Street and said she looked like a Cyndi Lauper wannabe, but old."

Sam snorted. "Isn't Cyndi Lauper in her seventies?"

Devlin shook his head. "I try not to confuse my dad with facts. It's not worth the argument. This Bellamy woman have any clue what it's gonna take to run the Mermaid?"

"Not a single one," Sam answered. "But she's enthusiastic about doing it. I see a lot of Curly's backbone in her. She can't do it alone, though."

"Isn't the daughter supposed to be helping?" Devlin grimaced again. "Oh, that's right. The daughter wants to dump the place. Probably wants to pocket a share for herself. That land is worth a pretty penny, even if the motel isn't."

"Curly did alright there for years. He just didn't want to change with the times and market it online or update the place."

Devlin looked around the small living room pointedly. "Yeah? Sounds like someone else I know."

Sam scowled into his whiskey. "Give it a rest. There's nothing wrong with this house."

"You mean other than the fact that nothing has changed in here since the last century?"

"Nothing *needs* to change," Sam grumbled. "This isn't some business that needs to stay current for tourists. It's just the place where I sleep and eat a few meals." He raised his glass. "And occasionally have a drink with my pain-in-the-ass cousin who thinks he's an interior decorator instead of a lobsterman."

"Part-time lobsterman these days. My real-estate work is taking over." Devlin sighed. "A lot of lobstermen are giving it up entirely. Between climate change and the market fluctuations, it's tough out there."

Sam grunted in agreement. Half of his business at the marina was with lobster boats, most of them multigenerational businesses like Devlin's. If that business continued to dry up, he'd have to pivot to more pleasure boaters. He didn't like pleasure boaters much. They were fussy and demanding when it came to marina services. Some of them were flat-out snobs. Some had no business being *on* a boat, much less owning one. At least the lobster boaters knew what they were doing. They never ran into another boat—or the docks—and the only things they demanded were a dedicated slip and power-and-water hookups. Sometimes they didn't even demand the hookups. Just a place to park the boat and no one to bother them.

"Some guys are backing out too soon," Devlin said. "Markets and lobster populations fluctuate all the time. But the expenses really eat into the profits. Fuel is high, insurance is high." Devlin sipped his whiskey. "And then you have the hobbyists out there interfering, and the thieves taking other people's traps… It's a lot of hassle for something that doesn't pay as much as it used to."

"Are you okay with selling houses to pay the bills?"

Devlin shrugged. He did that a lot. Especially when he wasn't comfortable. It was a *tell* in their weekly poker games at the family-owned Salty Knight. Devlin and his father owned 80 percent of the bar, and Sam owned twenty, as defined by his and Devlin's grandparents' wills.

"I don't mind it," Devlin finally said. "I'm good at it, and I don't come home smelling like shellfish. But lobstering's in my blood…*our* blood."

"Don't look at me. I know Knights have been doing it for generations, but I'm happy doing the occasional fishing charter and keeping the marina going."

The accident that took Sam's parents and grandparents had ended up splitting all the family businesses. Devlin's dad, Fred, took their grandfather's lobster boat and the building the bar was located in. There was a restaurant attached, but that had been closed for a couple of years. Sam got the marina and the house, as well as a few storefronts on Wharf Street that he leased out.

A gray cat strolled through the room. Smoke sat in front of the fireplace like he owned the place, as usual.

Devlin watched as he sipped his drink. "That cat's an indoor cat now, huh? I thought you didn't like pets?"

"I don't. Animals should earn their keep, and Smoke is a great mouser."

"Dude, you have mice in the *house*?"

"Well, no, but…"

"So he's a pet now."

"No! He's not an indoor cat. He's a…hybrid. He still goes out and patrols the marina with his buddies during the day." The marina had three or four cats hanging around most of the time. Most were near feral, having been dropped off by someone who figured the marina would welcome their unwanted cats. Smoke licked himself, one hind leg in the air, then curled up into a sleepy ball on the hearth.

Devlin raised an eyebrow. "Sure looks like an indoor cat to me. In fact, he looks like a pet. Does he have little food dishes with his name on them yet? Maybe a sparkly little collar?"

"You really are a pain in my ass," Sam grumbled. "You know damn well I brought him in when he got hurt fighting with something." That had been a pricey veterinarian bill—thirty stitches' worth. The vet thought it was a dog that had managed to grab Smoke. "And now he comes to the door in the evening and I let him in. It's no big deal." He had a hunch Smoke was hiding from whatever hurt him. Sam could relate.

Devlin was still smirking. "Not a big deal for most people. But for you? A cat is a major life change. Next thing you know, you'll be buying a new sofa made in this century and really living large."

Sam flipped his middle finger in the air in response. He looked around at the beige walls and worn gold carpeting in the living room. Paintings of old sailing ships lined the walls. The lamp on the end table had a ship inside a large glass wine jug. Devlin had a point—the place *did* look dated.

But his grandparents and parents had loved this house, and, sixteen years after their deaths, he still didn't have the heart to change anything. As he'd told Devlin, this old house was just a place to eat and sleep.

And talk to ghosts.

Chapter Four

Lexi leaned against the wooden railing of the overlook deck and watched the waves softly shushing against the shore. The rhythm was hypnotic. There was a small outcropping of rocks directly below the deck. Since their arrival on Cape Cod ten days ago, she'd learned the shoreline here varied between expanses of sandy beaches and places with rugged, rocky stretches. Their beach was a mix of the two.

Their beach. She straightened. It was *Mom's* beach. She wanted no part of this, no matter how pretty it was. She'd been spoiled by her years living in her downtown Chicago condominium. She loved the convenience and energy of being in the city, and she was giving the side-eye to a lot of what she'd seen on Cape Cod so far. All the big lobster and crab signs on businesses, as if the island was crawling with crustaceans. Every restaurant was a Lobster Shack, Clam Box, Crab Shed, Shrimp House or some other combination of those eight words. It made her think the whole place had become a caricature of itself. Nothing felt *real*.

The few towns she'd seen so far looked alike. A generic strip mall on the outskirts, with the downtown devoted to tourists with their colorful gift shops and seafood joints. A chilly breeze off the water blew her hair across her face, and she brushed it back behind her ears. Okay…

the *ocean* was real. The weather was still cool, but she had to admit it wasn't a bad thing to wake up to the Atlantic every morning.

Mom had certainly fallen head over heels with the place. She'd gone into town almost every day, and came back with stories about meeting some wonderful person and finding some fabulous business. Mom took long walks on the beach in the afternoons, bundled up against the cold and coming back with rosy cheeks and bright, happy eyes.

She didn't seem to care about the shabbiness of the Sassy Mermaid. Lexi reluctantly turned her back on the ocean and looked at the low-slung motel with its 1960s color palette. Washed-out white walls with the doors in alternating colors from the sixties. It wasn't falling down or anything, but it screamed its age. How many people in today's high-tech world wanted to bring their families to a time capsule?

There was a beat-up green pickup truck by the office door that hadn't been there when she'd returned from her run ten minutes ago. It belonged to Sam Knight. She knew that because he'd been here almost daily since their arrival. Showing Mom where everything was. Teaching Mom how to turn everything on and off if there was some plumbing or electrical emergency. Lexi almost—*almost*—wished there *would* be an emergency like that, just so Mom could see what she was getting herself into. But helpful Sam had already given Mom a list of people who'd done work at the motel, and some who'd worked at the motel for Curly during the busy summer months.

Sam didn't seem like that bad of a guy, but his mere presence irritated Lexi for some reason. Maybe because he was *so* small-town-aw-shucks all the time. It was too precious to be real. Maybe it was because he seemed as determined to get Mom to *stay* as Lexi was to get her to sell. Just yesterday, he'd helped her set up an appointment to have the pool opened for business before Memorial Day weekend.

That was apparently the official kickoff of "the season" here on the Cape. From what Lexi had seen on the reservation list, it wasn't going to increase the Mermaid's business by much. Maybe *that* would be enough to get Mom to see this place was never going to be a moneymaker.

She walked back to the office. Sam was behind the desk with her mother, and the two of them were laughing over something as he pointed to the screen. They paid no attention to Lexi.

"Here's where we went wrong, Phyllis." Sam tapped the screen. "Looks like Curly entered the Allens' reservation for *next* year instead of this year. That's why you couldn't find their reservation when they got here yesterday." He winked at her mom. "Fortunately, you had rooms available."

Mom snorted. "Availability is *not* our problem. We have way too many empty rooms."

Hmmm. Maybe her mother was already seeing what a money pit this motel was.

Sam's forehead furrowed. "It's still offseason. If you get the word out about new ownership and spruce things up a bit, the rooms will fill up. The website will be the key. Has Lexi updated it yet?"

Lexi started to point out that she was not a website designer, but her mother answered first.

"Lexi's been…busy with other things."

"Like *what*?"

There was something in Sam's huffed answer that made Lexi bristle. In just those two words, she felt more than heard an accusation that she wasn't pulling her weight at the Sassy Mermaid. She cleared her throat sharply and he glanced up at her. He'd known she'd been there. *Jerk.*

"I've been busy trying to convince my mother to *sell* this place." Lexi met his look, raising her chin. "Not that it's any of your business."

"Lexi." Mom's voice was firm. "He's here trying to help."

Sam still held her gaze, so she addressed her answer to him.

"Why is he here every day, Mom? His job ended when you arrived."

The attorneys had explained that they'd hired Sam and his cousin just to keep the place from closing up until her mother could take over.

"He's here because I *asked* him to be here. I even told him I'd pay him. There are too many things here I don't know how to do."

Lexi's mouth fell open as she turned to her mother. "Excuse me? You're *paying* him? Mom, he's just trying to take advantage…"

"He," Sam interrupted, "is standing right here."

"Sorry, Sam…" Mom started. But Lexi talked right over her. Yes, she was being cynical, but life had taught her she had to be.

"I thought you *had* a job, Sam. Boats or something, right?"

His gaze sharpened. Was that humor she'd glimpsed? Or anger?

"I own a marina. Look, I don't know why you're being so prickly, but here on the Cape, locals take care of each other."

"We're not locals," Lexi pointed out.

"Curly was, and you're Curly's family."

"Curly wasn't a *local*. He moved here from Iowa."

"Yeah, sixty years ago. He *earned* the title of being a local…" He combed his fingers through his dark hair, leaving it standing on end. His hands locked behind his head, as if he was trying to hold on to his patience. "Look, we're arguing over semantics. My only goal here is making sure the Mermaid survives. The motel is an institution in Winsome Cove, and I don't want it to fail. We're dealing with enough change around here as it is." His hands dropped to his side. "And even though your mom has *offered* to pay me, I told her I'd never accept it. I'm being a nice guy. Sorry if that offends you."

Her eyes narrowed at the insincere apology. *Great.* Another male ego for her to soothe. There was only one problem for Sam—she didn't give a damn about his bruised ego or his passive-aggressive nonsense.

"In my experience—" she made a show of examining her nails to show her lack of concern "—*actual* nice guys don't need to proclaim it to people."

Sam's fingers curled against his thigh. She'd gotten under his skin. Her mouth curved upward. She hadn't had this much fun in a while.

Her mother scowled, pointing back and forth between the two of them. "I don't know what has you two so snappy this morning, but I need you to knock it off."

Lexi took a deep breath, trying to step back from firing verbal daggers. Sam's suggestion that she wasn't all that busy around here had stung, but only because it was true. Mom kept telling her she didn't need Lexi's help in the rooms because so few were being used. But Lexi didn't have anything else to do, other than stewing about her future, which was still shrouded behind a veil of fog. None of that was Sam Knight's fault, even if it was fun to spar with him for some reason.

"Being nice doesn't offend me." She gave Sam a one-shoulder shrug. "But I'll admit it makes me suspicious.

Blame it on experience." Lots and lots of experience. But if he'd turned down Mom's offer to pay him, she couldn't imagine he was doing anything wrong by being here. "I won't interfere if you're *really* trying to help."

She'd tried not to emphasize the word *really*, but failed. She wasn't ready to say she trusted him, and he knew it. She saw it in the flare of emotion in his blue eyes before he gave her a thin smile and a nod of acknowledgement. Mom smiled at the two of them.

"That's better. Honey, we were just talking about the website. Have you…"

"I'm just the liaison. I sent the log-in information to the designer you hired, but I don't know if Olivia has started on it yet." If Mom was going to try to make this place profitable, Lexi felt obligated to do more to help her. Besides, it would only make it more valuable to sell. She'd have to stow her usual sarcasm. At least while her mother was in earshot.

"Good! Sam has some great ideas for the website, so why don't you two work on that together?" Mom stood and patted Lexi's hand. "Play nice now. I still have rooms to clean."

Her mother was out the front door before Sam or Lexi could say a word. They looked at the door, then at each other. He seemed completely baffled, and Lexi couldn't help chuckling.

"Welcome to life with Phyllis. She knows how to get her way without people knowing what hit 'em."

Mom had always had subtle influence on others, but she'd perfected the art since the divorce. She'd become bolder about it. Sassier. Like the grinning mermaid on the neon sign out front.

Sam's eyebrows rose and he shook his head. "I can see that. Look, the only thing I said to her about the website was that it needs a fresher look and new pictures. I'm no internet expert, but the whole thing looks dated. Curly paid some high-school kid to design it years ago, and other than the reservation software, I don't think he's updated it at all."

"Just like the motel, right?"

He started to argue, then shrugged. "Fair point. Curly let the place go. He couldn't keep up with it and, like I said before, he was too proud to accept much help." His voice dropped, as if talking to himself. "And he hated change even more than I do."

That was an interesting tidbit of information. None of her business, but...interesting. She mentally filed it away and scrolled through the website images.

"Yikes. This site really *is* bad. These pictures look like they're from 1974."

"Some of them probably are," Sam agreed. She liked the way his accent softened his words. *Are* came out more like *ah.* "My cousin, Devlin, is a decent photographer. He works in real estate, so he knows how to capture rooms at the best angle and all that. I'll ask him to stop over if you want."

"Real estate, eh? I'd definitely be interested in meeting him. Maybe he can convince Mom that it would be smarter to sell this place."

Sam stifled a curse. He never should have mentioned the real-estate angle. He leaned on the edge of the counter and rubbed the center of his chest, willing his tension— and heartburn—to ease.

"Why are you so determined to get your mother to sell? She seems happy here."

Lexi snorted. "My mother would be happy anywhere. She wanted a new start and she thinks this is it. A brown-and-gold-plaid gift from God." She stood and waved her arm around the paneled motel office. "But when the honeymoon glow fades and she sees this old place for what it is—a money pit—she'll want out."

"And if she doesn't?"

In his limited interactions with Lexi, she'd seemed pretty sure of herself. But a flicker of panic flashed across her face at his question, gone so fast he wasn't completely sure he'd seen it. For all her bravado about her mom selling the Mermaid, she had doubts it would happen. Maybe Phyllis was where Lexi got her grit from, which meant Phyllis could get her way.

"You…" Lexi's voice broke, and she cleared her throat. "You know she can't run a motel by herself."

"Are you trying to convince me or yourself of that?"

"Come on. She's sixty-two. She should be sitting in the sun somewhere, not working harder than she's ever worked in her life just to lose money."

He remembered what Devlin said the other night about Lexi's motives. Lexi knew the motel property was worth a small fortune. "Are you pressuring your mother to sell so you can get a slice of the sale money?"

She shot him a disgusted look. "I don't need her money, but *she* does. We're worried about her."

"We?"

"My brother and sister and I."

"So the three of you have already decided what's best for Phyllis? She's not some doddering old woman. Does she have some sort of condition I'm not aware of that makes her incapable of making her own decisions?"

"No…" Lexi frowned, then turned away and glanced out the window. A motel guest pulled out of the lot in a gray minivan. The Dempseys from Ohio. "Don't get me wrong— she's smart. Energetic. Friendly. She'll give it her all. But she doesn't know how cutthroat business can be." She turned to face him again. "What liars people can be."

"Talking from experience again?"

He didn't like the idea that Lexi had been lied to so badly that it had colored her view of mankind in general.

She fidgeted with the hem of her long sweatshirt. "Sadly, yes. But come on—you know how it works in the real world. And don't tell me it's not like that on Cape Cod. This isn't some fairy-tale place where nothing bad happens."

"Trust me, I know that." Sam knew that more than most. "But we all want the Mermaid to be successful, which means we won't let anyone cheat your mother." He couldn't help the edge that hit his voice. "So you're free to leave Winsome Cove. We'll watch out for Phyllis."

It wasn't like Sam to be rude or sharp with people, especially someone he barely knew. But something about Lexi Bellamy pushed his buttons. Made him tense. His rudeness didn't intimidate her, though, because she just laughed.

"I appreciate the oh-so-subtle suggestion, but I'll be judging my mother's safety here for myself, thank you. I tend to start on the side of caution and wait to see if I'll be proved wrong. So far, I haven't seen enough to change my mind about this motel, or this town."

"Other than your morning runs, you've hardly left the motel to see what Winsome Cove is like."

Her eyes narrowed dangerously. "Okay, Stalker Boy, how do you know about my morning runs?"

That had been a clumsy thing to say. Along with annoying him for no reason, Lexi also made him careless. But she ran past his house almost every morning, just as he was making coffee at the kitchen window.

"Not stalking. Just observant." That didn't sound much better. "I live in the house at the marina, just past the curve on Harborview. It has blue trim. I've noticed you going by a few mornings. And I haven't seen you other than that—not in town, and not here when your mom has reached out for help with anything."

She seemed to be digesting that, and she nodded, her shoulders easing as she decided maybe he wasn't stalking her after all.

"That's the big old house with the open porch and over-grown landscaping?" She didn't say it as an accusation, just fact. And she was right. His grandmother would hate to see the current shape of her beloved hydrangeas. "So you have a family, then?"

Sam blinked—once quickly in surprise, and then again more slowly as the pain settled in his chest. He rubbed it again.

"No. Just me."

"That's a big house for one person."

Some nights it felt bigger than others. Some nights the walls felt crushingly close. "I...I inherited it."

"Oh." She paused, her stance softening. "Well, it's close to work, I guess."

"Right out the back door. Comes in handy."

Lexi nodded. "You know, I *have* driven Mom around some. I'm just a city girl at heart. No offense, but I'm not into the overwhelming quaintness of Cape Cod."

Sam didn't respond right away. Conversations seemed to work like that between them—halting, as if they were both curious, but also both reluctant to share much.

"No offense taken," he finally said. That wasn't quite true. He liked the *overwhelming quaintness* of his home-town. "But I thought you were from Iowa?"

"I grew up in Des Moines, which is a pretty large and cultured city, believe it or not. Then I lived in Chicago for five years." She smiled, and more of the distrust faded from her eyes, which were more golden than green now. "I loved the energy and the diversity—there's always something interesting going on."

"You haven't seen the Cape in season yet," he pointed out, still feeling defensive. "The population explodes, and there's a festival or fair somewhere every weekend. The farmer's markets open up—the whole place really starts buzzing after Memorial Day."

She didn't look convinced. "For what…three or four months? And then what happens? The sidewalks roll back up again and everyone hybernates?"

He spread his hands wide in defeat. "I get it. Small towns. Simple pleasures. Not your thing. So when do you head back to Chicago?"

What kind of job did she have where she could take weeks away from it? There was a quick pinch of pain in her expression.

"Chicago's my past, not my future."

There was definitely a story behind *that* sentence.

"Where's your future, then?"

She gave a quick laugh. "Anywhere but here, Sam. Anywhere but here."

Chapter Five

Lexi was restless. Turns out you could only spend so much time feeling sorry for yourself before life ran you over and reminded you that it wasn't stopping for your pity party. It was early May, and she had decisions to make. Big ones.

Stay in the restaurant business? Find some other employment with normal working hours? Look for work on the Cape? Back in Chicago? Home to Des Moines? Some new city? Her conversation with Sam the other day made her realize she needed to start figuring out what was next for her. And where.

Sam had a way of asking questions that made her drop her guard. She was still sharp with him—and he was with her—without any idea why they rubbed each other the wrong way. And yet, he also had a way of getting her to open up. It was annoying.

Maybe it was the fake-feeling Mr. Wholesome routine that got under her skin. She didn't trust easily in the first place, and his golly-gee-whillikers act made her irrationally angry. Irrational, because he really *was* helping them with the motel. Mom thought he was a sweetheart, and she said everyone in town just adored Sam Knight. For some reason, that made Lexi view him with even more suspicion. No one was *that* nice.

She leaned on the railing of the overlook and watched a large mama seal nudging her baby toward the water's edge. She'd read about the sharks that had returned to the Cape Cod beaches in recent years, following the growing seal population for food. Was May too early for the seal pup to be in danger? Or was there a shark trolling the beach right now, waiting for its breakfast to slip into the water?

"This view never gets old, does it?" Her mom walked up and leaned on the rail next to her. "We need to get a picture of it for the new website." She nudged Lexi's shoulder. "We should take it before those great white sharks return and there's blood in the water. That wouldn't be good for business." Mom let out a sharp laugh. "Shelly at the decorating store told me they usually start showing up mid-June, but Crystal over at the post office says they've been seen as early as May."

Lexi marveled at how fast her mother was becoming part of the Winsome Cove community. She was on a mission to develop all the business connections she could for the motel, which was smart. But Mom was also making real friends here already.

The pink was fading in her hair, but she had an appointment to get it cut and recolored at the Shiny Shark Salon. Apparently, Crystal had recommended them. Mom was dressed in her usual skinny jeans—today's were heavily embroidered with flowers—and a low-cut red knit top, with a jaunty white scarf tied at her neck. Lexi shook her head. Who *was* this bold, hard-working woman and where had her sweet, homemaking mom gone? She couldn't decide which woman she preferred.

"Oh, look!" Mom exclaimed. "There's a baby seal down there!"

The pup was scrambling ahead of its mother, both of

them slipping into the waves rolling gently onto the beach this morning.

"What if the pup isn't safe?" Lexi blurted out, feeling a surprising lump in her throat. "What if it's not ready? What if there is a shark out there?"

There was a beat of silence before her mother's hand covered Lexi's on the railing. Her voice softened.

"Sweetheart, a mother *never* knows when her pups are ready. She just does the best she can to prepare them before they hit the water." Phyllis gazed at Lexi, searching her face as if gauging her daughter's panic level. Because that's what this was—*panic*. And she didn't know how to push through such an unfamiliar emotion.

"As far as sharks go—" Mom tucked her short hair behind her ear "—there are *always* sharks out there. You and I know that better than most, don't we?"

Lexi nodded, blinking back tears. As much as she'd vowed to herself as a teen that she'd *never* be like her mom, scurrying around the house to avoid one of Dad's temper tantrums, she'd fallen right into the predictable pattern. She'd almost married someone just like her father in all the worst ways.

Her former business partner and fiancé, Karl, hadn't started out that way, of course. He'd encouraged her to finish her culinary degree in Chicago and come work for him.

Then Karl began complaining that every time they switched restaurants, it was up to him to find another job. Never mind that *he* was the one who got them—or at least himself—fired. He complained when she spent a rare night with friends, or even with her family.

She'd offered to find another job—a normal job—so they wouldn't have to live *and* work together. He'd accused her of being a martyr. Of making him the "bad guy." He criticized her clothes, her hair, her body. Eventually, and too late, she'd realized he *was* the bad guy.

By that time, they were running the upscale downtown restaurant she'd dreamed of. They were making money, thanks to her growing reputation in Chicago. Instead of appreciating the success, Karl hadn't been satisfied. In his rush to make *more* money, he'd gotten the restaurant involved with illegal activity and ended up making her lose everything that mattered to her. She sighed, then straightened, pulling her hand away.

"Dad didn't exactly set the best example for reliable men, did he?"

There was a flash of regret in her mother's eyes. "I don't like you kids thinking of your father as one of the sharks. He loves all of you…" She hesitated. "In his own, flawed way. He's just… He's always lived in fear."

"Fear? *Dad?* He's one of the pushiest, most arrogant men I know. He spent years telling you everything you did wrong, then left you for someone his children's age."

Her mother nodded. "True, but your father has always been afraid—of losing his status, losing the business. Maybe because he took over the car dealership from *my* father, and that made him insecure. It isn't something *he* built, even though he's been successful with it." Mom's smile was sad. "And he fears getting older more than just about anything else."

"Well, bubble-headed Tiffany isn't going to be his fountain of youth. She's already running him ragged."

"And spending all that money he worked so hard for," Mom agreed with a sad smile. "I'm afraid he's headed for a fall."

"Is that why you were so eager to leave Des Moines? You didn't want to see it?"

"That was part of it, yes. When it happens, he'll reach for something he thinks he knows—me. And if I'm there, I might give in and take him back. And that would be bad for me."

Lexi studied her mom and realized she definitely preferred *this* version of her. Still warm and kind, but stronger and wiser after being broken.

Mom gestured broadly toward the motel with a laugh. "And look at this wonderful place that landed in my lap! It was fate, Lexi. This is where I belong." Her smile softened. "But it may not be where *you* belong. It's time for you to start figuring that out. And it won't happen with you sitting around here and moping by yourself all day, every day."

"Well, you won't let me help with the rooms," she muttered petulantly.

"I'd let you if I thought it was what you wanted—" she winked "—and if you were any good at it. But, honey, you're a chef. A *wonderful*, award-winning chef. You need to get back into a restaurant kitchen." Her face brightened. "You know, I saw a vacant restaurant on one of the side streets in town. We should check that out. Let's you and I go to dinner tonight and scope out the dining scene. We'll see who your competition might be."

Lexi cringed inside, but she gave her mom a smile and agreed. It *was* time to get back out there. But the odds of there being a so-called *dining scene* in Winsome Cove were mighty slim. There was an old guy on one of the side streets selling big quahog clams that he was steaming in a giant pot right beside his gas station. She needed *actual* competition to keep her skills sharp. Fast-food joints and gas-station clams didn't count.

Or maybe she was just scared.

There was a brief cacophony of sound from the beach.

The small cluster of seals were barking sharply as the mom and pup came back out of the water and joined them on the sun-warmed sand. Lexi and her mom watched as the tired pup stretched out and quickly fell asleep.

"You see?" Mom pointed at them. "Baby ventured out and returned alive. It's time for you to do the same thing."

Sam was mowing his front yard when he saw Lexi jogging down Harborview Drive. He glanced at his watch—she was later than usual. He stopped pushing the old mower as she got closer. It had been almost a week since they'd talked in the motel office, but she'd crossed his mind daily. Which was weird.

She'd made it clear she thought Winsome Cove was some little hick town not worthy of her presence. It sure wasn't Chicago, but come on—it wasn't the boondocks, either. Boston was only a forty-minute drive away, depending on traffic.

Her auburn hair was pulled back into a ponytail. She was in shorts and a faded T-shirt, with a pair of well-worn running shoes. He'd thought of her as a snob, but to be fair, she didn't look like one now. She looked like any other woman out for a run.

Lexi didn't notice him standing there until she was in front of the house. She slowed to a stop, pulling earpieces from her ears and draping them around her neck.

"Hey," she said.

"Hey," he answered back.

Their conversations were always so sparkling. She looked past him at the lawn. "Trying to tame this yard of yours?"

He patted the handlebar of the rusted push mower. "Time for spring cleanup. I had to get this thing working first, then I sent the blades out to Hank's to be sharpened. Then it rained last week, so...here I am."

One corner of her mouth lifted. "Thanks for that abundance of information."

"Well, you asked."

"I asked a yes-or-no question."

Irritation rose inside him. Why had he even bothered to attempt polite conversation with a woman who clearly didn't know what that was? Time to switch subjects.

"How's your mom doing? I haven't heard from her in a few days." At first, he'd been at the motel daily, but it seemed Phyllis was gaining more confidence in herself.

"She's fine." Lexi wiped her brow with the back of her hand. It was one of those days that hinted at the warm summer weather to come. "I really can't figure it out."

"Figure what out?"

"Why she's doing so fine." She gave a *what-the-heck* gesture with her hands. "My mother knows nothing about running a motel. Nothing about the hospitality business. But here she is, insisting she's going to keep the place." She looked at him, her hazel eyes dark with concern. "Thank God, I'm here to help her."

"Why?"

She scowled at the abrupt question. "Excuse me?"

"You keep saying *she's* never run a motel, but what's *your* experience?" He held up a hand to stop her, shaking his head. "I know, I know. It's none of my business."

She opened her mouth to answer, then stopped. "I haven't run a motel, but I *have* run restaurants." She straightened. "I know the hospitality business. I know *business*, period—the ups and the downs."

"Run restaurants? Like...a manager? Hostess?"

"A hostess…" She rolled her eyes, her voice cooling. "Try a trained head chef."

Well, *that* was unexpected. "And you think being a cook qualifies you to advise on running a tourist-town motel? The Mermaid doesn't have room for a restaurant, if that's what you were thinking."

She wiped sweat from her forehead and sighed. "I don't know *what* I was thinking, to be honest. If my mom wants to make a go of it, I guess I need a plan for myself. And a job somewhere."

So she *was* unemployed. Bad cook? Bad employee? Bad luck? He was inexplicably curious, but he knew he'd be pushing things if he asked. She looked at him.

"Know any places on the Cape looking for a five-star chef?"

Five-star? Full of herself much?

"Didn't you say you're from Iowa?"

Her eyes narrowed again. "You think Iowa doesn't have fancy restaurants? The breadbasket of the nation? Ever hear of corn-fed beef?" She reached up to adjust her earpieces. "To be fair, I got those five stars in Chicago, where there *are* a lot of fancy restaurants."

Sam winced. Why did he keep stepping in it with this woman?

"That didn't come out right…sorry. The only thing I know about Iowa is from the movie *Field of Dreams*. I just think of small towns and cornfields."

"That's what most people think of, and it's true to a point. But we have cities and universities and fine dining and—"

"Of course, of course. I didn't mean to sound like some east-coast elitist."

"That would be ironic, wouldn't it?" Sarcasm dripped from her voice as she made a point to look at the house behind him. He followed her gaze. The cedar-shake siding needed a fresh coat of stain. The blue paint on the trim and the porch was peeling. The hydrangea bushes were overgrown to the point of being out of control. He'd known all of that, but seeing it now through *her* eyes made it more stark. The place really was looking neglected. But it was a solid old house. And it was his.

"Sorry if we're not up to your Chicago standards around here."

"Winsome Cove just looks worn-down once you get off the main drag. Mom and I were on one of the side streets the other night, and that dead-end street looked like a ghost town. Businesses shuttered. Paint peeling…"

Was she talking about *Wharf* Street?

"You know what…" he began, turning back to face her. "This place may be a dump to you, but it's my home. My house. My town."

Lexi blinked. "I never said it was a dump. It was just that one street. The rest of the town is cute enough. *Cute* just isn't my style."

"Yeah, I've noticed." He cringed. That was unkind.

There was a beat of silence before she answered.

"Wow. You and I really bring out the snark in each other, don't we? I guess it's a good thing we don't have to worry about it for long, since I'll be leaving." She gave him a soft smile, and he felt something shift a little inside his chest. "This town is *your* home, not mine. If you don't care how it looks, that's fine."

"How soon are you going?"

Lexi barked out a laugh. "Can't wait to get rid of me?"

"No, but…" He sighed. He'd stepped in it again. "I just… I mean… I was curious. You're not doing anything for work…" Why did he care? For all he knew, she was independently wealthy. "And once again, that's none of my business."

"You're right. It's not." She shook her head. "You're stuck with me for a few months. I promised Mom I'd give her the summer. Then I'm outta here."

She put one earpiece in place and gave him a pointed look. "I told her I'd help organize the office today, so I have to go."

Sam watched her jog away, her ponytail swinging back and forth between her shoulders. He shook out his hands, trying to release the zap of electricity he felt whenever he was around Lexi Bellamy.

She was right—they brought out the snark in each other. He'd spent years perfecting the art of holding his feelings in. It wasn't like him to be so testy, but around her...

He shouldn't give a damn what she did or what she liked. So why was he so powerfully curious? Why did he want to know *everything* about the woman?

And why did he both love and hate the idea of her being in Winsome Cove this summer?

Chapter Six

Lexi had to admit that Winsome Cove had its share of charm for a tourist town. After her run-in with Sam that morning, she'd felt guilty about disparaging the guy's home. She'd always been one to speak her mind, but not to be intentionally hurtful. Her self-imposed penance was to spend time in the small downtown area and look for the positive.

Most of the businesses on Main Street were painted cheery colors, and baskets of flowers hung from the rustic iron lampposts designed to look like upside-down ship's anchors. But she couldn't help feeling it was a bit of a facade. It was too cutesy to be real.

The shops were what you'd expect to see—souvenirs, art galleries, T-shirts and more souvenirs. A national chain coffee-and-doughnut shop at the outer edges of town. A small restaurant called Sal's Seafood House, with the front covered with fishnet and a stack of colorful painted lobster traps on the sidewalk by the door. A sign in the window boasted it was the home of The Largest Clam Platter on the Cape. It didn't claim to be the best…just the biggest. There was a bar named Crabby Pete's, and a tiny coffee shop next to that.

One of the artsy shops was a store named SeaShelly Designs. It was owned by another of Mom's new friends,

Shelly Berinson. Mom said it was Shelly who'd redecorated
Great Uncle Tim's apartment when she was just starting
her business ten years ago. He'd been one of her first customers. Lexi probably had Shelly to thank that the apartment wasn't as brown and gold as the motel rooms were.

The interior design shop was at the corner of Main Street
and a short dead-end street that ran between Main Street
and the harbor. She and Mom had started walking down
Wharf Street the other night, but it felt a little shady. There
weren't many storefronts open there. She could understand
why—it was hidden and the buildings looked as tired as
Sam's house. There was a small townie bar at the bottom
of the street, next door to a vacant restaurant.

She paused at the window of a place called Admiral Tees.
The nautical theme was apparently the *only* theme around
here. But she supposed that was why people came to Cape
Cod—to immerse themselves in the rustic fishing villages.
She'd seen the commercial boats heading out in the early
morning light, so it wasn't *all* fake.

There were several stacks of folded T-shirts in the shop
window. One stack had a very drunk-looking cartoon lobster holding up a beer mug. The words read *Get Wrecked
on Cape Cod*. It was a perfect gift to send her brother and
sister. She wanted to be sure Max and Jenny didn't forget
her sacrifice, or the promise they'd both made to take a turn
watching out for Mom if Lexi couldn't get her back to Iowa.

That was looking less and less likely, especially since
Mom told her last night that the sale of their family home
in Des Moines was closing next week.

To be fair, Jenny's life had been upended, too. As the
only one still in Des Moines, Jenny had been pressed into
a series of frantic tasks, organizing the packing and stor-

age of whatever anyone wanted to keep from the house, and the sale of everything else through an auction service.

Max was, as usual, off wandering the nation's Renaissance fairs in his motorhome, towing his portable forge, without a care or responsibility in the world.

Neither Max nor Jenny had been as upset as Lexi when she'd told them Mom was selling the family home. They knew that Lexi was keeping an eye on Mom so she didn't get in over her head with this motel project, so they seemed fine with all of it. As long as they didn't have to uproot their own lives. How nice for them.

Lexi couldn't hang out in cutesy little Winsome Cove— even the name was sugar-sweet—forever. Mom, on the other hand, seemed to be planning exactly that. She was putting down roots here like a plant starved for water. She'd already filled a notebook with plans for updating the motel. Mom was happy. She got up every morning and cleaned rooms, running the commercial laundry machines like she'd been doing it all her life. Then again, maybe owning a motel was the perfect job for a woman who'd been doing laundry and keeping a house spotless her entire married life.

Lexi pushed open the door to the T-shirt shop. Her mother was excited about making her fresh start hundreds of miles from where anyone knew her. Hundreds of miles from where Phyllis Bellamy had been a homemaker extraordinaire…and not much else. Now she was running a business. Lexi held in a laugh. Mom *owned* a business. How well she was going to be able to *run* it was still up in the air.

"Good morning!" A young woman came out of the back room to greet Lexi. She was wearing a colorful tie-dyed T-shirt emblazoned with the words *Cape Cod*. "How can I help you?"

Lexi took two T-shirts from the pile near the window.

"I'd like these two shirts, please." A hot pink one for Jenny, and a black one for Max…to match his grumpy soul.

"Of course. Will that be all today?" At Lexi's nod, the woman started ringing them up. She had long, narrow, beaded braids and mahogany skin. She was petite and curvy. Her accent sounded Caribbean, tinged with a hint of French—she enunciated each syllable distinctly. She gave Lexi a bright smile. "Are you a visitor to Winsome Cove?"

She hesitated. "I guess you could say that. My mother is the new owner of the Sassy Mermaid Motor Lodge…"

The woman gasped, her eyes going wide. "You're *Phyllis's* daughter? Oh, then you are not a visitor, but a new resident, no? She talks about you often. That Phyllis Bellamy is making her mark in town already." She extended her hand. "I am Caroline Curie. This is my mother's shop, along with her wife. I work here on days when I am not at school."

Lexi shook her hand, wondering how Caroline knew her mother already, and why she made Mom sound like a movie star. "I'm Lexi. Do you go to school here on Cape Cod?" She remembered passing signs to a community college the other day when she'd driven to Yarmouth for groceries.

Caroline shook her head. "No, I attend Berklee in Boston."

"The music school? Wow. What are you majoring in?"

"I play the cello," Caroline answered with a small, but proud, smile. "I also sing. Opera, mostly."

"Wow again. Very impressive. You won't be selling T-shirts for long with that education."

Caroline handed her the small shopping bag. "Well, you know what they say about starving artists. There's not a huge demand for classical musicians, much less opera singers, but if I can make it into a major company in a big city, I'll happily give up my T-shirt gig."

"How do you know my mother?"

"Your mother *makes* herself known. She is a bit of a force of nature, no?" Caroline laughed. "She has been up and down Main Street several times in the past few weeks, introducing herself to everyone and handing out business cards for the Mermaid. She had lunch with my mother, Genevieve, and Amy just the other day. A savvy marketer, that woman!"

Lexi was at a loss for words. She knew her mom had made friends here. But it sounded like there was a plan behind all her socializing. She'd been getting to know the locals in a way that already had them talking about her *and* the motel. They were going to have to change the name to the *Savvy* Mermaid.

"I heard Sam Knight is helping you and your mom, too." Caroline leaned forward and lowered her voice, looking ready to drop some gossip. "He is *such* a sweet man. He and his cousin, Devlin, are almost too nice to be true, y'know? Always so hardworking and chivalrous, those two." Caroline winked. "And easy on the eyes, right?"

"I haven't met Devlin yet, but Sam has helped Mom with some things."

She couldn't figure out why Mom, and apparently everyone in Winsome Cove, thought Sam was so amazingly sweet. She couldn't argue about his looks, but his personality around her was far from this wholesome image he had around town.

"You live with Phyllis, no?" Caroline asked. "But I haven't seen you before. Do you have one of those remote jobs you can do from anywhere?"

"Um…" Lexi straightened. "I'm a chef, so video conferencing doesn't really work for me. I'm here to help my mom at the motel. Just to get her settled." Although it seemed

Mom was doing a good job of that on her own. "I'm actually…between jobs at the moment." She caught herself and lifted one shoulder with a half grin. There was no need to dance around it. "In other words, I'm jobless with zero prospects."

"I understand that!" Caroline laughed. "That's where I'd be if my mother hadn't given me this pity job. What kind of food do you cook?"

Everyone here wanted to call her a *cook*. She'd had too much training to accept that title.

"I was the head chef at a popular restaurant back in Chicago. Upscale Italian cuisine." She didn't know why she'd added *upscale*. It probably made her sound like a snob, but that job had made her immensely proud before it ruined her.

"Ah…" Caroline's smile faded to sadness. "Not a lot of upscale cuisine in Winsome Cove, I'm afraid. The old Waterfront Restaurant on Wharf Street was a nice family place, but it closed during the pandemic. I'm not sure if Fred and Devlin plan to reopen it or not."

There wasn't *any* upscale cuisine here, from what Lexi had seen. The dining options consisted of Sal's Lobster House for fried clams and a couple of bars. There were other towns nearby for food, of course. No one was going to starve. The Cape consisted of three strings of connected little towns—one strand on each coast and one up the middle until the Cape grew so narrow that they merged into one.

There was money here, judging from the property values she'd seen, so there had to be fine dining *somewhere*. People couldn't be driving all the way to Boston for dinner on a regular basis. She just hadn't found those restaurants yet. Even if she did, they surely already had head chefs. Lexi blinked. Not that she cared. Thinking of finding a job in this postage stamp of a tourist trap made no sense.

She wasn't staying.

* * *

Sam walked down Wharf Street early Friday morning and wondered where the week had gone. In fact, where the *Spring* had gone. It was mid-May already. Of course, since Phyllis and Lexi's arrival in April, he'd spent a lot of his time at the Sassy Mermaid Motor Lodge. Phyllis had called him for help on a regular basis at first. It was his own fault—he'd made a big deal of telling her to call him anytime with questions. And she'd done just that. Maybe that's what had made time go so swiftly—he'd been nudged out of his usual routine. He finally had something to think about rather than sit at home in his usual funk, doing his best to ignore the world.

Phyllis had given him some laughs since her arrival. With her spiky pink hair and those torn jeans and her love of animal-print boots… She was one of a kind. She knew nothing about running a motel, but she'd jumped into the task full force, with enthusiasm and humor. That was one of the things he liked best about her—she approached everything with a smile and a laugh. There was no prim and proper Midwesterner in her. Although she *was* what people called "Midwest nice." He never arrived at the Mermaid when she didn't have a plate of cookies or pan of brownies ready, or even burgers frying on the grill outside.

Her daughter, on the other hand, had more of the prim and proper in her. Lexi was…aloof. He'd seen her a few times by herself on the overlook deck, staring out at the ocean like she was waiting for a long-lost lover to come sailing home. She seemed detached from what was going on. He should be able to relate, since he'd been accused of being the same way more than once over the years.

Phyllis's questions came fast and furious at first.

How did she turn the washing machines on?

Flip the water lever up to open it, Phyllis, then turn the machines on. Turn the water lever off afterward to avoid a flooded laundry room.

Where are the extra bathroom toiletries stored?

Curly kept a low inventory on stuff like shampoo and soap, especially in the offseason. You'll need to buy more, and no, I don't know where he ordered from.

How did she know if anyone's made reservations?

The reservations are kept in this program, and should automatically transfer to the room schedule in the calendar in this program here.

After the first few weeks, the everyday stuff was sorted out. His visits were down to once or twice a week. Less because Phyllis called, and more because he wanted to check on her and see how she was doing. She was determined, but he didn't like the thought of her getting in over her head just because she wouldn't ask for help with something. And Lexi was staying very hands-off.

Maybe that had more to do with her general disgust over the entire motel itself, and her mother's plan to maintain ownership of it. Maybe she was trying to prove to Phyllis that she couldn't—or shouldn't—do this alone.

To be fair, Sam understood Lexi was protecting her mother by being suspicious of everyone. She was determined not to trust or embrace anyone or anything in Winsome Cove, other than perhaps the ocean itself.

It looked like she'd be staying awhile, since her car had arrived on a flatbed truck last week. The Mini Cooper was bright red with a white racing stripe from front to back. A little more playful than he'd pictured for someone as uptight as she seemed to be.

Phyllis had explained the other day that Lexi's sister was originally supposed to drive the car to Winsome Cove, but the sister had ended up busy taking care of the sale of the family home back in Iowa. Phyllis was committed to keeping the motel, and she'd cut her ties with Iowa completely.

The Bellamy women were both strong, but also very different. Phyllis was as freewheeling and open as the Atlantic Ocean on a summer day. While Lexi was more like the ocean in midwinter. A little gray. Not dull, but nowhere near as colorful as her mom. He had a feeling Lexi could be stormy, but it was below the surface. He thought of the way she'd put herself between her mother and him that first night.

Sam didn't care, of course. He and Devlin had been paid by the attorneys to keep the motel operational until the heirs took over. They'd done that and now he could move on. He wasn't going to get involved with the Sassy Mermaid Motor Lodge, or the Bellamy women, any more than he had to. His life revolved around the marina and Wharf Street and that was fine with him.

"Well, well—look what the cat dragged in."

Sam looked up, then grinned when he saw his uncle.

"Hey, Uncle Fred, how's it going?"

His father's brother was sweeping the sidewalk in front of the Salty Knight. The Salty was a small townie pub that had been in their family for generations. It had never catered much to tourists, being on Wharf Street instead of the more populated Main Street.

Wharf Street was a short dead-end road running along the harbor's edge—behind and below the businesses on Main Street. It had once been Winsome Cove's main thoroughfare, a hundred years ago. The town leaders at some point after World War II decided it was too narrow—and the buildings on it too rough-looking—to represent the wholesome Winsome Cove they wanted tourists to see. So they'd cut off one end for a parking lot and pushed most of the businesses up to Main Street.

But Sam *liked* the buildings on Wharf Street. Maybe that was because he, Devlin and his uncle owned most of the ones that were left. And the Knight family had never been big on change. If It Ain't Broke, Don't Fix It could be on their family crest. Still, he had to admit that Wharf Street was looking a little tired these days. A few of the storefronts were empty, and even those that were occupied had faded paint and dusty windows. Sam stopped, turning around to look at the row of nineteenth-century clapboard buildings as if seeing them for the first time.

Damn. This might be something in his life that actually *needed* fixing. Sure, the locals liked to joke that Wharf Street was *their* Main Street. Off the main drag. No souvenir shops. No trendy coffee houses. No crowded sidewalks during the summer season, packed with sunglasses-wearing children clutching the hands of exhausted-looking adults.

"What the hell are you looking at?" Fred demanded. "D'you lose someone?"

"If I did, they'd be pretty easy to spot on an empty street, Fred." Sam turned to face his uncle. He was the literal definition of a *salty Knight*. Patriarch of the family, he was a short and sturdy spark plug of a man who often had the temperament of a pissed-off junkyard dog. Sam looked at the front of the bar, which was just as old as the other buildings. He reached out to wipe the salt film on the window with his finger. It was a constant battle with places this close to the ocean. "This is looking a little grimy, don't you think?"

Fred jabbed at Sam with the end of the broom. "Quit touching it, you doofus! No one looks close enough on Wharf Street to worry about that stuff." He shooed at Sam with a sweeping motion toward Sam's feet. "And mind your own business, Mr. Fancy Pants."

Sam laughed. He'd never been called fancy *anything*. "I didn't mean the Salty specifically," he explained, sidestepping the broom Fred was still threatening him with. "Just because we're not the center of town doesn't mean the street has to look...neglected."

The buildings—even the empty ones—were clean, for the most part. It's not like the Knights were slum lords. But suddenly everything looked...*old*. Not old and quaint. Just old.

Fred squinted up at him, his morning stubble silver where the sunlight hit it. "Who put a bug up your ass? Let the ritzy shops up there worry about impressin' people." He jerked his head up at the backs of the businesses on Main Street, fifteen feet above Wharf. "That ain't for us."

Normally, Sam would agree. But something was itching at him this morning. Something that had him seeing the storefronts he and Fred owned through different, more critical eyes. He realized those different eyes were a spicy blend of gold and green. He was seeing the street through the eyes of Lexi Bellamy. And damn if she hadn't been right about how things looked.

The fancy tourist traps up on Main hid what he'd called the *real* Winsome Cove. But the real Winsome Cove wasn't some hidden gem at this point. It was just hidden. Wharf Street had been a hopping place fifty, or even twenty, years ago. The Salty Knight had anchored a line of thriving businesses, from a nice restaurant to the fish market. There'd been a local hardware and dry-goods store. Hell, there'd even been a gardening shop at the top of the road—his mom used to buy her plants there.

Now? Now the Salty was one of the few places open for business on Wharf Street. The attached restaurant closed during the shutdown and never reopened. The coffee shop had moved up to Main Street, where it was now struggling to compete with the national chains.

The hardware store had been put out of business ten years ago by the big-box stores that had popped up around the Cape. Devlin was using that building as his real-estate office now. Joseppi's Fish Market was still there, and the original Joseppi's granddaughter, Carmen, ran the place. Carm catered to restaurants more than to the general public, so it didn't generate much foot traffic. There were small apartments above most of the shops, and they were always at full occupancy. Affordable rentals were a challenge on the Cape these days, especially for the service workers who kept the tourist businesses going.

His uncle folded his hands on top of the broom and rested his chin there. He grumbled something about "Fancy Pants" again and scowled at Sam. "I'm not saying it wouldn't be nice to get the restaurant opened again, but I haven't found anyone I like to run it, and I'm sure as hell not gonna do it myself. The bar is enough work for me." He straightened and cleared his throat with a great deal of noise, then spit on the sidewalk. A real charmer was Uncle Fred. "If you're so worried about it, why don't *you* get some tenants in here, or open something yourself? You know how to cook, right?"

Sam barked out a laugh, holding his hands up. "Not *that* kind of cooking, Fred. Nothing any customers would want to pay for. And honestly, the marina keeps me as busy as I care to be. I've been letting the apartment rentals cover expenses here and haven't been worried about the properties, but all these empty businesses don't look good. We need a plan."

"You mean *you* need a plan," Fred answered, going back to sweeping. "I'm happy just the way things are."

A month ago, Sam would have said the same thing.

A month ago, he'd figured his life was going to play out in the same predictable way it had been going. Work the marina, do the occasional charter, eat, sleep, repeat.

A month ago, he hadn't met Lexi Bellamy with all of her annoying opinions about the place he called home.

He looked at the empty restaurant window. Lexi claimed she was some fancy five-star cook. Maybe she could give some guidance to Fred and Devlin, or even recommend a cook to hire. If she cared so much about how bad Wharf Street was, maybe she'd help them spiff it up. It wasn't like she was doing anything else.

"Hey, Fred, I might know someone who could help you with the restaurant…"

Chapter Seven

Sam groaned as he arched his back and stretched. It had been a while since he'd spent a day with Devlin on the *Suzie Q* picking up lobster traps. They'd tossed all the legal-size lobsters into the boat's tank, then put fresh bait in the traps and reset them, each marked with a small buoy so boats could avoid them. It didn't always work, of course, with the weekend boaters beginning to return for the season. They always lost a few traps during the summer months to someone's propeller. There was a bit of solace in knowing the propellers probably didn't survive the encounters, either.

"That's the last of them. What's wrong, cuz?" Devlin snickered behind him. "You getting too old for this line of work? What would our ancestors say?"

"I'd advise you not to pick on the hired help, especially since you hired me for *free*."

"You're the one who volunteered, pal. You takin' her in? I could use a beer."

Sam stepped to the helm. They'd made plans to clean up at Sam's house and grab drinks at the bar. He aimed the boat toward the entrance to the cove and the marina. The air had a crispness to it that said it would be a chilly night. It wasn't summer yet, regardless of how warm it got during the day. Memorial Day was still a week away.

"Yeah, I've got it."

He docked the big boat easily. He'd been operating boats since he was a little boy, starting with a dinghy, then a small sailboat, then on up to the commercial fishing boats.

He and Devlin headed up to the house to shower and change. Devlin was tapping on his phone screen as Sam held the door for him.

"Who are you texting?" Sam had a smartphone, but he used it sparingly. He thought of himself as old-school, but Devlin often said Sam was just old. Sometimes he agreed.

"I'm letting Carm know how many lobsters we pulled in and getting today's price. Looks like I can pay my mortgage for another month."

Sam snorted. "Yeah, right. Like you couldn't already pay *three* mortgages between the boat and the real-estate gig."

"Yeah, sure." Devlin brushed past him, moving toward the staircase to be the first in the shower, probably hoping to snag the hot water before the old water heater ran out. "Don't forget my mortgage is based on *three* incomes—the boat, the real estate, and the restaurant and bar. Without the restaurant open, the bar is turning into a loser." He stopped on the bottom stair and turned back to Sam. "Hey, Dad said you're the one who suggested Lexi Bellamy might help with the restaurant. We met with her yesterday and she was really impressive. She had some great ideas. Looks like we'll be reopening by the end of June."

Sam had been regretting that suggestion ever since he'd made it to Fred. Lexi hated this town so much that he worried she might offend the old guy and tell him the place was hopeless. Devlin's smile made that possibility seem unlikely.

"That's great, Dev. She was able to recommend someone to run the place?"

Devlin slapped the newel post at the bottom of the staircase before going upstairs.

"Even better. She took the job herself. Lexi's our new cook…er, chef."

Lexi stood inside the front of the restaurant and looked around in satisfaction, feeling just a hint of terror. This was only temporary, so she shouldn't get too excited. She took a deep breath and allowed herself a smile. The place looked good.

She wasn't sure what had been more surprising—that Fred and Devlin made the offer to her to run the restaurant, that she'd said *yes*, or that it was *Sam* who'd come up with the idea for her to meet with them.

Five weeks ago, she'd had zero interest in doing this. But as soon as she'd walked into the tidy kitchen area, she saw herself working in it. Maybe any commercial kitchen would have done that to her, because it had been so long. But once she stepped into the Waterfront's kitchen, a plan had begun to sprout in her mind. Start small. Cook her socks off. Get some good press. Use that good press to build a résumé for somewhere new. Somewhere bigger. Better.

She'd been honest last month with Fred and Devlin about her intentions. She wouldn't be staying past the summer, but it would be easier for them to find a chef to come into an established business than to try to start from scratch. She'd help put the Waterfront on the map again, then let someone else take the reins. But she'd wanted permission to change a few things, including the name.

Her enthusiasm for the idea, selling it as a fresh new start, swayed Devlin into agreeing. Fred was far less enthusiastic. She had a feeling not much in this world made Fred Knight enthusiastic. But they'd worked out a deal—

she'd leave the bar, which was connected by a short hallway where the restrooms were, alone. That was *his* turf and he liked it just the way it was, but he was glad to provide drinks for the restaurant. She'd agreed to that and things had been set in motion.

And here she was, ready for the grand opening of 200 Wharf—the address of the building—tonight. With a little help from Mom and Shelly Berinson, the dining room had been transformed from dark-paneled walls, dark floors and dark pine tables into a fresh, bright, inviting restaurant. They'd whitewashed the pine walls and replaced the dated sailing-ship paintings with more modern art by local artists. Shelly knew several painters who did images of local interest, from pelicans, to the beaches, to a lobster boat in the harbor. There was a small, neat tag on each painting with a sale price, just in case a diner fell in love with one of them.

They'd removed the heavy brown curtains from the front windows overlooking Wharf Street and, most importantly, from the large picture window in back, overlooking the cove and marina.

The tables had blue-and-white-checked tablecloths, with slender white bud vases holding a single chrysanthemum from the flower shop up on Main Street. The flowers were in an array of pastel colors, and it felt as if they brought sunshine inside.

Shelly had accomplished exactly what Lexi wanted—it was a waterfront restaurant without beating the diners over the head with plastic lobsters, dusty fishnets on the ceiling, or old paintings of sailing ships on paneled walls. She had some seafood dishes on the menu, but 200 Wharf was *not* a seafood restaurant. There was too much competition on the Cape in that category for an Iowa chef to tackle.

She glanced at the front window, where the new name

had been painted in blue-and-gold contemporary lettering, along with a tagline: Locally Sourced American & Italian Cuisine. Devlin hadn't said a word when he saw it, but she couldn't miss the sideways glance he gave his dad. They hadn't completely bought in to her plans.

It was a risk, but she hoped it was one that would work, if only to get people talking. The place had been called the Waterfront for decades. The name was as tired as the restaurant was. And it had been closed for two years, so there was no great attachment to the name locally. Once she had the place up and running, and had moved on, Fred could change the name back and hire a new chef to cook whatever the hell he wanted.

Her mom thought the whole plan was wonderful, of course. Lexi could always count on her to be a cheerleader. It didn't hurt that Mom clearly hoped Lexi would fall in love with Cape Cod and decide to stay, but that wasn't going to happen. She was here to get some good press, then she was off to a vibrant metropolis somewhere with an actual nightlife.

The only person to rain on her parade so far, other than Fred's constant griping about the noise and mess, was Fred's nephew. The guy who'd brought her into this deal, then acted offended when she'd accepted the job. The guy who'd barely spoken ten words to her since she'd signed on. The man who'd just walked through the doorway from the bar.

Sam looked around the room, his face a portrait of disinterest. Or dislike. Or disgust. Whatever it was, it was some form of diss. As usual. He hadn't been in the restaurant—at least not that she knew of—since the artwork went up and the tables had been set in place. He took it all in before finally looking at her.

"Where did the old paintings go?" His voice was sharp.

"I sold 'em on eBay." She knew that lie would fire him up. Not that she wanted... Oh, who was she kidding? Of *course*, she wanted to fire him up. It was easy. And fun. Her new little Cape Cod hobby. Especially since he'd been such a brat over the past month.

Sure enough, his cheeks went ruddy and his eyes narrowed. "You *what*?"

"Yeah, they were old and dusty, and I didn't want them near my food or my patrons. Some guy paid me twenty bucks for the whole lot." She shrugged, biting back a grin at his now horrified expression.

"Those paintings didn't *belong* to you," he growled. "You had no right..." He must have seen the laughter in her eyes, because he stopped abruptly. "You didn't really sell them, did you? You're just trying to piss me off."

She stared up at the ceiling, placing her fingers on her chin, pretending to be deep in thought. "I'm not sure *trying* is the right word. There's very little effort involved. My mere existence here annoys you for some reason, so it only takes the slightest little push to get you over the edge." Her hand dropped. "Your uncle put the paintings in a storage room, so stop fretting. You've avoided me for weeks. Why are you here *now*?"

He snorted and looked around again. "Just wanted to see what all the fuss was about. Was there *anything* you liked about the old place?"

"Sure. The kitchen is great. The dining area just wasn't my style—sorry." She wasn't sorry, of course. And he got her sarcasm right away.

"So you just change anything that doesn't suit you?"

"Um...yeah." His question confused her. "That's the joy of being an adult—you figure out what doesn't work for you and remove it from your life."

"If only it was that simple," Sam muttered. He walked over to examine one of the new paintings. It was a long, horizontal watercolor, framed and matted in white, with a large wash of bluish green behind the small brown silhouette of a man standing on a dock, with a boat floating nearby. The man had a fishing hat on, with his hands in his pockets. It was one of the larger pieces in the room, and the simplest. It had a peaceful vibe to it, capturing the quiet end of a day.

"That looks like…" He spoke the words softly, then cleared his throat with a cough. "The old paintings were bought specifically for the restaurant." His eyes went hard again. "You *do* realize you don't own this place, right?"

She let out a heavy sigh. "You *do* realize I didn't change anything without Fred's or Devlin's approval, right? I was under the impression *they* are majority owners in—" she raised her fingers to make air quotes "—'this place.' Why the hell are you so irritated about me working here? *You're* the one who recommended me to Fred and Devlin for the job!"

"No." He folded his arms and glared at her. He hadn't learned yet that she didn't intimidate easily. "I did *not* recommend you for this job, and I sure didn't expect you to *take* it. I thought you'd give them some advice or know someone who could do the job. I thought you were *leaving.*"

So that's why he was so mad. He didn't want her to have the job at all.

"I *did* know someone. Me. I'm here, and this is happening."

Sam grumbled and stared down at a table, set with bright white porcelain place settings. "Where did all this stuff come from? How much did it cost?"

"Oh, my God," she said, rolling her eyes. "You're like a grumpy old man coming in here and carping about everything. All you need is a monocle and a walking stick to pound the floor with! The white china was in boxes in the storage closet. I assume someone bought it for here at some point in the past, which *should* make you happy. It's *old*. Just your style."

Sam had to be pushing forty, but sometimes he acted like he was eighty with all of his grousing and clinging to the past. She was beginning to think it wasn't *her* he didn't like, but the change she kept bringing into his life.

Chapter Eight

A grumpy old man?

Lexi thought he was a *grumpy old man*? Just because he honored family traditions and believed in embracing history? Of course, he was grumpy—she was steamrolling over everything that was familiar to him. The restaurant looked… Well, it looked…

Aw, hell. He pinched the bridge of his nose.

It looked nice. Clean. Bright. Inviting. Customers would love it. If Lexi's cooking was anywhere near as good as her design choices, the place would turn a profit as soon as the doors opened. He had no reason to be angry about that.

But he was fuming.

Like a grumpy old man…

He blew out a slow breath. "I'm very much a minority owner here, but I'm still invested in the decisions that are made. This place has been in my family for three generations. And what's with the new name? 200 Wharf? It sounds… I don't know. It doesn't sound like a restaurant."

"It's the address. It's a trendy thing right now. Remember when I told you that you didn't know what *hip* was? Well, this is hip."

Sam couldn't care less what was trendy. Wharf Street had never been about trends. He looked around the restaurant again, his eyes resting on the watercolor painting. Even in silhouette, the man on the dock looked so much like his dad that it hurt. Sam couldn't decide if he hated the painting or loved it. "It just feels like you're throwing away the things my grandparents loved."

A rare swell of emotion made his voice break. Saying the words out loud clarified his thoughts on the restaurant. This wasn't the place his grandfather had created, or that his grandmother had managed so proudly. He didn't recognize the restaurant at all, and that pissed him off. If that made him a *grumpy old man*, so be it. He faced Lexi again, bracing for her to tell him why change was wonderful.

Instead, she was very still, staring at him with something worse than anger. She had pity in her eyes. In her large, sad, hazel eyes. She took a step forward. Her hand touched his arm, and the heat from it made him wonder if she'd just come from the kitchen.

"Sam…" There was something in the way she breathed out his name that made his chest go tight and cold. No… hot. Just like her touch. Burning him. She looked up into his eyes. "I'm not trying to erase your family's history. I'm trying to…" She paused. "Look, *they* wanted a successful business, right? They wanted people to enjoy their meals here. They wanted it to be welcoming, and they wanted to serve good, local food. Not too fancy. Not too casual. Someplace the locals could enjoy as well as the tourists. Right?"

She'd never spoken to him in this voice before. Soft. Velvet-smooth. Warm. Almost as warm as her touch, which was still making his skin burn where her hand rested. He found himself unable to speak, so he just nodded abruptly before she continued.

"Those are all the things I want, Sam. It's a face-lift, not a demolition." She moved closer. "Trust me with this. It's what I do."

An angry response was stuck in his throat, refusing to come out. All he could do was stare into those eyes, losing himself in the colors there—chocolate, emerald, gold.

Damn. Had she cast a spell on him? Why wouldn't his words come? How had they gotten this close? He yanked his arm away before taking a moment to think. Actually, he *had* thought. And his only thought was…*Danger! Escape!*

He stepped back, breaking the moment and blinking away his confusion. With that little bit of space between them, his anger rushed back in. It felt different. A little desperate. But it was far more familiar than the tidal wave of emotions he'd felt while trapped in her gaze.

"From what I've heard," he snarled, "what you *do* is get in bed with criminals and use businesses for your personal gain."

It was a cheap shot. One he'd had no intention of flinging at her like this, furiously and without warning. But it succeeded in immediately dousing the glow in her eyes. It killed the softening of her mouth, the warmth in her voice. She sucked in a harsh breath, absorbing the blow. Then her chin rose and the fire returned. This time it was in her eyes, not her touch.

"You know, people around here keep telling me what a great guy you are, but you've clearly got them all conned. You're actually a total asshole." Her mouth, so pretty a moment ago, was pressed into a thin, straight line. "Did you run an internet search on me, or did your cousin tell you?"

"Devlin? He knew?" He hadn't said a word about it to Sam.

"Did he know the *facts*? Yes. Not the conjecture you

found online. Have you told all your friends yet? Does *everyone* know?"

She spat the last question at him, and he heard a thread of panic behind her rage. She was afraid he'd sabotage the restaurant opening by outing her past. That was something he'd *never* do, but she had no way of knowing that from the way he was behaving.

"Oh, hell, Lexi. Of course not. I shouldn't have said that…" He jammed his fingers through his hair. "It just came out." *Because I needed to put distance between us.* "You may not be doing things the way I'd choose to do them, but I don't want you to fail." He paused. "But I *was* going to ask…"

Her anger cooled slightly, but he could tell she wouldn't be letting her guard down around him anytime soon. That was probably for the best. She crossed her arms, then unfolded them and let out a heavy sigh.

"My partner in the Chicago restaurant was laundering money for some drug dealers. I had no idea until the feds showed up and shut us down. I managed to convince the investigators of my innocence, and I testified against Karl." The words came quickly, as if she was reciting a story she didn't like telling. "I still lost everything—the business, my investment, my reputation."

Sam said exactly what he was thinking.

"That sucks."

The corner of her mouth lifted as she nodded in agreement.

"To say the least." She looked up at him. "Especially since we were engaged at the time. I had no clue what he was up to. I can cook rings around anyone, but my ability to judge someone's character is deeply flawed." She shrugged. "At least he didn't try to drag me into his schemes. That's something, I guess."

"But he *did* drag you into it. You lost the restaurant because of that jerk." Sam was surprised at the way his fingers curled into fists at his side. Usually he was mad *at* Lexi for whatever reason, but right now he was angry *for* her. "And he was your fiancé on top of it?"

"I really know how to pick 'em." She stared straight ahead. "I was looking for a daddy figure and forgot my daddy was a skirt-chasing jackass who made my mother miserable." She stopped, her head snapping back. "Wait... Why do you care about my exes? And why am I *telling* you?" She turned away and straightened the silverware on a nearby table.

Another piece of the Lexi puzzle fell into place. That was what it felt like—he was adding bits of information to form a clearer picture of who she was. What made her tick. And maybe figure out why she pushed his buttons so easily. Like now, when she looked over her shoulder at him.

"So now that I've spilled *my* story, why don't you tell me about *your* biggest life mistakes, or maybe the trail of broken hearts you've left all over Cape Cod?"

His biggest life mistake wasn't something he ever wanted to discuss. With anyone. It was a hell of a lot worse than trusting the wrong person. It was even worse than a business loss. His mistake left him without a family. And yet... he almost told her. The idea that she could get him to that point made him bristle with annoyance.

"I don't owe you a life story just because you spilled yours. And I doubt any woman is nursing a broken heart over me. I'm very clear about what I expect from relationships, and what I don't. They're in or they're out—their choice."

"Gee, you sound like a real charmer, Sam." She straightened and checked the time. "As scintillating as this conversation has been, I have work to do. Thanks for stopping by to let me know everything you disapprove of. I hope you're not disappointed when I tell you I don't care."

"Not disappointed and not surprised." His voice was flat. "Good luck tonight." Her eyebrows rose in surprise, so he explained. "It's a family business. I want the place to succeed."

"But...you're not coming to opening night?"

"I..." He hadn't really thought about it. "I don't know. Probably not. I have a boat engine I'm working on. In fact, that's what I should be doing now."

He turned to leave, and she didn't stop him. Didn't give him any of her verbal jabs. She just let him go. This whole conversation had been weird. It had started with their usual sparring, but that odd moment when she'd tried to be sympathetic to him had knocked them both off their game. Then he'd taken a flame thrower to her in response. He was almost in the hallway when he paused, not looking back.

"I liked the walls better dark."

She didn't answer, but he heard soft laughter behind him as he left.

"Of course, you do."

"This truffle risotto is *amazing*."

"I don't know if I've ever had a steak this tender."

"Girl, how did you learn to cook shrimp like this in *Iowa*?"

"If this brown sugar Italian chicken doesn't bring people to Wharf Street, nothing will!"

Lexi had been listening to compliments all evening. Well, at least whenever she took a minute from the busy kitchen to make a pass through the restaurant. Tables had been full all night, with the overflow waiting outside or over in the Salty Knight. Which naturally made Fred miserable.

"I didn't bank on this kind of traffic," he'd grumbled

to her when she checked on the bar halfway through the evening. Fred's New England drawl was even heavier than Sam's. "I'm running out of the *tahp*-shelf stuff that I don't usually sell. And they want fancy drinks. I ain't making mojitos for no one!"

It was her mom who'd shut down the complaints, as she swatted her towel at him.

"Quit bitching, old man! You'll be able to buy all the top-shelf booze you need after you tally up your receipts tonight. And there's nothing *fancy* about a mojito—it's rum, sugar, soda and mint leaves."

Mom had volunteered to be an extra server tonight, and quickly declared herself in charge of drink orders. She was a pink-haired pixie, running back and forth between the restaurant and bar. Instead of looking exhausted, Mom looked…excited. Happy. Energized.

She'd probably been the biggest surprise of the night. Not only had Mom handled the bar business, but she'd also handled it really well. Lexi commented on it earlier, and Mom had leveled her with a look.

"Do you know how many country-club dinners I was in charge of in Des Moines through the years? All the charity events I've hosted? I didn't sit on some throne and order people around—I *worked*. Who do you think made the margaritas at Acapulco Night every year?" Mom had put her hands on her hips. "Do you kids really think I'm so incompetent?"

"No, of course not…" But the truth was, they had missed a lot of what their mother was doing when she wasn't being "Mom" at home. Lexi found herself being shooed back to the kitchen at that point, but it was a conversation worth continuing at a better time.

She accepted a hug and congratulations from a few more

diners, including Shelly and Devlin. She wasn't sure if they were a couple or just friends, but she liked them both. They looked cute and comfortable together. Shelly was tall, with deep red hair. She wore a long flowing skirt in a swirl of colors. Devlin was shorter, but had the same rugged good looks his cousin had.

"Don't take this the wrong way—" Shelly held her at arm's length after their hug "—I know you're a chef, so I shouldn't be surprised, but holy cats, that was delicious! Did you see the food guy from the Cape Cod paper was here?" Shelly had the accent of a Cape Cod native, so *paper* sounded more like *pay-pah*. "That man was smiling when he left. This place is going to be a smash success!"

"I hope so." She wanted that for Devlin and even for cranky old Fred. And she needed it if she was going to break into the restaurant market somewhere else.

Devlin rested his hand on her shoulder. "It's a whole new restaurant, Lex. I don't even recognize it. And the food..." He shook his head. "I wasn't sure about you moving it away from being strictly a seafood place, but I think this is exactly what Winsome Cove needs. I even caught my dad grinning earlier, if only for a second."

Lexi chuckled. "I definitely missed that. I only saw him complaining about all the drinks he was making."

Devlin rolled his eyes. "Bitching is Dad's happy place. Besides, your mom made most of the cocktails. Dad poured the beer and wine. The two of them were a sight behind the *bah* together."

Lexi had only seen a few minutes of the bar action, but she imagined the two of them arguing all night must have been pretty entertaining.

The last table of diners left, promising to be back again. Lexi excused herself from Devlin and Shelly and went to lock the door. She was exhausted and still had cleaning to do in the kitchen before she headed back to the Sassy Mermaid.

The door opened just as she got to it. She started to say the restaurant was closed when she met familiar blue eyes. As usual, Sam looked around before settling his expressionless gaze on her.

"The place is empty."

"No shit, Sherlock. We stopped serving an hour ago. I'm just locking up."

"Whoa, okay…" Devlin chuckled awkwardly and gave Lexi a look. "Uh, hi, Sam. You missed one hell of a night here at 200 Wharf. Full house all evening!"

Sam didn't say anything. Despite all his talk about wanting the business to succeed, he'd probably been secretly hoping she'd flop tonight. She turned the key in the door behind him and clicked off the Open sign. She was still stinging from their earlier exchange, and wasn't in the mood for more negativity. Devlin stopped her, though. "Got any leftovers for Sam to sample?"

She wanted to say that if Sam wanted her food, he could damn well show up when the restaurant was open and *pay* for it. But he was a partial owner. And he was Devlin's family. And she liked Devlin.

"I have some chowder left over. I'll heat some up."

"Don't bother," Sam said. All she could think was that he didn't even want to try her food, and it fired her temper. He was good at that. She turned and sneered at him.

"Afraid I'll poison you? Or afraid you might like it and have to lie about it? God forbid I should be good at what I do."

Sam gave a harsh laugh, his eyes narrowing. "Sorry to disappoint you, but I already ate. You'll have to poison me some other night."

Devlin raised his hands and stepped between them,

while Shelly watched, wide-eyed. "O-*kay*. That's enough, you two. What the hell?" He faced Sam. "Not that your attitude would be acceptable with *anyone*, but she's our *chef*. And not a throw-everything-in-the-deep-fryer kind of cook like the last guy was. Lexi is an *artist*. And an employee. So straighten up your act." Devlin rubbed the back of his neck and chuckled softly. "I don't think I've *ever* had to tell you to behave, Sam."

Sam just glared in her direction. "She started it!"

Lexi folded her arms. "Seriously? You sound like a five-year-old."

Devlin turned to face her. "I don't know where *your* attitude comes from, either. Maybe it's time for both of you to turn it down a notch."

Over Devlin's shoulder, Lexi saw the speculation in Shelly's eyes. The last thing the restaurant needed was some gossip on the grapevine about Lexi and Sam fighting. Despite Lexi seeing *no* explanation for it, Sam was a beloved local son.

If people thought he hated this place—and he clearly did—it might tank her plans to get out of this town.

Chapter Nine

Lexi's eyes were like windows, and Sam watched as she battled with herself. She wanted to light into him, but then her expression leveled, going carefully neutral. She'd thought better of it. Probably because Shelly was so obviously enjoying this little show. Lexi wouldn't want people talking. That wouldn't be good for business. He frowned.

It really wouldn't be. Fred and Devlin were counting on the restaurant doing well. Sam didn't want to blow that up.

Lexi started to speak, but he talked over her, speaking to Devlin first. "I'm just in a mood because of that damn boat of McBride's. I spent three days on the thing before figuring out the problem. It's got me cranky." He gave Lexi a quick nod. "Sorry."

She stared for a minute, then nodded in return. "Me, too. I've been on my feet for hours and I still have cleanup to do in the kitchen. I should get to it."

Devlin was still staring at Sam. His expression clearly said he was expecting more. *Oh, for crying out loud.*

"Can you warm some chowder for me while you're in there?" Sam got an approving grin from his cousin. "I had a sandwich earlier, but I've got room for a little more. If it's not a bother."

The words were no different from what he'd say to anyone in Winsome Cove. Even-toned and polite. Good old Sam Knight—Mr. Nice Guy. But they felt weird when he said them to Lexi. Unnatural. Like he was playacting at being nice.

"Of course, Sam," she answered, her tone just as careful as his. "I'd be happy to."

Liar.

He said it with his eyes, and she raised an eyebrow, her answer clear.

Right back atcha, pal.

She left their little show of friendliness and went into the kitchen. Devlin waited until the door closed before he rounded on Sam.

"What the hell is wrong with you? And don't tell me any BS about you being stressed about a boat engine. You work on boats for a living, and you *love* solving a challenge." Devlin looked at the door to the kitchen. "Did you two have a fight or something?"

Shelly scoffed, reminding Sam she was still there, soaking this up like a sponge. Sam, Devlin and Shelly had grown up together. She and Sam had even dated for a bit. It had been brief, one of those things where they were great friends who hung out with the same friends, so it somehow seemed logical to be a couple. *Logic* was not a good reason to date someone. Shelly had ended it pretty quickly, accurately pointing out that they were much better as friends than lovers.

"Sam doesn't do fights, Dev." Shelly smiled smugly. "Sam does silence and avoidance. Fighting means caring, and Sam…doesn't let himself do that. Not about people, anyway."

Damn straight.

Devlin let out a beleaguered sigh. "Right. You're just

ticked off about all the changes she made to the place, aren't you?"

Ignoring Shelly's gloating, Sam nodded. "You know me and change."

"You're not a fan. I know." Devlin clapped Sam on the back. "Give it a chance, though. We had lines down the sidewalk tonight of people waiting to get in. It was nuts, but in the best way. And everyone *loved* the food."

He couldn't rain on Devlin's happiness by reminding him that Lexi wasn't hanging around to keep the restaurant going. As soon as she got a job in the city—*any* city—she was done. Then what? He swallowed hard.

"I'm glad it was a success. And not just because of my cut of the profits. I'm happy for you and Uncle Fred." Sam leaned to the side to look down the connecting hall to the bar. "How did he handle being so busy?"

"The same way he handles everything else—by complaining all night. But he'll be happy when he sees the bank-account total in the morning. He couldn't have done it without Phyllis. She was a godsend."

"Phyllis? Lexi's mom?"

Shelly moved closer to the conversation. "Phyllis was a dynamo all night long. She literally shoved your uncle out of the way and started making cocktails behind the bar, as well as delivering them to the customers. Didn't take any of Fred's guff and charmed everyone."

He grunted. "Yeah, I can see that happening. Phyllis is one of a kind. Too bad her daughter didn't get more of that charm."

Shelly stared at him. "What are you talking about? Lexi is one of the nicest people I've ever met. She's direct, but that's no big deal on the Cape. Everyone's direct around here. She's funny, too."

Lexi had a sharp tongue, and he supposed that could be seen as having a sharp wit. She was quick at sending zingers at him. But *nice*? She hated Winsome Cove. Looked down her nose at everyone here. At least...that's how it seemed to him. Had he missed something?

"Here you go, Mr. Knight." Lexi came through the kitchen door, carrying a small tray with a skewer of shrimp, a cup of steaming bisque and a slice of crusty bread. Damn, it smelled good. "A late-night meal for the boss. Well, *boss* may be a stretch, but..." She paused, then put a bright— and fake—smile on again. "Anyway, I hope it meets with your approval."

He sat at the table and stared into the bowl. It wasn't a traditional white New England clam chowder, but it wasn't the abomination called Manhattan clam chowder, either. Even Lexi knew better than to serve *that* on the Cape. This soup was somewhere in between. It had a creamy tomato base, not too thick and not too runny. He could see chunks of shrimp and clam, along with diced tomato. There was a sprinkling of crumbled bacon and chopped basil across the top. He took a spoonful and barely managed not to swoon over the flavor. It was fancy and rustic all at the same time, and it was delicious.

There was a thick slice of French bread, served with roasted garlic cooked to the point where it was soft enough to use as a spread. It was like make-your-own garlic bread, but...better. The shrimp was garlicky and lemony. There was no sense hiding how delicious it all was, especially with three people standing over him, watching his every bite.

"It's good." Understatement, but it was as much as he was willing to concede.

"Careful, you might strain yourself with such a big compliment." Lexi said.

Devlin was laughing. "*Good?* It's incredible and you know it."

"I saw the way his eyes glazed over in ecstasy," Shelly agreed. "The question is why lie about it?" She looked between Sam and Lexi. "Why are you two so weird with each other?"

Lexi turned for the kitchen, her hands in the air. "Don't look at me—I just cook food, and I couldn't care less what Sam thinks."

"That's what I mean," Shelly replied. "It's your *business* to care what people think, and I know you do."

"People who matter, yes." And with that, she was gone.

While attention was directed elsewhere, Sam took the opportunity to enjoy his food. He wasn't sure when he'd tasted anything as good. The silence that fell after Lexi went into the kitchen forced him to look up.

"What?" he asked.

"That's *my* question, cousin. What have I missed between you two?"

"Nothing."

Shelly scoffed. "And there's the denial we know and love. Come on, Sam. You're not rude with *anyone*, so…why her?" Her eyes went wide. "Oh, my God, do you *like* her? You haven't *liked* a woman in—"

"Are you crazy? I can't stand…" He paused. He'd never get away with lying to Shelly, and he didn't hate Lexi. "I mean, I don't like her that way. Or…in any way. I'm Switzerland when it comes to her, but let's be real—Lexi only took this job so she can make a name for herself and get out of here."

"You say you're *Switzerland*, but you don't sound very neutral to me." Devlin grabbed the last bite of bread, which Sam had already spread with garlic. *Jerk.* "And everyone knows why Lexi took on the restaurant." Devlin began counting off on his fingers. "One, she's only in Winsome Cove until she feels right about leaving her mom running the motel alone. Two, in the meantime, she's bored. Three, we're close enough to Boston that she just might get a fabulous write-up in the *Globe* or even a viral TikTok review and be able to get a job somewhere she *does* want to be."

"Because they'll finally overlook what happened in Chicago."

Devlin's eyebrows rose. "She told you about that?"

Sam shrugged. He wanted to lick the soup bowl clean but didn't want to give Devlin and Shelly the satisfaction of knowing how delicious he thought it was. "I got an overview, yeah."

He didn't want to admit he'd done an internet search on her first.

"So what's the problem?" Shelly asked. "Lexi wants to rebuild her career, and she needed a starting point right at the time Devlin needed someone to reopen the restaurant and create some publicity. It's a win-win."

It didn't feel like a win of any kind. Not when it kept Lexi in Winsome Cove. And in his family business. Changing things he didn't want changed.

Changing him.

Lexi didn't see Sam again for almost a week. She'd been too busy with the restaurant, which had gotten off to a great start since the opening and right over the hectic Fourth of July weekend. That was good news, but also a stress on her supplier relationships. When a restaurant claimed to sell locally sourced ingredients, they needed to actually *do* that. Ethically it was the right thing to do. Some restaurants claimed their menus were *locally sourced* and only bought their eggs locally. Or considered the local supplier—who got their food from wherever was cheapest—as a *local source*.

Lexi couldn't do that. Not if she wanted a prayer of rebuilding her reputation. But Cape Cod was not a big place, and also not known for food production, other than cranberries and seafood. That didn't mean there weren't farms on or near the Cape, but the number was limited. She'd discovered relationships were tough to build as an outsider. The only reason she'd made any deals was that she'd used the Knight family name and people knew Fred, Devlin and Sam.

Now that she was increasing her orders substantially, she was running into some resistance. Especially from the seafood suppliers. The lobstermen, the clammers, the oystermen. They were a tight-knit and distrustful bunch. She wasn't an idiot—she knew seafood and knew what she needed. But these men and women were giving her lots of side-eye now that she wanted more of their catches. The same way Joe Toscanio was looking at her now. As if her offer to buy *more* lobster this week was suddenly suspect. Fred Knight had told her Joe owned several lobster boats, and his daughter, Carm, owned the fish market on Wharf Street. They were *the* seafood suppliers in town, and, according to Fred, Joe was the boss.

"From what I *he-ah*, you might not be around much *long-gah*." Joe leaned against the gunwale of his lobster boat and took a drag from his cigarette. His New England drawl was so heavy that every word that should be one syllable sounded like two. "Now you want me to commit to sell you *mo-ah* at the same price? I don't know…" He scratched his neck and stared out at the water in the cove.

They were at Knight's Marina. Sam's marina. It was

neat and tidy, just like him. And somehow...neutral like him, too. Serviceable. Efficient. But nothing that would be considered more than what was absolutely necessary. A metal barn stretched over the water near one dock, and she assumed that was where he serviced the boats he worked on. There was a small building that looked like it housed an office, or a ship's store—maybe both. His house was up by the road, overlooking the marina. The view of the harbor must be pretty from there. She wondered if he ever appreciated it.

Joe was still pondering the heavy burden she was placing on him by asking for a few more of his lobsters each week. She wondered if he'd consider it such a difficult decision if she was a local. Cape Cod could be more cliquey than high school. She paused, pulling her shoulders back. Time to remember that she'd navigated high school just fine.

"I may not be here for the long haul, Joe, but the restaurant will be. Fred and Devlin Knight will make sure of that." Joe watched her out of the corner of his eye, not saying a word. But he was listening. She pressed on. "They know I'm short-term. I'm just trying to help them get the restaurant up and running again. Create a little buzz. Then they'll find someone else—" she stepped sideways until she could look him in the eye "—someone *local*, I'm sure. And my mom is helping. Phyllis Bellamy? From the Sassy Mermaid Motor Lodge?"

After a beat, Joe's rigid expression softened. "That Phyllis is quite a gal."

She barely managed to suppress her laughter. She was trying to use the Knights to win Joe's favor, and it was *Mom* who made the guy all soft and gooey. What was that woman doing to mesmerize this town?

"Yes, my mother is quite a woman, alright," she answered. "Did you know she's waitressing part-time at the restaurant? She's charming everyone on Friday and Saturday nights."

Joe laughed. The gruff old lobsterman actually tipped his head back and started laughing. Because of Mom. "Yeah, I heard that. I hear she and Fred have been gettin' into it at the bar." That last word sounded more like *bah*. He winked at her. The crusty old dude *winked*! "I'd like to see that."

Bingo.

"I can arrange that, Joe." She tried to remember what Fred had told him about the guy. "Why don't you come to 200 Wharf on Saturday? You and your wife, Loretta. My treat. I'll even make sure Mom takes your drink orders."

He hesitated, but not for long. "Are you trying to influence our deal, Miss Bellamy?"

"Absolutely, Mr. Toscanio."

"Do I need to wear a tie or somethin'?"

"No dress code other than shoes and shirt required."

"Do you know how to cook *lob-stah*?"

"I haven't had any complaints, but I'll let you decide for yourself."

"My wife likes her desserts. You make those, or buy 'em frozen?"

"What I don't make myself, I buy fresh from the bakery in Chatham."

"You got good coffee?"

"The best—from the roaster over in Barnstable."

Silence. Then Joe nodded.

"Saturday then." He turned away to start doing whatever he was doing with the traps that he'd been doing when she'd arrived. "And I can probably give you what you need through the *mah*-ket. Just remember, I don't control how many lobsters come in every week, on my boats or anyone else's."

"Understood."

She stepped toward the boat to shake his hand, but he brushed her off.

"Don't need that 'round *he-ah*, and you don't want to shake my dirty hands right now." He started the boat's engines and asked her to hand him the heavy lines holding him to the dock. Joe may have thought the request would intimidate her, but her dad had kept a boat on the Mississippi in Des Moines. Nowhere near this big, of course, but she knew what she was doing on a boat dock.

Lexi watched the *Mystic Madam* head away from the marina with a sense of satisfaction. She'd done it. She'd worked out a deal with the Cape Coddiest of Cape Cod natives. She walked up the dock toward her car, but pulled up short when she saw Sam standing in the open doorway to the office, leaning against the doorjamb, arms folded on his chest. He'd probably been hoping Joe would send her packing, but she'd won the old guy over. Or at least, her *mother* had—she'd have to figure out what Mom was doing to these Winsome Cove folks.

She walked over, feeling smug about her bargaining powers.

"Good morning. Nice place you have here." And it was. She could see the office and ship's store through the big window, and everything was neat as a pin. It was dated, with the knotty pine paneling Sam apparently loved so much. She suspected he'd *never* paint over it here the way she had at the restaurant. "Is that… Is that an antique cash register? Do you still use it?"

"No reason not to use it," Sam answered, stepping aside so she could enter for a better look. "It's been sitting there for fifty years or more and works just fine."

It was the type of cash register where the numbers popped

up on tabs at the top as you entered them. She guessed it was more than fifty years old—probably closer to seventy. *No reason to change.* That seemed to be a theme with Sam. He was stuck in some past life instead of in the present one. He watched her intently.

"Saw you talking to Joe out there."

"Yes, we just negotiated a deal for more seafood for the restaurant."

"You negotiated a deal with *Joe*?"

Something in his eyes made her pause. Was that… amusement?

"Well, yeah. He owns the lobster boats."

Now Sam looked truly entertained, and she got a queasy feeling in her stomach. He grinned at her.

"Joe?" he scoffed. "Joe barely owns his house and wouldn't have *that* if his wife and daughter hadn't taken over the books. He drives to the casinos way too often, and let's just say he's not very good at winning. They put the two boats in Carm's name to protect them, and she's got one of them for sale because they're losing money. Whatever you think you negotiated, think again. Carm's the decision maker, not Joe."

"Fred told me…" Her voice dropped off as she realized it was probably some big joke to the bar owner.

Let's make the newcomer look like a fool.

That's what she got for trusting anyone in this town with the last name of *Knight*.

Chapter Ten

Sam watched Lexi's expression fall and felt a pang of guilt. Usually, he got some small pleasure from bursting her high-and-mighty bubble, but not now. Not when she'd walked up to him all proud and sassy, tossing her hair back like she'd just negotiated world peace.

He'd been watching her from the office from the moment she'd pulled in with her little red car. She'd walked out to the *Mystic Madam* like she owned the place, with long, confident strides. She'd been getting some time in the sun over the past few weeks, and her skin had a golden glow. Had she dressed this casual on purpose, to appeal to the old lobsterman? He had to give her credit if she had. Her simple tennis shoes and denim capris, with a dark blue sleeveless top, made it look like she was ready for a day on a boat. When Joe pulled away from the dock, she'd handled the lines like a pro for him. She'd been around boats before.

And now, she was in his ship's store. The space wasn't very big, and it felt like the walls were getting even closer.

Sam noted her last words. "Wait…my *uncle* told you to talk to Joe about a business deal?"

Her cheeks flushed pink. "Big joke, right? You Knight men are so very funny." She straightened her shoulders, regrouping. He liked the way she could do that—whenever she felt at a disadvantage, she'd pull herself up and flip things around to run offense. Her mouth thinned. "Congratulations—you fooled the city girl. But the joke's on you, because I'd rather negotiate with a fellow business*woman*, anyway. Men are just as unreliable in small towns as they are in the big city."

She started to turn away, but Sam grabbed her forearm to stop her. The surge of energy he felt from his fingers right to his scalp reminded him why he tried not to touch Lexi. They had this weird energy that seemed to increase exponentially if they were in physical contact.

What would ever happen if they kissed?

What? No! Dumbest idea ever.

He forced the unwelcome thought back into a far corner of his brain. He'd examine where it came from later. Not now. Not when his hand was still touching her skin. Not when she was glaring up at him, lips parted, eyes all fire and ice, and…

But what *would* it be like to kiss Lexi Bellamy?

"Are you just going to hold me in here all morning or can I go now?" Her question, and the sharp tone, snapped him back to reality. He released her arm, ignoring how reluctant he was to do it.

"There's no Knight family conspiracy to get you, Lexi," he said, looking into her hazel eyes to let her see that he meant it. And because he'd realized he really liked looking into those eyes. He blinked, trying to remember what he was trying to say. "And, uh… The truth is, my uncle can be an ass sometimes. To anyone. He gets a kick from pushing people into uncomfortable spots. Don't ask me why, because I have no idea."

His fingers still tingled, and he rubbed the back of his neck, hoping it would rub off whatever energy she'd left behind. "And honestly, if you made any headway with winning Joe over, that'll go a long way with Carm. He's a tough nut, especially with outsiders, and she'll appreciate that you took the time to deal with him. So you didn't completely waste your time."

"But I'm probably wasting the free dinner I promised him and his wife." Her shoulders dropped in defeat. "Giving away free food is not usually my approach to doing business."

"Did Joe say he'd take you up on it? With Loretta?"

"Yeah. They're coming Saturday night. Why?" She rolled her eyes. "Is that some kind of joke at my expense, too?"

Sam smiled. "No, Joe's not like that. But for him to agree to take his wife out to dinner at a sit-down restaurant? They don't do date nights very often, especially since he racked up those gambling debts. That news will make Carm's day. And probably Loretta's, too."

"So…not a waste of my time?"

"I think your chances for a discount from Carm just went up substantially." She started to turn toward the door again, but he didn't want to let her leave just yet. "Hey, I saw you handling the lines for Joe. Looked like you actually knew what you were doing. Where'd you learn that?"

She looked out at the boats at the docks. "My dad always had a boat of some kind."

"In *Iowa*?"

She rolled her eyes again, but this time she was laughing.

"I keep telling you people that Iowa isn't all cornfields! And the east coast isn't the only place in the nation with water. Des Moines is on the Mississippi River. And we have lakes, too."

"Ocean boating's a little different than boating on rivers or lakes."

"And now we're back to competing again. Honestly, Sam—" She put her hands on her hips. "A boat's a boat and a wave is a wave. Once you know the basics, what's the difference?"

Was she serious? "It's not a competition, but if it was… Well, come on—the ocean is a lot more challenging than some lake." He'd faced some harrowing storms out on the Atlantic.

Lexi considered his claim for a moment—or at least pretended to—tipping her head to the side and moving toward him slightly. Was it a step or just a lean? He wasn't sure, but it brought her close enough for him to smell clean soap and a touch of floral cologne. Her eyes shone with humor, and her lips were pursed together, almost in a kiss. A surge of something strange washed over Sam. With a jolt, he realized what it was.

Absolute naked desire. For *Lexi*. What was wrong with his brain today? And why was something deep inside of him so obviously in agreement? He coughed, trying to pull himself together, then cleared his throat. Then coughed again. *Come on, body—get things under control down there.*

Lexi shook her head. "Do you know how strong the current is on the Mississippi? How many hazards there are lurking right below the surface? And as far as lakes go, does the *Edmund Fitzgerald* ring a bell?"

Any sailor knew the story, and probably knew the song about it, too. The *Edmund Fitzgerald* was a ship that had gone down in a November storm on Lake Superior back in the 1970s, taking twenty-nine souls with it. The somber thought took care of his sudden case of lust. But Lexi wasn't finished.

"Of course, the ocean's bigger by far, so you could probably rattle off a hundred wrecks. I'm just saying…boating is dangerous wherever you are."

He frowned. "I didn't say boating was dangerous. I said

it's more *challenging* on the ocean. But boats are made to
float, and they'll fight to do that as long as some human—
or Mother Nature—doesn't do something stupid."

"Maybe, but I'm not a fan."

"Not a fan of *boats*? Why? You can swim, can't you?"

Familiar anger flashed in her eyes. "Of *course*, I can
swim. I'm in the motel pool every morning. I just don't
like boats that much. Bobbing around in the water, relying
on one little motor with currents pulling at you and God-
knows-what beneath you and having to watch the sky all
the time for storms. It's not exactly relaxing."

Boating not relaxing? He suddenly felt sad for her.
"You've been boating with the wrong people, my friend."

Her right eyebrow arched high. "I'm your friend now?"

I'd like to be more than friends...

Dammit! What was wrong with him today? Maybe he
shouldn't have skipped breakfast. At least he'd managed
not to say it out loud.

"I just meant that you don't have to worry about all that
stuff on a boat. We have tools to spot the *God-knows-what*
beneath us, and tools to tell us where the weather is, and
if you're lucky, your boat will have *two* engines, so if one
quits, it's an inconvenience, not a crisis." He shrugged.
"And frankly, being out on a boat on a nice day with the
anchor dropped is about as relaxing as it gets. It's even better at night, with the waves gently rocking the boat and the
stars so bright you feel you can almost touch them. It makes
you feel...small, but grateful. It's one of my favorite things."

Uh-oh. She was giving him that look again. The same
one she'd given him in the restaurant last week when he'd
let down his guard and admitted his dislike of change. That
soft look. Like she cared. About him. And damn if she

didn't put her hand on his arm again, just like she'd done then. His skin twitched at her touch.

"You make it sound tempting." Her voice was soft, too. "I didn't picture you as the poetic, philosophical type." She patted his arm, then dropped her hand.

But somehow—and he truly didn't know how it happened—her fingers tangled with his on the way by… and stayed there. Even worse, his hand wrapped around hers and held on to it. Not only did she not pull away, but her hand also tightened on his in return.

"Do you like poetic, philosophical men?" His voice was strange in his ears—low and rough. If she answered *yes*, he'd have to immediately start reading some of his grandmother's poetry books.

Lexi's mouth opened slightly, her lips soft and full and pink. One corner lifted into a half smile.

"Not usually, no."

Thank God. He lowered his head, no longer caring that this made absolutely no sense. They were *holding hands*, for heaven's sake. Like a couple of bashful middle-school kids. And she was looking up at him as if she was expecting…something.

When had she moved so close? When had she tipped her face up toward his? Her warm breath moved across his cheek, and he stopped caring about the hows and whens. He turned his hand to intertwine his fingers with hers. His other hand reached up, then hesitated just an inch from her face. He couldn't just stop caring. Not when he was getting ready to kiss the woman.

"Lexi…" Her eyes had fallen closed, but they swept open again at the sound of her name. He swallowed hard. What was he going to say again? He couldn't remember. His fingertips brushed her cheek, then he cupped it in his palm.

She leaned into his touch. Their noses just barely brushed, and they both inhaled at the contact. Her mouth was right there beneath his. Her lips against his were so warm. So soft. His fingers wound into her hair and he was pulling her in to make this a *real* kiss.

The sound of tires crunching on the gravel parking lot took a moment to sink in for both of them. They were in a bubble of sweet, hot desire. But the impact of a car door closing right outside the office propelled Sam and Lexi backward, out of the embrace and against opposite walls in the store. Did he look as shell-shocked and dazed as she did? He had a feeling the answer was a firm *yes*. His chest rose and fell in sync with hers, like they'd both just had the fright of their lives. And they had. Talk about a close call.

"Hey, Sam!" Devlin strode through the door. "Did that gasket come in for…? Oh, hi, Lexi. I thought that looked like your car out there. In the market for a boat?"

Sam had never in his life wanted to punch his cousin the way he did right now. Or thank him. He wasn't sure which.

Lexi was silent, looking a little panicked. It's not like they'd been caught—they were nowhere near each other when Devlin came in. Maybe it was the near kiss that had panicked her. He could relate.

Devlin gave her a curious look, and Sam jumped in.

"She stopped to talk to Joe. About lobsters. For the restaurant."

Dev chuckled, still talking in Lexi's direction. "Are you aware that I, too, harvest lobster?"

"Your *dad* sent her to Joe," Sam explained. "Probably figured she'd get chased off the dock, but she managed to soften the old bastard up and convince him to come to the restaurant this weekend." She looked at him in surprise. Yeah, he was impressed. *Deal with it, babe.*

Devlin was frowning, looking back and forth between them. "And that success has rendered her mute? Are you guys going at it again?"

Lexi's eyes slammed into Sam's, and she was holding back laughter, same as him. She pressed her lips together so tightly that dimples appeared, and her cheeks went crimson. They'd been ready to go at it for sure, but not in the way Devlin was referring to. Sam started to speak, but she finally found her voice.

"You know how it is with us, Devlin." Lexi pushed away from the wall, carefully steering clear of Sam as she headed to the door. "Sam thought your dad's prank with Joe was hilarious. I didn't. End of story. I need to get to the restaurant."

"I'm sorry about Dad. His sense of humor has always been a bit...off. He's not a bad guy. He just..."

"Acts like one?" Lexi said, finishing for Devlin, then held up her hand. "Sorry. I've known my share of bad guys before and you're right—Fred isn't one of them. A pain in the ass, maybe. But not *bad*. Anyway, I really do have to run."

She was gone before either of the Knight cousins could respond. Sam was rolling her words around in his head, and he didn't like them one bit.

"What is it with you two?" Devlin rounded on him, his arms spread wide. "It's bad enough I have to worry about my father chasing her off, but your insistence on firing her up all the time might do that before Dad does. Why can't you just be nice to the woman? Or...leave her alone?"

That last bit wasn't an option. Getting her off the Cape would be best for both of them. But he had a feeling he wouldn't be able to leave her alone until then.

Not after coming that close to kissing her.

* * *

When Saturday night arrived, Lexi sensed that most of the diners were there in anticipation of something. They were whispering and winking from table to table, watching the clock and the door. She was in the dining area when Joe and Loretta Toscanio walked in, and the energy jumped. Joe was in a blue striped button-down shirt. The width of the white lapels screamed that it was from the 1990s. But it was clean and pressed with tight creases down the sleeves. His thick hair was flat on his head, as if he'd run a wet comb through it. Loretta was a heavier-set woman who was beaming at everyone. Her silver hair was short and curly, like a fluffy halo. She wore a brightly colored floral dress and greeted many of the diners by name.

So that was it—they were all there to watch the Toscanios on their date night. That was sweet. Or…were they there to see what Joe thought of the menu? Lexi gave them a quick wave before scurrying back to the kitchen. The lobsterman's opinion of her cooking might be more pivotal than any on-line review, at least with the locals.

Their order came in—French onion soup and lemon peppercorn chicken for Loretta. Shrimp bisque and steak with lobster sauce for Fred. Of course, he wouldn't go for something as basic as steamed lobster. Lexi smiled to herself as she shouted out the order to the line cooks. She knew her skills, and she had this.

She avoided the dining room until she knew they were near finishing their dessert—they'd decided to split an order of her champagne-soaked strawberry shortcake made with fresh buttermilk biscuits. She hadn't even peeked through the window in the kitchen door. She didn't want anyone thinking she was nervous. Because she wasn't. Nope. Not her. She glanced in the small wall mirror by the door. Her hair was still neatly twisted in the back, with only a few strands breaking free. Time to get the verdict.

Joe and Loretta looked up from their dessert when she got to their table. A hush hung in the air—the whole dining room seemed to be waiting with bated breath to see what Joe had to say. Lexi gave them a bright smile.

"Hi, Joe! And, Loretta, so nice to meet you!" She shook Loretta's hand. "Did you enjoy your meal?"

Joe wiped his mouth slowly with his napkin, staring at the empty dessert plate. "Well… I'm not much of one for ritzy food, but I enjoyed it. Lobster and steak is always a good combo, and the shrimp bisque was…different." He paused, and she wondered if it was intentional, for dramatic effect. "But the shrimp was *tend-dah* and the spices were good. Loretta?"

Loretta beamed at Lexi. "Honey, that's some of the best chicken I've had, and that's sayin' something. And the dessert… Oh, my God, it was good. Were those strawberries really soaked in champagne?"

Everyone in the room let out a collected sigh of relief, including Lexi.

"Yes," she said, nodding. "I slice them and put them in champagne or Asti Spumante in the morning. It gives them some nice, crisp sweetness, don't you think?"

Loretta raised her hands like she was praising the Lord. "Oh, yes! And did you make these biscuits? What's your secret?"

Lexi leaned forward, pretending to whisper. "One drop of almond extract and a dash of sea salt." She looked back to Joe. "Does the food pass muster, Joe?"

"It'll do, young lady. It'll do." He winked. "I'd be proud to have my lobsters wind up on these tables."

She nodded and managed to say some sort of thank-you

to Joe, but she was distracted by the sight of Sam sitting at a corner table with the Toscanios' daughter, Carm. There was a time when she would have assumed he was poisoning Carm against Lexi and the restaurant, but the moment their eyes met, she knew that wasn't the case. He'd said she'd need to win over Carm, and somehow, she understood that he was doing his part to make that happen.

Her skin tingled at the memory of what happened at the marina a few days ago. They'd been having their usual sparring match, and then…they were touching. Their hands were together, fingers entwined. And his hand was on her cheek… She flushed hot at the thought of how close they'd come to kissing. Technically, their lips had briefly connected before Devlin's arrival. She licked her lips now, then walked to the corner table.

Sam watched her approach, his gaze sweeping from her feet to her face, coming to a rest on her lips. His eyes were dark and intense. The corner of his mouth twitched. He was remembering, too. And enjoying the memory as much as she was.

The two of them having chemistry was some crazy cosmic joke. He'd seemed to actively dislike her from the get-go. He thought she was some kind of snob, just because she hadn't been impressed with the tiny tourist town of Winsome Cove. It wasn't personal. The people here were fine, if a bit protective of their own.

Sam hated change, of course. Like…*really* hated it. Almost to the point of phobia, judging from his reaction to what she'd done to the restaurant. But he didn't seem to have any objection to the way their relationship had shifted the other day. From sharp-tongued retorts to their breaths mingling together as the distance between their faces shrank.

She wasn't going to apologize—not even to herself—about her desire for the man. Sex didn't have to be tied to any sort of defined relationship. But an affair with Sam would be…messy. It might interfere with the restaurant or cause issues with members of his family. She returned his slanted grin.

But it sure would be fun.

"Lexi!" Carm jumped to her feet and embraced her. Carm was tall and muscular, as if she could handle a day hauling in lobster traps with no problem. Her short, dark hair framed her dark eyes and broad smile. "There's already so much buzz about the restaurant." She gestured to their empty plates. "And for good reason! The food… oh, my God." She sat back down, gesturing to where her parents sat. "And I see you got the Joe Toscanio seal of approval. Thanks for giving them a nice night out. Mom was so excited when she called me about it."

Lexi tried to focus on Carm. Tried to ignore the pull of knowing Sam was… Sitting. Right. There. Carm was as talkative as her father was taciturn. "Dad said you wanted an expanded agreement for our seafood. It'll mean juggling some of our other accounts, but I want to support a neighboring business and Sam and Dev both vouch for you. Stop by the market sometime next week and we'll get an agreement on paper. I'd love to be affiliated with a restaurant of this caliber."

Sam had vouched for her? She met his gaze as Carm continued. His expression was once again carefully neutral. Back to bland Sam, who hated change. The same man who'd twisted his fingers into her hair and pulled her in for a kiss. Nothing neutral about *that* Sam. He looked away, avoiding the way she was studying him. She caught up with what Carm was saying.

"…Shelly thought we should do something for Wharf Street businesses during Old Harbor Days this summer. Our own little festival, you know? The market could sell quahogs, Shelly and Devlin could do raffles and you could offer food samples. Maybe Fred could hand out virgin cocktails. Wouldn't that be fun?"

"When is this?" Carm talked in such a rush that Lexi had lost track of a few details. Sam answered.

"Old Harbor Days is in August. Loads of that small-town stuff you love so much." He said the words matter-of-factly, but she still felt the sarcastic jab. He spoke to Carm next. "Lexi may not even *be* here in August."

Carm's head snapped back. "August is next month. I'm pretty sure Lexi will still be here. Right, Lex?"

It wasn't as if she had an inbox full of job offers. She shrugged. "I'm guessing yes. Give me the details on Old Harbor Days when we meet next week. I'll run it by Fred and Devlin and see what they—"

There was a loud burst of laughter behind her, and she turned to see her mother standing at Joe and Loretta's table, one hand on her hip, the other resting on Loretta's shoulder. She was wearing a pair of short shorts that made her tiny apron look like a skirt. She'd opted for flats, which made sense with all the running she had to do between the bar and restaurant. But the flats were shiny metallic silver with narrow straps that crisscrossed up her legs. Her low-cut top was the same pink as her hair. That pink was pretty intense at the moment. Mom's new hairdresser had touched it up and added even more spiky layers.

The diners at the tables around them were watching and laughing as Mom told the Toscanios a story about the year a bat flew into their house when Lexi was a baby. Her mother didn't have many fears, but bats and mice were at the top of the short list.

She was telling how she'd been getting baby Lexi ready for bed when the bat swooped into the bedroom right over Mom's head. Mom had run from the house into the backyard, screaming at the top of her lungs. She'd breathlessly told her then-husband what happened. Dad had reportedly stared at her for a moment, then asked, *Where is Alexa?*

That had been the moment when Mom realized she'd left her naked infant on the bed while she'd saved herself. It was a funny story, but Lexi couldn't help wondering how Mom had just…forgotten she was there. Probably the curse of being the middle child.

No one else seemed to think it was a sad story. The whole restaurant was laughing, including Carm and Sam. *Lovely.*

Sam grinned. "Alexa?"

She gave a heavy sigh. "Yes, that's my given name. Chosen long before the popular artificial-intelligence gadget adopted it." She leveled a look at him. "And, no, I won't obey your commands or tell you what time it is, so don't even try it."

Carm was biting back a smile. "Got tired of the jokes pretty quick, huh?"

"It didn't take long at all," Lexi agreed. "When it was new and all the commercials came out, everyone—and I mean *everyone*—greeted me with 'Alexa, what's the temperature?' or 'Alexa, what should I wear?' or 'Alexa, order dinner for me.'" She rolled her eyes. "I can't even blame Mom or Dad for it. They had no idea that my name was going to become a common household assistant. I started calling myself Lexi after college, and fortunately it stuck pretty quickly."

"It suits you." Sam's comment made both women stare at him. He just shrugged. "What? It does. It's not as stuffy as Alexa sounds." He paused, a twinkle of humor appearing in his eyes. "Although you *can* be a know-it-all."

That hadn't seemed to stop him the other day at the marina. She didn't say it out loud, but he must have read her mind, because his smile grew. His eyes went a shade darker, and Lexi almost gasped.

What *was* it about this guy? How did she just...*know* when he was thinking about kissing her? And why did that make her knees tremble and her pulse jump? She licked her lower lip and his gaze went straight to her mouth. He wanted more than a kiss. She felt a warmth growing deep inside. *She* wanted more, too.

How much would be enough with him? She pressed her lips together tightly, moving back as panic rose. Maybe this thing they had between them was too dangerous to explore, after all.

"Uncle Fred, it's not a bad thing to be making money."

"Bah..." Fred waved off Sam's comment with a grimace. "I was happy when this bar was just a place for me and my friends to get together, play some cards and solve the problems of the world with no one bothering us."

"Dad..." Devlin rested his arms on the old bar. "You and the guys could drink beer in your living room if that's all you want." He held up the receipts from the past few weeks. "Hell, if this keeps up, you'll be able to afford to fly your pals to Bermuda for a beer. We haven't had a Fourth of July weekend that good in a long time."

Fred grumbled as he grabbed a bar cloth and started wiping the surface, forcing Devlin to grab the pile of receipts to keep them dry.

"It's not the same. Everything's changing. And that Bellamy woman is enough to drive anyone crazy."

Sam straightened. "What has Lexi done?" Other than make Fred a boatload of money in a short time.

"Not *her*. She's fine. She sticks to the kitchen and mostly minds her own business. But her *mother*…"

Sam and Devlin stared at each other in surprised amusement.

"Phyllis?" Devlin asked. "What did *she* do?"

"Bah!" Fred tossed the bar cloth into the sink beneath the bar. "What doesn't that woman do? She's everywhere, spouting opinions about whatever she doesn't like. Helping herself behind *my* bar and making drinks for customers. Do you know what she did last week? She ordered plastic drink stirrers in purple, with a goofy lobster at the top!" Fred leaned toward his son with a scowl. "A *lobster*. In *purple*. In *my* bar."

Devlin's jaw worked back and forth as he tried not to laugh. He carefully avoided looking at Sam for the same reason. Phyllis Bellamy was a firecracker. Sam had noticed the new drink stirrers over the weekend.

Devlin winked at Sam. "Dad…you haven't changed the drink stirrers since 1982. Or the inside of this bar, for that matter. And we *do* come from a long line of lobstermen, including me." He held up a hand when Fred started to argue. "They're *purple*. I get it. But she asks the customers who wants what, and people are asking for the lobster."

"And since when do I give a damn about catering to people?"

Fred said it in complete seriousness. Sam choked on his coffee, and Devlin started laughing so hard he had to wipe tears from his eyes. Sam managed to speak first.

"Two months ago you were afraid you'd have to close

the bar because you weren't covering the overhead. Now you're complaining about too many happy customers?"

Fred glared, then pointed a finger directly at Sam. "*You* don't like change, either, so why are you stickin' up for that bossy, pink-haired woman? What's next—her telling me to paint the inside of the bar purple, too? Wharf Street is changin' too much. We used to keep the tourists up on Main, and I don't like all these new people down here. All those preppy snobs."

He had a point. Sam *didn't* like change. But he was also practical. Without the restaurant, the family bar may have had to close its doors. And they were only talking about plastic drink stirrers. He couldn't help thinking Fred was overreacting.

Devlin regained his composure. "I don't think *preppy* has been a thing since the twentieth century. And progress isn't all bad. The bills are paid. I've picked up two new real-estate clients since the restaurant started bringing people past the office. Carm and Shelly say their businesses are up, too."

"Yeah, but at what price?" Fred demanded, his voice rising. "The price of my sanity, that's what! I can't keep up with it, and I don't have time to talk to the guys anymore. They're sitting in a back corner to avoid the foot traffic, and I'm working my ass off at the bar."

"Oh, my God." Phyllis Bellamy walked in from the connecting hallway. She was in skintight leopard-skin capris and a black top that looked as if it had been painted on her. Sam couldn't remember how old she was exactly, but he knew it was older than she looked. And *definitely* older than she dressed. But she had the brass to carry it off. And she sure knew how to handle his uncle.

"You were bitchin' when I left yesterday and you're *still*

bitchin' this morning," she said. "I'm trying to clean and I can hear you all the way over in the restaurant! If you don't want to work so hard, hire someone to cover the bar. Lord knows, you're making enough money to pay someone. You'd be doing both of us a favor—I'd appreciate not having to make all the cocktails you refuse to learn."

"She's got a point, Dad." Devlin drained his coffee and slid the empty mug across the bar. "If you hired someone for the busier nights, you'd be able to sit with your cronies like old times."

"Why should I pay someone to do my job?"

Phyllis spread her hands, as if to say *well, duh.* "Look, old man, if I can hire a part-timer to watch the motel desk while I work here, you can hire a real bartender."

Fred scowled. "I *am* a real bartender."

"Give me a break. A real bartender would know how to make a freakin' mojito without panicking."

Devlin caught Sam's eye and mouthed *wow.* Sam nodded. He couldn't think of the last time anyone gave Fred Knight this much pushback, especially a woman. Phyllis poked holes in his dour persona and set the guy back on his heels. But he didn't back down an inch. Despite his red face and raised voice, Sam had a feeling his uncle was *enjoying* this.

"Lady, you'll never see *this* guy in a panic over anything. If I don't know how to make something, the customer will just have to drink something else. No panic involved, except maybe for you. Heaven forbid you disappoint some tourist. Try not to cry about it."

"Dad..." Devlin warned, but Phyllis talked over him.

"You say that word like it's a curse...*tourist.* But I make my living off those tourists now, and you do, too. The whole town does this time of year. So get over yourself, swallow your stubborn pride and hire some help. It won't make you look weak, it'll make you look smart." She turned to leave with a snap of her towel. "For a change."

A stunned silence fell over the bar after she left. Phyllis had left all three men speechless. Must be a Bellamy woman trait—the ability to level a man with words.

And damn if all three men weren't smiling at the empty doorway.

Chapter Eleven

Lexi had managed to avoid Sam for over a week now. Was it immature of her? Of course. But ever since that quasi-kiss at the marina, she'd had no idea how to act around him. Seeing him in the restaurant with Carm had just reinforced that. The way his eyes had scorched Lexi's skin as his gaze traveled up her body. The slanted grin that told her he was thinking about that kiss, too. That he wanted more. And, God help her, so did she.

She stepped out of the shower and changed into shorts and a Stay Salty T-shirt. She didn't need to be at the restaurant for a few hours yet.

She and Devlin had talked about opening for lunches, too, with a limited menu. She knew they'd do good business, but once she left, would the new cook, or the staff, be interested in such long days? Besides, having mornings relatively free allowed her to help her mother at the motel. She'd just finished cleaning six rooms before her shower.

Business at the Mermaid had picked up nicely. They'd had a full house over the holiday weekend at the beginning of the month, and had been nearly full ever since. Mom decided to lean into the funky midcentury vibe of the motel. She'd used the money from selling the family home to buy old-fashioned princess phones for the rooms, and bedspreads covered with colorful daisies, with curtains to match. She'd also invested in more modern features, like flat-screen TV monitors and upgraded Wi-Fi. People seemed to like it.

They wouldn't be able to do any heavy remodeling until business slowed later in the year, but they had plans to paint the rooms and add framed posters from the sixties to make the motel look like a throwback to an era of hippies and beatniks. Lexi paused on her way downstairs to the office. There was no *they* in this plan. She'd be gone by then. The motel was Mom's project, not hers.

That had been made clear by her mother's refusal to listen to any of Lexi's advice, particularly when it came to finances. Pouring so much of the profits from the house sale into the old motel didn't seem like a sound business plan, although Lexi had to admit that bookings had been well above what Curly had done last summer, according to his records. She'd had a video call with her brother and sister that week, and they'd made it clear they thought Mom would be better off investing the money rather than throwing it into a money pit of a motel. Max had been especially outspoken.

"You were supposed to get her to dump the place, Lexi, not spend her last dime to preserve it."

"How much time have you spent with Mom lately, Max?" she'd demanded. "She isn't the mousy little housewife we grew up with. I honestly don't think she was *ever* that woman, but now she's…embracing it."

"It was your job to *stop* that," Max answered. "She can still dump that stupid motel and move home to Iowa… maybe get a nice condo near the river."

Jenny had joined in. "I know Mom is enjoying her freedom, but Max is right. It's time to be practical. It's time for her to come home."

Neither Jenny nor Max wanted to hear what was becoming more evident to Lexi with every passing day. Mom *was* home. She'd outgrown her Iowa cul-de-sac and found a place where people appreciated her as the person she was *now*, instead of constantly comparing her to the suburban soccer mom she *used* to be.

Lexi walked into the reception area just as Mom walked by outside, bopping to the music in her earbuds while she pushed the linen cart. She was wearing a bikini top under a see-through white shirt and extremely short cutoff denim shorts that barely clung to her hips. She looked more like someone headed to a beach cabana than the laundry room. It was still jarring at times to see this new version of Phyllis Bellamy. But Lexi was beginning to appreciate her fearlessness.

Mom started waving to someone, then removed her earbuds and put them in her pocket. Lexi groaned when she saw the tall form striding across the parking lot. *Sam.*

It was possible he'd been avoiding Lexi, too. Since their last conversation at the restaurant, he hadn't been back there, or to the motel, as far as she knew. Mom hadn't mentioned calling him for anything today, but she was giving him a tight embrace now, standing on tiptoe to kiss his cheek. Lexi inhaled sharply. She was *not* going to be jealous of her own mother. Not even when Sam wrapped his arms around Phyllis and lifted her off the ground in an embrace.

He released her mom and immediately looked to the window, giving an awkward half wave. She went outside, deciding that keeping the window between them was silly. They were two adults who had a couple weird moments of attraction, but that didn't mean anything significant. Speaking for herself, it had been months since she'd been with any man, so it was natural that when one as good-looking as Sam Knight came near, she'd feel…something. Maybe he was just lonely, too. Maybe their moment had passed.

"Hi, Sam," she said, making sure her voice sounded perky and welcoming. But friendly. Nothing more than friendly. "What brings you to the Sassy Mermaid?"

"Phyllis texted me about some loose boards on the overlook. I had some time today and figured I'd check it out." She realized he was carrying a small toolbox in one hand. He scanned the motel, noting the planters hanging on the railings in front of each room, overflowing with geraniums and wave petunias. There were only ten rooms occupied for tonight, but they had reservations for a full house by Thursday. "The place looks good. I hear business has been up."

"It's been wonderful, Sam!" Mom exclaimed. "The new website is getting a ton of traffic, and we're getting great reviews from people staying here. One woman called it a 'quaint and quirky time capsule back from Cape Cod's glory days.' I guess that's a compliment."

He smiled down at her. "It is, Phyllis. An accurate one, too. I like that you've decided to hang on to what makes the Mermaid special."

Lexi couldn't help rolling her eyes. "Of course, you do. Because it means nothing changes, right?"

His smile faded, but not too much. "Change isn't always for the best, especially when it's change just for the sake of change. Still think your mom should sell?"

Her mother looked more expectant for her answer than he did.

"I think, regardless of my opinion, that she's staying here. At least for now." She wondered how Mom would like the quieter winter months on the Cape. "And I respect that."

Mom beamed at those last words. It was true—Lexi might think the decision was impractical and expensive, but she'd come around to the fact that it was Mom's decision to make. If her brother and sister didn't like it, they could come try to change Mom's mind.

And Phyllis Bellamy had proven she could do the work, hire help and manage the business side of things. Sam just nodded and started walking across the lawn toward the overlook. Lexi didn't remember seeing any loose boards out there, but she hadn't been inspecting the construction. She went there to watch the sea, the beach and the noisy seals, who still gathered on the rocks below to catch some sun. She'd miss the deck when she left Cape Cod. She'd miss the ocean. The cute baby seals. And Sam Knight's fine backside as he walked away.

No. Not that. She was not watching his backside. She turned and found her mother giving her an oddly amused look.

"What?"

Mom shrugged. "Oh, nothing. I was just wondering if your eyeballs were ever going to be finished devouring that man's ass."

"Mom!" Lexi didn't know if she should laugh or gasp in horror. "No offense, but Sam's a little young for you to be noticing his backside. And I wasn't… That's not what…" *Ugh. What's the point?* "Okay, the man is very nice to look at. But that's all I'm doing—looking."

"O-kay." Mom's voice was singsongy and sarcastic. "But you're both single and there's no harm in—"

"No." Lexi couldn't say it any more firmly. "Do *not* go playing matchmaker for me. The last thing I need is some torrid affair with a—a fisherman."

Her mom put her hand on her hip. "Alexa Bellamy, I did not raise you to judge people like that. And he's *not* a fisherman—

that's his cousin, Devlin. And Devlin is delightful. Sam's a business owner. You could do worse."

She didn't trust this attraction to Sam. She had good reason not to—her judgment when it came to men was suspect at best. She straightened her shoulders, ready to end this conversation.

"I've *done* worse, Mom. I have no desire to make the same mistakes over and over again. Anyway, my rooms are finished. I was going to vacuum the reception area and neaten things up in the office."

"Thanks, honey. I just need to finish the last load of linens and then I can help with the office."

It was an hour before Lexi saw her mother strip down to her bathing suit and jump in the pool. It almost felt like being home, having a pool right outside the door. Max, Jenny and Lexi had spent their summers swimming in their backyard pool. She didn't remember seeing Mom in the water that often, but as she watched her dive in and swim powerfully back and forth across the length of the pool, it was obvious that Mom had spent a lot of time in the water, too. Was it when they weren't home, or had they just not paid attention?

Mom grabbed a towel and came into the office, brushing her wet hair off her face.

"Oh, my, I forgot how nice it was to dive into a pool after a long morning of housework." She dried her hair vigorously. "It's getting hot out there. Why don't you take a bottle of water out to Sam?"

Lexi was pretty sure Sam was capable of getting water for himself, and said so. Her mom was *not* amused.

"The man is doing us a *favor*. He shouldn't *have* to take care of himself. Take the man a bottle of water." Mom paused. "Unless you're afraid of the hot guy with the pretty behind?"

Lexi grabbed water from the small fridge in the lobby. "Puh-leeze. I've seen my share of men and their pretty backsides." Although Sam's was exceptionally nice. "You're right about him doing a lot of favors here. Maybe it's time for you to stop relying on him so much." That way, she wouldn't be running into him when her guard was down.

"I don't know. I think we're doing *him* a favor, too," Mom answered. "If not for us, he'd just be sitting at that marina all by himself every day. He liked helping Curly, and Devlin says he likes helping us."

"You talked to Devlin about Sam?"

"More like the other way around. Devlin said he was glad to see Sam coming over to the Mermaid, because he's half a hermit."

"Half a hermit?"

"Well, yeah. He stays at the marina all the time, he works on boats by himself. It's a solitary life for a man his age. Devlin said he's tried to get Sam involved in the bar or the restaurant, but he always retreats back to the marina. Did you know their great-grandparents built that place? He's been determined to keep it the same. He's a man of routine, and doesn't want anything changed or moved."

"Trust me, I've learned that much. Where are his parents?"

Her mother's face went very still. It was the same face she'd worn when she'd sat them all down to say she and their father were divorcing.

"Mom?"

"His parents are gone, honey. There was a plane crash. They and the grandparents on his father's side were on the plane."

The air left Lexi's lungs without a sound. Just…emptiness that refused to be refilled.

"All of them died at once?" Her mother nodded, her lips

pressed into a straight line. "How…awful." There was no word that could adequately define what that must have been like. Two generations gone. "How old was he?"

"College age, I think. So he was grown, but still young. Still tragic."

Knowing this changed her feelings about Sam, but she wasn't sure why or how. She'd called him a *grumpy old man*. Said he was afraid of change. Made fun of him. Knowing about the tragedy didn't give her any sudden clarity about why he was the way he was. But it had to be connected. Losing a family that way had to change everything for a person. It was none of her business, of course. There was absolutely nothing she could do about it.

But…there was a small part of her that wanted to try.

Sam rocked back on his heels and wiped his brow. There'd been a breeze that morning off the ocean, but it had faded in the heat of the day, and he was seriously regretting not grabbing a hat before hopping in the truck and driving to the Mermaid to work on the deck.

The structure was as solid as the rock cliff it was built on, but a couple of the newer boards had come loose. It looked like Curly had tried to attach them with nails too small to hold securely. In Curly's younger days that never would have happened, but as the man had gotten closer to ninety, he'd made a few misjudgments. But he'd also made some decisions that hadn't ended badly. Like leaving the Sassy Mermaid to a niece Curly hadn't seen in half a century. That decision, unlike these deck planks, had worked out really well. Phyllis was like a breath of fresh air everywhere she went.

She was an outsider, and it usually took a long time—often years—for outsiders to become locals. But there was something about Phyllis and her joyfulness and humor that struck a chord with people. It was odd, because New Englanders were known for being gruff and prickly. And it was an accurate stereotype a lot of the time. Uncle Fred was a perfect example.

But Phyllis, with her pink hair, leopard prints and sharp laugh, just seemed to brush right past that defensive front and hone in on people's hearts. She was genuinely happy to be here. Happy to run a motel. Thrilled to be a part-time barmaid, working with a man who would never admit she was good at it. She was just…happy.

He was surprised to see Lexi walking toward him. Lexi's attitude about Winsome Cove was the exact opposite of her mother's. She was *un*happy here. Restless. She didn't like the Sassy Mermaid. She didn't like the town. She didn't like him much. Whatever it was that kept buzzing between them, she was fighting it even more than he was.

Smart girl.

Her hair was swinging in cadence with her long strides as she crossed the lawn. She was in shorts. Not micro shorts like her mom, but there was plenty of long, lean leg exposed. She was carrying two bottles of water, and he smiled.

He'd worked up a sweat out here. And getting some refreshment would clear his head. He was a simple man. Wake, work, rest, repeat. He had his small—tiny, really—group of friends in Devlin, Carm and Shelly. He had his grumpy uncle. He had his boat. That was enough for him. At least it had been, until Lexi showed up. Now, he found himself examining his life more than usual. Over the past couple of months, he'd found himself questioning his isolation. He'd even wondered a few times what he might be *missing*, which had never been a worry before.

"Mom thought you might be hot." Lexi shoved a bottle of water into his hand. He had a feeling she would have let him roast out here if her mother hadn't spared a thought for him.

"Tell your mom I said thank you." Only a slight ruffle of an eyebrow showed that she'd picked up on his sarcasm, but she didn't have her usual snappy comeback. Instead, she looked at the large deck.

"So is it safe now?"

Phyllis had told him that Lexi often brought her coffee out here so she could sit and listen to the surf below.

"It was always safe," he answered, standing with a stretch. "Looks like Curly used some short nails to secure a few boards, and they popped up a little. I pulled them out and screwed the decking down good and tight."

She sat in one of the Adirondack chairs and stared over the calm sea.

"What was he like?"

"Who...? Curly?" To his surprise, she nodded. She hadn't expressed any interest in her great uncle other than a few random questions that first day. He sat on the chair next to her, draining half the water bottle before he answered.

"Curly was... Well, he was like a cross between your mom and my uncle. He was funny and kind like Phyllis, but could also be stubborn and salty like Fred. He was a character, for sure. He was already here when I was born, so to me he was always a part of Winsome Cove." He finished his water. He didn't often let his mind wander back to childhood, but memories of Curly made him smile. "He welcomed anyone who lived in Winsome Cove to use his beach and this deck. He wanted to share everything he had with others. And he loved having us local kids around. He'd put us to work for an hour or two picking up around here and doing odd jobs, then let us use the pool to cool off."

She was still staring at the horizon. "I just don't understand why he never reached out to Mom after he left Iowa, yet still left everything he owned to her."

Sam frowned. "Curly was a great guy. But he never talked about what happened between him and his brother way back."

"He never married?"

"Nope. I heard he was a rascal when he first moved here. He had a special friendship with Winnie Hempstead for maybe twenty years, but it was hard to put a label on it. They spent a lot of time with each other—playing cards, walking the beach or stopping by the bar for a drink. She passed away three years ago." He hesitated. "My grandmother always called them a *Golden Pond* couple, from an old movie she loved. She said they got along like Fonda and Hepburn—feisty and independent on the outside, but they took good care of each other."

Just mentioning his grandmother made his heart begin to ache. That pain was why he stored those memories safely away. Opening that box just a little let some of the razor-sharp pain hit him again. It was a mistake. He went silent, his focus on packing that all away. Trying to erase Grandma's laughter from his mind. It was sweet, but it just hurt too damn much. That's why he didn't talk about them... any of them.

Lexi made a soft, strangled, sympathetic sound, like clearing her throat and sighing at the same time. Her gaze met his and it felt...different. Uncomfortable to him. A warning that he wasn't going to like what came next.

"I heard...how you lost your family. I'm sorry. That must have been brutally hard to go through." Her even voice said she was treading carefully, instead of her usual snark.

"I don't talk about it." The words came out in a snarl, which wasn't fair. He was more angry with the memory than with Lexi. But he sure as hell wasn't going to discuss it with her or anyone else. He'd barely managed to push away Grandma's laughter. The box was closed and locked down.

"O-kay…" She blinked, then looked back at the water. "I was just saying that—"

"Don't say anything at all, alright?" He stood abruptly, pushing his empty water bottle at her. "I'm serious when I say I don't talk about it." His chest tightened, and he jammed his fingers into his hair, pulling it to the point of pain. The pain was what he needed. His tension eased a bit. He let out a long sigh. He was being a jerk. "Look, I'm sorry. I didn't mean to snap at you. I just don't…" His voice trailed off.

"You don't talk about it?" Lexi asked. "Yeah, I got that. But…do you think maybe you *should*?"

His brow furrowed. "Should *what*?"

"Talk about it. With someone." She held her hand up. "Trust me, I'm not saying it should be me. But…someone."

"No, thanks." He'd tried that once, and it hadn't ended well.

There was a beat of silence.

"Okay, then." She stood, calmly looking him in the eye. He'd been rude to her, but her expression held only concern. Where was the testy exchange he looked forward to—or rather, expected from her? "Well, thanks for helping with the deck, and for filling in a few blanks about Great Uncle Curly."

She turned to walk away, and Sam realized she was doing exactly what he'd asked. He didn't want to talk. So she was leaving him alone.

Perfect.

Except…it didn't feel perfect at all.

Chapter Twelve

"Do you think you'll have a good supply of soft-shell crabs this week?" Lexi asked Carm. "I'm thinking of doing an upscale crab sandwich with thick toasted bread as a special."

"So far, the harvest is looking good this season. I can take care of you." Carm jotted a note on her tablet. "You want them for the weekend?"

"Yes, I'd like to serve the sandwich on Friday and Saturday, and maybe a more casual po'boy version on Sunday if we have leftovers."

"You got it. I think we've got this week's order handled." Carm set down her tablet and smiled. "The restaurant seems to be staying busy. How are you doing with the rest of your local sourcing for food?"

"It's easier in the summer because I can get local vegetables from the Cape. I'm doing my best to source in Massachusetts, or at least in New England for as much as I possibly can, and I want to build good relationships. Last week I visited my beef supplier near New Bedford. Great place—grass-fed, hormone-free Angus beef."

"Relationships are key on the Cape." Carm handed Lexi a sample plate with the shop's seafood salad on it. "So… are you still leaving us?"

"Eventually." Lexi paused. She was enjoying running

200 Wharf far more than she'd expected. But she had a plan. "I mean, yes. But these relationships are for the business, not me personally."

Carm studied her for a moment, then nodded. "Of course, they are. Hey, speaking of good business, *our* business is picking up since you opened. For the first time ever, we ran out of seafood salad last Friday. Even the locals seem to be remembering we're here." Carm looked up and smiled. "Speaking of locals…"

Lexi turned to see Sam walking into the market. She straightened, not sure how to react. She hadn't seen him since their awkward conversation a few days ago. Was he still angry with her? Or would they be okay as long as she didn't mention his family?

The way he'd shut her down made it clear he hadn't managed to deal with his losses in a healthy way. Not that anyone just *got over* something like that, but many years had passed since the accident, and he still couldn't even *discuss* it.

She kept wondering how that loss shaped the man he was today. Every time she wondered, though, she reminded herself that it was none of her business. If Sam wanted to live in denial about his obvious failure to cope with the past, that was his problem, not hers. It's not like there was anything she could do about it. She'd given him an opening to talk, and he'd very firmly shut her down. *Fine.*

"Hi, ladies. Did I interrupt any good gossip?" Sam's gaze barely met Lexi's before jumping away. He may not be angry, but…he was feeling awkward, too. She didn't like it. They were out of sync, but she could fix that.

"About you? Don't flatter yourself."

He barely hesitated before his comeback. "I hardly think I'm a topic of gossip in this town. My life is too boring."

He'd made the comment with his trademark easygoing smile.

"That's for sure," Lexi huffed.

"Okay, you two." Carm held up her hand with a laugh. "Back to your corners."

That was fine with Lexi. She didn't trust the Mr. Nice Guy performance Sam gave everyone in town. Friendly. Easygoing. Bland.

She liked it better when he was on guard like this. Sharp. Funny and annoying at the same time. They technically weren't opponents over anything, but if they were, he'd be a worthy one.

Carm seemed satisfied that they were going to behave. "We were talking about Lexi getting to meet some of her local sources for the restaurant. She was up at the cattle place near New Bedford, getting to know the operation. I think it's smart, don't you?"

"I guess." He gave a half-hearted shrug. "So when are you going to go out on a fishing boat? Or do some clamming in your bare feet?"

"I hope the clams I serve aren't coming anywhere near anyone's bare feet."

"Probably not," Sam said, "but it's the most fun way to find them. Walk out into the low tide and feel the bumps under your feet. Might be a rock, might be a clam. Use a rake to dig down and find out." Sam was staring off, as if reliving a moment that made him smile. "Steam a basketful over a bonfire and eat until you can't eat any more. Good times."

There was a beat of silence in the market. He was obviously somewhere else, but she saw the moment the memory became too painful. He winced slightly, then gave a tiny shudder. She wondered how he coped with all those memories he had, but refused to enjoy. It was as if he was punishing himself with them instead.

"Don't forget to get a license first," Carm said.

"Wait." Lexi looked at Carm in amazement. "You mean people really just walk out in their bare feet and get clams to eat?"

"Well, I personally don't recommend bare feet, because I cut my heel once on a rock trying that," Carm said. "Most people wear boots or water shoes."

Sam's mouth twisted in mock disgust. "You can't feel the clams under your feet if you're wearing wading boots."

Carm waved him off. "You should take Lexi clamming, Sam. Or lobstering—I hear you're taking Devlin's run while he's visiting his sister in New Hampshire."

"That's not until next week. Today I'm running a lobster boat I worked on back out to P-town and picking up my boat."

Carm grinned. "Let me guess, for the Molloys?"

"Yeah. Barb offered to give the *Katydid* a full detailing and cleaning as partial payment on the engine work, so I left it there when I picked up the lobster boat. Today I'm doing the exchange."

He looked at Lexi. "But Lexi doesn't want to go on a boat. She's afraid of them."

"I am *not*!" Her temper flared.

"You think they're dangerous, remember? All those scary things under the water?"

"Well…boats *can* be dangerous. I never said I was *scared*." Did she sound childish? Maybe. But she'd never admit her fears to Sam, of all people. He appraised her for a long moment, a mischievous gleam in his eye.

"Okay. Then come with me today."

* * *

Sam had no idea where those words came from, or why he'd spoken them out loud. Him and Lexi on a boat? For hours? Worst idea ever in the history of ideas. He was an idiot.

Lexi was frozen in place, mouth open, as stunned by the words as Sam had been. She'd say no, of course. They weren't pals or anything. Especially after the way he'd snapped at her a couple days ago.

But then, her mouth closed and her chin raised, her eyes narrowing. Oh, no. She was taking the invitation as a challenge, probably because he said it in front of Carm. He had a feeling Lexi didn't back down from challenges very often.

"Fine." The word was tight and firm. "I'm off today and don't have anything else planned. When do you leave?"

"Fifteen minutes." He took in her outfit—pink shorts and a floaty white top with strappy sandals. She looked terrific, but not for a lobster boat. "I'll make it twenty so you can run home and change."

She didn't want to do this. He could see it in the tightness of worry around her eyes. But she'd already accepted, and wasn't about to back down. They stared at each other in silence.

Carm jumped in. "Fabulous! Now you'll see how a lobster boat operates, without the mess or early hours of actual lobstering. And Sam's one of the best, so don't worry about a thing. You're probably gonna want to wear jeans, and grab a sweatshirt or jacket—it's always cooler out on the water. If you don't have deck shoes, a pair of sneakers will do." Lexi didn't move, and Carm laughed. "Girl, you better hurry, because he's not kidding about when he's leaving."

Lexi blinked, then started toward the door. As she passed him, he spoke.

"Meet me at the marina—I'll have the boat running. Look for the bright red lobster boat, the *Stella Dare*." She still looked stunned about what was happening. *Same girl. Same.*

"Oh—okay. See you there."

He watched her hurry to her car. Carm spoke up behind him.

"I don't have to worry about either of you tossing the other overboard, do I?"

"I can only speak for myself, but…no." He shrugged. "I wasn't planning on having a passenger, you know."

"And yet the invitation came from your lips. Funny how that happened." Carm was giving him an odd, speculative look.

"What is your problem?" he demanded.

"I don't have any problem at all, sweetie. But you might. I didn't realize you two were always so…feisty together. It's very entertaining."

"What the hell are you—"

"I'm just saying—" she held up both hands "—Lexi doesn't seem to fall for your phony Mr. Placid act you usually put on around town." She clasped her hands under her chin dramatically. "'Oh, that Sam! He's such a sweet man! Always so kind and pleasant, blah, blah, blah.'" She stuck her tongue out at him and folded her arms on her chest. "And when you're not all sweetness and calm, Lexi doesn't take any crap from you. Almost like you've met your match for once."

"*You* never took any of my crap," Sam pointed out.

"I've known you since we were in diapers. Neither one of us can intimidate the other easily. But this new girl has you figured out already. It makes my romantic heart go pitter-patter."

Sam grabbed the door in a sudden temper. "Jesus, Carm.

You've been reading too many romance novels, and they've addled your brain. There sure as hell aren't any damn happily-ever-afters in the future for Lexi and me."

The 750-horsepower engine was idling at a pleasant rumble as Sam prepared the boat for departure. When he'd brought it in last week, the engine had an annoying clicking sound every once in a while. It was just enough to be worrisome. He'd tracked the issue down to a valve going bad.

"Permission to come aboard, captain!" Lexi was on the dock. She'd changed to trim, ankle-length jeans and a yellow Salty Knight T-shirt, which was big on her, but she'd tied it at her waist. She had a ball cap on, with her hair pulled through the back opening in a ponytail. Sunglasses rested on top of the visor, and she carried a small canvas tote bag.

He motioned for her to step up on the side of the boat, where there was a rubber pad, then held her hand as she jumped in. She tossed her bag into a sheltered corner.

"Sweatshirt and jacket," she explained. "And Mom insisted I bring bottled water and some of the cookies she'd just baked." She looked around the wide-open deck at the back of the boat. There was no wall across the back. "How big is this thing?"

"She's forty-eight feet long and almost twenty wide."

"Wow—that's a big boat to captain alone, isn't it?"

"Not if you know what you're doing." He sounded pompous. And technically, she wasn't wrong. On a rough day, a man could get in trouble alone on a boat this size. But he'd grown up on commercial boats, and manning them was second nature to him. Besides, the seas were fairly calm today.

"Well, ex-*cuse* me, Mr. Perfect." Lexi rolled her eyes. "I guess you don't need my help with the lines, then?"

He'd forgotten she had some boating experience. On *lakes*, but still.

"Sure. I've loosened them already, so once I'm in the cockpit and give you the nod, you can pull them in. And maybe pull up the fenders when we're underway and put them in the baskets there?" He nodded at the wire baskets inside the boat. She nodded and hopped up on the gunwale—the narrow area that allowed a sailor to walk from the back to the front deck of the boat. Sam gave the gauges one last check and, satisfied, told her they were ready. She flipped the loop of rope off the iron cleats on the dock and pulled it onto the boat.

The boat was moving slowly as he backed out, turned and carefully worked his way out of the harbor, around other boats on moorings, making sure he stuck to the marked channel. The tide was just heading out, but the levels were high enough to avoid trouble in here…for now. Lexi worked on pulling in the thick fenders that protected the boat from rubbing against the dock.

Once he got out to open water and made sure she was standing nearby and hanging on to the rail, he picked up speed, smiling at the steady sound of the engine below.

"You love it out here, don't you?"

He glanced at Lexi before he went back to scanning the horizon for other boats. It was a Tuesday, so there weren't many pleasure boaters, but there were still enough to keep an eye on. Boats didn't have brakes and could not stop on a dime like a car. Even if he cut the engines, momentum would carry the boat forward.

"It's what I know best," he answered. "Generations of Knights have boated these waters. I guess it's in my blood."

She was watching the shoreline fade behind them. "How far out are we going?"

"We'll be two or three miles offshore most of the way."

Lexi frowned. "So…in the middle of the ocean."

He chuckled. "Hardly. The ocean's a very big place." He looked her way again. "Lexi, we'd be in more danger *close* to the shore, from sandbars and rocks. Out here all we have to worry about is idiots like that."

A sleek powerboat to their left was skimming the waves as it raced out to sea, set to cross their path too close for Sam's comfort. He slowed the *Stella Dare* to give the guy plenty of space. The man at the helm never acknowledged their presence as they sped by, but three bikini-clad women waved enthusiastically.

"Don't you have the right of way as a bigger boat?"

"I had the right of way, but not because we were bigger. I was to that guy's right, which meant I had the right of way. But he wasn't even looking, so I gave him a wide berth. I don't know if he ever saw us. There's no need to be dead right, as my dad used to say."

Sam bit the inside of his lip, hoping the pain would push away the memories that kept popping up when Lexi was around. It's not that she *reminded* him of his family—his grandmother may have had some of Lexi's sass, but that was it. Grandma had been short, round and blue-eyed, with long pewter-colored hair she'd worn in a twist behind her head. His mother had been taller and more slender, with stylishly short blond hair. Mom had been more introverted than Grandma. She'd been happiest when she was working in her garden or curled up with a book, although she did like joining his father for a sunset cruise in nice weather.

Emotion clogged Sam's throat, choking him to the point where he could barely breathe. What the hell was happening? He could actually *see* them in his mind—the people he'd worked so hard to avoid remembering, because it hurt so damn much. And now...his chest was on fire and he realized he was gripping the ship's wheel to the point where his knuckles were turning white. He blinked a few times, forcing himself back under control, his teeth grinding tightly at the effort.

"What did your dad mean by that?" Lexi asked. "What's *dead right*?"

"I don't talk about my father." The words came automatically. A defense mechanism. He knew that, and was grateful for it.

"But you just said..." Lexi started to argue, then turned away, grumbling. "Never mind. Can I go below to check out the cabin?"

He gave a quick nod. "There's not much of a cabin on a commercial vessel, but go ahead. Just be sure to hang on to something so you don't get thrown if we change speeds or hit a bigger swell."

She went below without answering. He'd made her mad again. Or, worse, hurt her—again—with his blunt refusal to answer her questions. This trip really was the worst idea ever.

Chapter Thirteen

The *Stella Dare* was bigger than any boat Lexi had been on before, and far less luxurious. She understood it was a commercial boat, but there was *nothing* comfortable about it. The tiny cabin consisted of a small table, a barely there counter with a miniature sink and a microwave bolted down so it was secure during rougher seas. The head—she knew enough not to call it a *bathroom* on a boat—was the tiniest of wooden closets with a small marine toilet inside. The very front of the cabin held bunk beds in the V-berth. *Beds* was a stretch. More like wooden sleeping shelves with a thin cushion on them.

It was rustic. Serviceable. No frills whatsoever.

A lot like its current captain.

She peeked up at where Sam was sitting. He was busy watching the horizon, so she was able to study his profile without him noticing. There was no denying he was a good-looking man, but there was nothing soft about him. The muscles on his upper arms and shoulders were lean, hard and defined. She knew, from the night he came down the stairs to greet her and her mother with a fireplace poker, that his abdomen was the same.

His face was square-jawed and creased with lines from the sun. His nose would have been aquiline and classic, except for the slightest bend in it, indicating it had been broken sometime in the past. His hair, the color of dark chocolate and never exactly in place, was windblown now, showing his high forehead. Sam was squinting, creating deep crow's feet. His mouth was firm, in a straight line at the moment. Was he concentrating or was he angry?

It's not like *she'd* brought up his family. He was the one who'd shared something his dad had taught him, then bit her head off when she asked what it meant. The man was damn confusing!

Just then he looked down and saw her at the bottom of the steps. He'd caught her staring, so there was no sense looking away. His expression softened just a bit—the lines were less set in stone.

"You might want to hang on to something," he said. "I'm going to give her a run at full throttle to see how the engine sounds."

"Can I come up on deck first? It's a little...depressing down here. And noisy."

The corner of his mouth twitched as she came up to stand near him. "I told you it wasn't fancy." Once he saw her holding the metal bar in front of her, he pushed the throttle and the big boat lurched forward. The momentum made her clutch tightly.

"There are grab bars all over," she said. "Is there a nautical term for them?"

He had a real smile now, but barely. "We call them *oh-damn* handles. On rough seas or when the speed changes, even good sailors need to grab on."

The boat was slicing through the waves now. The engine was louder, but it didn't sound like it was straining. She cast another look at the wide-open back of the boat. It was like riding in the rear of a pickup truck with no tailgate. The boat was running level, but it still felt like it would be easy to just slide off the back if you weren't careful.

"It looks like something is missing…like the whole back of the boat." She felt her cap loosening in the wind and grabbed the brim to pull it down tighter.

"This boat will hold sixty or seventy lobster traps, stacked," Sam answered. "The traps are tied together, so once the first trap and marker go off the back, the other traps get pulled in one after the other like a chain as the boat goes forward. It's a lot easier than someone lifting each of those traps individually and tossing them over the side." He looked over his shoulder at the back of the boat. "And if the boat is rigged for tuna fishing, it makes it easier to get the bigger fish in the boat."

"How many people fall off the back?"

His eyebrows shot up. "Uh, not many. These guys—and women—know what they're doing and where the back of the boat is. If the seas are rough, they'll use lines to hook themselves to those bars on the side of the boat. I'm not saying commercial fishing isn't dangerous, because it is. But falling off the boat is generally a rookie move, or the sign of a bad captain."

The two of them seemed back on solid, noncontroversial ground now. Lexi hoped they could stay that way for the rest of the day. Sam seemed to feel the same way. He relaxed into the captain's chair and motioned for her to come closer. He'd throttled back on the engine a bit, but they were still moving at a good pace. There was a rocking motion that she hadn't felt in her river and lake boating experiences. Sam explained that ocean water moved in rounded swells rather than peaked waves, at least on mellow days like this.

"Trust me," he said grimly, "the ocean can be cruel and

unforgiving. I've been in twenty-foot waves before, and it's not something you want to do on purpose. Commercial fishermen see far worse than that."

She nodded. "I remember watching *The Perfect Storm* in the theater."

Sam stared out at the horizon for a long moment. "My dad lost a good friend in that storm. He'd been the best man at my parents' wedding."

Lexi was quiet. He'd made it very clear he didn't want to talk about his family, but...he kept doing it himself. She let it slide, and Sam began explaining the instrument panel in front of him—the depth finder, the gauges, the navigational screen that showed them as a small blinking dot off the southern shore of Cape Cod. They'd rounded the bend in the Cape, heading for Provincetown at the very tip.

She'd been to Provincetown by car twice. Once with her mom and once with Shelly, who was going there on a Friday afternoon to buy some art from a sculptor friend for her shop. It was a popular spot, with far more tourists than Winsome Cove saw. There were a lot of whale-watching cruises that left from there, as well as commercial fishing and pleasure boats. The heart of the town, though, felt like so many Cape Cod towns—small, with curving roads and clapboard shops in pastel shades.

And the traffic! It took Shelly and her well over an hour each way to make what should have been a half-hour drive at best. Shelly told her that in the offseason, it was a much easier trip, but like the other Cape towns, a lot of businesses closed up for at least part of the offseason. She'd enjoyed that day, and Shelly was becoming a good friend.

She hadn't expected that to happen this summer— making friends in Winsome Cove. But Shelly was funny, full of energy and told great stories. Carm was becoming a good friend, too. Widowed three years ago, she was the opposite of Shelly in many ways—quiet and bookish, but kindhearted to the core. The two women had grown up in Winsome Cove, but they'd welcomed Lexi into their circle without hesitation.

Sam pointed out the Cape Cod National Seashore, nearly forty miles of beach and dunes that started not far from Winsome Cove and stretched to Provincetown.

"When you get out on the beaches there in the offseason, it's like seeing Cape Cod in her natural state—windblown and pure."

She smiled. She liked it when Sam got poetic like that. He loved this place. It was part of him somehow, especially being out on the water. This was Sam in his element. A Sam not many people got to see. He'd moved her into the captain's seat—really the only comfortable spot to sit out on deck. But she wasn't fooling herself into thinking she was driving the boat. He was standing at her side, one hand on the wheel near hers, and the other near the throttle.

He pointed out a couple of commercial fishing boats farther out from shore, explaining how the riggings worked to pull in the nets or traps or fishing lines, depending on what they were fishing for. He slid her out of the seat when they rounded the end of the Cape and approached one of the marinas in Provincetown.

Bringing the big boat into dock was no problem for Captain Sam, but Lexi liked to think she helped a little. She put the large rubber fenders on the side of the boat to protect it, then went up to the front deck to toss the line to the two men on the dock who'd come to help. The large, heavily bearded older man was near the front of the boat, and his eyes went round when he spotted Lexi with the line.

"Damn, Sammy boy," he called out. "You've upgraded your crew! Toss it over, miss."

She did, then hurried to the back, but Sam had brought the boat so close to the dock that the young boy had already grabbed the rope and tied it to the dock cleat.

Sam introduced her to Callum Malloy and his grandson, Jacob, owners of the *Stella Dare* and two other lobster and tuna boats. Callum took her hand as she stepped from the side of the boat up to the dock.

"So Sam's teaching you how to run my boat, eh? Don't go gettin' any ideas, young lady. That girl's like my lucky penny, and she's not for sale." He turned to Sam, who'd joined them on the dock. "Did you get her back to purring again?"

Sam's eyes met Lexi's, and she blushed. Yeah, she had a feeling he could make her purr without trying very hard. But as close as they'd been on the long ride, the heat level had remained in the acceptable range. And, of course, Callum was talking about the boat.

He and Sam walked away to settle the bill. Jacob, in his early teens, gave her a bashful smile. "Never known Sam to bring any woman with him, on his boat or one of ours. You and he dating or somethin'?"

A bubble of laughter rose in her throat. "Not even close. I'm a chef at a restaurant in Winsome Cove, and I like to source my ingredients locally so I know who and where they come from. Sam offered to give me a ride on a genuine lobster boat and I accepted. We're barely friends." It was true. The boat ride had been friendly enough, but they still hardly knew each other. "You might say we're business associates."

Someone cleared his throat behind her. *Sam.*

"We are *not* business associates," he said. "You don't

work for or with me, and I definitely don't work for you."
He looked at Jacob. "She and I are just acquaintances. We
have mutual friends."

The boy, with his shaggy black hair, was at that weird
phase where his arms and legs seemed disproportionately
long and awkward in connection to his body. He looked
back and forth between Sam and Lexi.

"O-kay. I didn't need a podcast episode explaining what
you two *aren't*."

Sam gave Jacob a playful shoulder bump. "Sorry, kid.
Hey, where's my boat?" Jacob pointed to where a sleek, older
boat was docked.

The boat was as long as the *Stella Dare*, but was built
for pleasure, not commerce. Long, narrow windows lined
what must have been a spacious interior cabin. The boat was
white, although it had faded to ivory with age. There was a
fly bridge above deck, where the captain's console was located. There was an elegance to the boat that Lexi honestly
didn't associate with Sam. The name on the back, in elegant
blue script, was *Katydid*.

"*That's* your boat?" she blurted out. "All that boat for
one guy?"

One eyebrow rose. "Are you suggesting it's too much
boat for me to handle?"

Jacob laughed behind them. "Too much for Sam? That's
a good one! Mom and I waxed her from stem to stern, and
Mom shampooed all the carpeting and upholstery. Chuck
power-washed the engines. Should be good as new."

Sam said that he'd offered to accept a full detailing of
his boat as partial payment for the engine rebuild on the
Stella Dare. It was a service the Provincetown marina offered and he did not. On the way here, he'd explained that

the Malloys were having a tough time keeping their operation going, so he hadn't minded bartering.

"Chuck took us out on her for a spin," Jacob said. "For an antique, she runs great."

Sam laughed. "Watch how you use that word *antique*, kid. The boat's from the 1980s, not the 1800s. She might qualify for *vintage*, but not antique."

Sam helped Lexi onto the boat. It was easier than getting on the lobster boat because there was a wide swim platform across the back. Jacob began loosening the lines from the dock. The back deck was small compared to the length of the boat, but there were two upholstered chairs bolted to the deck. She assumed they were for deep-sea fishing, since they had chrome fishing-pole holders and seat belts.

"Did you see the new Hatteras over at the long dock?" Jacob asked. "They're just here for the week." He pointed at a dark blue yacht, even longer than the *Katydid*. His voice rose with excitement. "Gramps says it cost over a million dollars! Is yours worth that much? If so, you should sell it and retire."

Sam was headed up to the bridge to start the engines. He stopped at the top of the steps and looked down at Jacob in disbelief. "A minute ago she was an antique, and now you think the *Katydid*'s worth a million dollars? Not even close, buddy. Also not close? Me and retirement age."

Jacob threw up his hands and laughed. "Sorry, Sam! For an old… I mean *vintage* boat, the *Katydid* can fly at full throttle. Oh, and Chuck topped off the fuel tanks for you, so you don't have to worry about that."

Lexi could tell from the way Sam's body went still for just a split second that he wasn't happy. He'd had the same reaction the first time Jacob mentioned this Chuck guy. But he smiled back at Jacob, not showing the boy his concern.

"That's great, Jacob. Tell him I said thanks. You gonna cast us off?"

There was something in his tone that told Lexi that Sam didn't think it was *great* at all.

Sam did his best to hide his annoyance from the kid. Jacob's stepdad wasn't a skilled boater by any means. Chuck had married into the business and was trying…sort of. But Chuck was cheap, and the Malloys didn't sell fuel at their marina. He was willing to bet Chuck bought the crappiest fuel he could find. The fact that Chuck had taken it upon himself to take Sam's boat out for a joy ride didn't sit right, either, even though everything looked fine. The engines started right up with a familiar purr. Sam started to relax.

Jacob unlooped the lines off the dock cleat and handed off the back line to Lexi, then ran up front to untie the ropes, fastening them to the loop on the railing of the front deck. The boy was getting good training from his grandfather and was a natural around boats. Sam waved goodbye, smoothly backed the boat out of the slip and headed out to the open water.

Lexi was bringing in the fenders and placing them in the baskets attached to the rails. Sam frowned at the sky. They'd be lucky to get back to Winsome Cove by dark, but at least the seas were relatively calm.

Lexi came up the chrome ladder to the bridge to join Sam. There were two captain's chairs side by side up at the helm, and she slid into the seat next to his.

"Wow, this boat has just as many gauges and computer screens as the lobster boat had," she said. "It's a pleasure boat, right?"

He nodded. "She's rigged for deep-sea fishing, and I do the occasional charter day trip on her."

"Why are boats and ships always *she*?"

"My grandfather said it was because ships are unpredictable, just like a woman." Sam noted how unimpressed Lexi was by that answer, and went on to explain. "Different generation, sorry. He meant it as a joke. But ships have been female for centuries. They were originally named for goddesses, and the feminine just sorta stuck. Maybe because, like a mother, a ship protects you."

"Okay." They cruised for a while in silence before Lexi sat back and put her bare feet on the railing. She'd pulled off her cap now that the sun was lower in the sky, and her hair was waving around her face. She ran her hands on the side of her head to tame it long enough to look at him. "Where did the name *Katydid* come from?"

Sam swallowed hard. He should have anticipated that question and steered the conversation away from boats and women and mothers. But he'd already barked at her once today for an innocent comment. And, honestly, looking into her eyes, it didn't feel quite so scary to talk about his family.

"My grandmother's name was Katherine. Everyone called her Katy, with a *y*. My grandfather bought this boat new in 1987, and named it after his nickname for Grandma—*Katydid*."

The only sound was the rumble of the engines and the wind moving through the bridge. The bridge was partially protected, with a low windshield, and was covered with a solid fiberglass roof above. On rainy days, there were zippered canvas sides that dropped down for more protection. It was warm enough today to leave it open. Sam thought he heard a little sputter from below, but only for a moment. The gauges looked fine.

"Why don't you like Chuck?"

The question surprised him.

"What makes you think I don't like Chuck?" He *didn't* like the guy much, but he thought he'd kept his feelings to himself.

"Your body language changed when his name came up—especially when Jacob said Chuck had taken your boat out and topped off the engines with gas."

"Diesel, not gas."

The answer was automatic. He was still thinking about how Lexi had picked up on his feelings. He wasn't sure how he felt about that. But she had noticed, and she was waiting for an answer. He checked the gauges again—had the tachometer on the starboard engine just wiggled? No, it looked okay now. Sam blew out a breath.

"Chuck's okay. He's good to Jacob and Barb. He's just not the best with boats. Or with me, for no good reason."

Lexi's right eyebrow arched. "There must be *some* reason."

He shrugged. "Barb's first husband, Ken, was my best friend from grade school, or maybe even before that. My parents were good friends with Callum and his late wife, Susan. Ken died when Jacob was a newborn."

"Oh, no," Lexi said softly. "What happened?"

"Afghanistan happened." Sam frowned at the gauges. The tachometers kept wavering, and he'd heard a few small breaks in the engine's rumble. He'd rebuilt those engines himself—they shouldn't ever knock or skip. Then everything steadied again. "Ken joined the marines right out of high school. Met Barb and moved her to P-town to be with his parents while he deployed. He came home for Jacob's birth, then had to go back, and…a roadside bomb killed him a few months later."

There was a long beat of silence between them.

"That's horrible," Lexi finally said. "But why is Chuck mad at *you*?"

"I don't know if he's *mad* at me, but I think he's got it in his head that I'm some sort of rival. I've known the family longer than him. I've known Barb longer than him. I'm Jacob's godfather. I grew up around boats and marinas, and Chuck grew up somewhere in Pennsylvania." The gauges faltered again, and he definitely heard a skip in the engines. Both of them this time. Then they smoothed out. *What the hell?*

"What's wrong?" Lexi heard it, too.

"Nothing. Everything's fine." *He hoped.*

"So you lost your grandparents and parents, and then your best friend? I can't imagine…"

"No, you can't." Tension rose in his chest, and his voice was sharper than he intended. He didn't want to revisit those awful years. Not ever. Before he could apologize, the boat slowed abruptly and pulled hard to the right. The starboard engine had stalled out completely. *Son of a…*

"What's happening?" Lexi asked. "And don't tell me *nothing.*" She sat up and slid into her deck shoes. Sam didn't answer, too busy trying to restart the engine. It caught, then sputtered, then stopped.

"The starboard engine cut out, and I have no idea why." He looked at her. "Can you keep us going straight for a few minutes while I go check it out?"

"How are we going anywhere with no engine?"

"There are *two* engines. The boat will tug to the right with only the left propeller turning, so you'll have to keep correcting it. Keep us about the same distance off the shoreline." He stood, indicating Lexi should slide over to his seat behind the wheel. "We're going slow. Just keep it going straight. That's it."

She didn't look convinced. "Can we get home on one engine?"

"Sure, but it'll take longer."

A lot longer.

"Why don't we pull into a marina and get it fixed?"

Sam reminded himself that she was new at this, but he didn't manage to keep all the sarcasm out of his voice when he gestured toward the sandy shoreline in the distance.

"Do you see a marina anywhere? It's just the national seashore for miles. Take the wheel and let me see what the problem is."

He had a hunch, but if that was the case, both engines would be...

The port engine began to skip and sputter.

Oh, shit.

There was silence as the boat rocked to a stop, turning just enough to take the waves from the side. The bridge was well above the center fulcrum of the keel, meaning a little sway on the lower deck translated to several feet of swaying up here.

"Sam..." Lexi wasn't panicked, but he heard the worry in her voice. He put his hand on her shoulder.

"We're okay. We don't need the engines to float." The boat rocked some more, and Lexi grabbed the rail, her face pale. "Lexi, I've been in seas so rough this bridge was almost laying in the waves, and this boat never came close to sinking. I promise you, we're safe."

When a boat took waves along its side, it created a weird sliding motion. If she was going to be seasick, this would be the time. But Lexi didn't look sick. Just scared. He wanted to check the engines, but he could see she wasn't going to let him out of her sight right now.

He looked at the electronic charts overlaying their GPS coordinates. There was a bay not far from their location. It was more like a bend in the beach, but it looked like it would be enough to protect them from larger waves, so they could drop anchor. It was in a part of the national seashore that wasn't inhabited, but it would provide shelter overnight. He just had to coax the engines to run long enough to get them there.

He put his hands on Lexi's waist and gently moved her back to the other seat. "I've got an idea. Cross your fingers, okay?"

She gave a quick nod. The starboard engine fired, but sounded like someone had put rocks in it. It managed to propel the boat for a few minutes before sputtering out. He immediately started the port engine and did the same until it died out. Back and forth, with each engine getting more and more resistant to starting. For one five-minute stretch, he had *both* of them running, and that's when he made the turn toward shore, holding the boat in line despite the waves now pushing at the back corner. The small bay was straight ahead. The starboard engine quit, but he gave the throttle a push on the port engine to shoot the big boat forward.

For one scary moment, both engines died as the boat was cutting through the surf. It started to turn sideways, then he got the starboard engine going again and shot into the bay, stopping as soon as he'd cleared the rougher water. He checked the depth finder and winced. There was barely a foot of water beneath the *Katydid* right now. Thank God, the tide was coming in instead of out. They should be able to stay afloat and keep from grounding overnight.

He turned the boat to face the ocean and dropped anchor before turning off the engines and letting out a long sigh of relief. That hadn't been easy, and could have gone wrong a dozen different ways. He wasn't sure if Lexi's silence the entire time was because she was trying to help him concentrate, or because she was terrified. Maybe both. Now he had to break the news to her.

"I don't suppose you brought a change of clothes?" he asked, trying to sound lighthearted.

What color she'd had left in her face drained completely.

"What are you saying?"

"I'm saying we're here for the night."

"Why can't we just call someone to come pick us up? Mom can drive to the park. Or someone could come by boat…"

"Lexi, I don't want to spend the night here any more than you do. But no one's getting anywhere close to this beach by car, so we'd have to walk out, and it's going to be dark soon. If I'm right, we'll need a tow, and that's best done in daylight." Her mouth opened, but no words came out. She looked out over the front deck of the boat, which was pointed toward the open water, bobbing gently against the anchor line. He'd drop a smaller anchor off the back, too, so the boat wouldn't spin while they slept. He smiled at her expression, keeping his voice low and calm. He didn't need Lexi panicking out here.

"This boat is a floating cottage. She's made for over-night trips. The weather's supposed to stay quiet until later tomorrow. You can have the bed, and I'll sleep on the sofa. We'll be safe and comfortable, *and* I'll have a chance to check the engines and see exactly what happened. But I have a feeling I already know. *Chuck* happened."

"You think he sabotaged the boat?"

"No, no, not on purpose." Sam quickly dismissed the idea. "It sounds like there's water in the fuel. Chuck probably topped off the tanks with the cheapest diesel he could find. Not maliciously, but because he's a tightwad."

That meant Sam would have to drain the tanks when

he got back to Winsome Cove, making this an expensive business barter. But there was nothing he could do about it now, other than let Devlin know that he was going to need a tow in the morning.

His cousin was definitely going to bring this story up for the rest of their lives. Actually, he and Lexi would probably *both* hear about this from their friends and families when they got home. But that didn't mean anything had to happen tonight other than sleep. They were two adults who could behave themselves for one night.

Some of the tension left Lexi's posture. "What are we going to do for food?"

He chuckled. "Barb always sends me back with a few meals in the fridge. Jacob said something about shrimp scampi. I promise we won't starve. This isn't ideal, but it's not a disaster, either."

She didn't look convinced, but then again, she hadn't seen the inside of the cabin. The generator ran off the same fuel tank as the engines, so they wouldn't have electricity, but that wouldn't be a big problem on a warm night like tonight. He had some LED lanterns they could use for light. "Come on, I'll show you how *un*rustic tonight will be."

Spending the night on the boat was not a problem. Spending the night on the boat with *Lexi* was going to be…interesting.

Chapter Fourteen

With a drink in her hand and the gentle rocking of the *Katydid* under stars so bright it looked like she could reach up and touch one, Lexi came to a bit of a revelation.

"It seems—" she tipped her red plastic cup in Sam's direction "—that I like boats after all. Quite a bit, actually." She leaned back on the slanted large window, with a cushion behind her for comfort. Sam was in a similar pose at her side, legs stretched out. They were reclining on the front deck, with a bottle of chardonnay between them.

Barb had put a large enough container of shrimp scampi in the refrigerator to feed both of them easily. Luckily, she'd included cooked linguine. Lexi warmed it all in a skillet on the propane stove, adding an extra splash of wine. She'd toasted some crumbled garlic bread in a separate pan and sprinkled it over the scampi for texture. Barb had also sent several squares of her blueberry-lemon cake.

Sam was right about this boat being a floating cottage. She'd been amazed not only at the tiny, yet fully functional, galley kitchen, but also at the rest of the living space on board.

From the back deck, they'd entered the salon, with windows all around—the ones they were leaning back against now—and a low navy blue sectional occupying two sides.

There was also a recliner, a flat-screen TV and various tables and cupboards. Down four steps was the galley, and beyond that was a bathroom—or *head*—and the main cabin, complete with a queen-size platform bed. In and under every nook and cranny was storage space—doors, drawers, even narrow closets. The boat wasn't over-the-top fancy, but extremely comfortable and practical. She glanced sideways at Sam. Everything Sam owned was just like him.

Sam's eyes were closed and his head was resting against the window. He was holding his red cup in his lap. It hadn't spilled, so she assumed he was still awake, or amazingly coordinated. He had to be exhausted after hours at the helm, and then the stress of both engines failing.

Once he'd gotten the boat double-anchored, they'd both called and texted everyone who needed to know where they were. It was Tuesday night, so thank goodness the restaurant was closed, and Sam had assured her she'd be back in time to open it tomorrow afternoon. Devlin would bring his lobster boat to the bay in the morning and tow them back to the marina.

They both heard and read their share of childish comments about the circumstances, with several people wondering what the sleeping arrangements were. Carm, an avid romance reader, had even texted Lexi, "OMG Just One Boat!"

It felt like the whole town must be buzzing with delight over the situation. But there'd be no funny business out here, because neither of them wanted that. Sure, they'd had a couple of close calls before tonight. And now, they were here on this boat. It was a big boat, but not *that* big. And they'd be here all night.

With nothing but starlight and this strange tremor in the

air between them right now. It was almost shimmering. Pulsating. Did he feel it, too?

"Why are you staring at me?" Sam didn't move as he spoke, but clearly his eyes hadn't been as tightly closed as she'd thought. Her cheeks burned when she realized she couldn't even deny it. She *had* been staring. And why not? He was one fine specimen of a man. Even in starlight. *Especially* in starlight. His head turned to look at her now. "Is there something crawling on me or what?"

She snapped her gaze away. "Sorry. No. And I wasn't staring *at* you, just looking in your direction. But not really thinking about anything, just..." She was the world's worst liar.

"Thinking about how much you suddenly enjoy boats now that you're stranded on one?"

She returned his half smile. "I enjoy *this* kind of boat." She glanced up at the sky. "This kind of night." *And this kind of man...*

Sam sat up with a sigh. "We lucked out in a lot of ways, especially the weather." He followed her gaze up to the stars. "It's a nice spot to drop anchor. The meal was great." He paused. "And the company's okay, too."

"Only okay?" she teased.

He shifted to face her, his eyes dark and intense. "Let's just say the night sky and wine seem to have calmed your usually sharp tongue. And mine, too, I guess. We haven't snapped at each other once since we anchored."

It was true. She'd had some opinions on the condition of some of the cooking utensils in the galley, including one pot that had *rust* on it. He'd laughed it off, and after dinner, they'd come up onto the deck, where the air was cooler.

With food in their stomachs, their moods had mellowed even more. The wine hadn't hurt, either. She took a sip of hers, and Sam pulled the cork out of the bottle and poured more in both cups. *Good job, Sam.*

They'd been up here for over an hour. They'd hardly spoken—which might also explain the lack of snark between them—but the silence had been relaxed and easy. There was something about the warm salt air that was nearly hypnotic. Almost sensual.

"It's hard to feel testy out here," she agreed. "It's sort of magical the way it clears your head and erases your worries. It's like being in a time warp. With no civilization in sight, it could be the twenty-first century or the eighteenth."

"Yeah." Was his voice huskier than before? She glanced at him through her eyelashes. He was the one staring this time. His gaze wandered from her face down her body, and she felt goose bumps rise on every inch of skin his eyes took in.

There was another long moment of silence. It wasn't as easy as before, though. It hung heavy between them. Maybe it was the wine. Maybe she was just tired. Maybe her imagination was running wild because she'd been without a man for so long.

What was Sam thinking over there? Did he feel the same vibe going on that she did? The corner of his mouth lifted.

"I know today—*tonight*—is way more adventure than you'd planned on. You've been a good sport about all this, Lex."

She took another sip of her wine, trying to keep her hand from shaking. She didn't usually like her name being shortened even further than it already was, but hearing him calling her *Lex* gave her full-body shivers. She tried to clear her throat. If he wasn't feeling this ridiculous heat, she'd make a fool of herself if she made a move. *Keep things light, Lexi.*

"You don't need to keep sounding so surprised, you know."

"Sorry." He leaned close above her. *So not helping.* "It's just that... I like it."

"What...?" What was he saying? "You like *what*?"

"You," he answered. "I like this softer you." He grimaced. "That sounded condescending as hell, didn't it? That's not the way I meant it. It's just...different. And... I like it. But I like Strong Lexi, too."

He was even closer now. He took the cup from her hand and set it aside. She looked up at his face, with the starry sky behind it.

What. Was. Happening?

Sam stared down at her, but didn't come any closer. Neither of them moved. All her senses were on fire. She could hear her pulse swooshing through her veins. She felt the heat from his body, now even closer to hers. He'd jumped in the water briefly after they'd anchored to wash away his sweat, but she could still smell it on him, mixed with diesel and saltwater. She took in a long breath, closing her eyes. Everything was perfect. Except for the fact that they weren't touching.

She opened her eyes and gave him a saucy grin.

"Are you gonna kiss me or not?"

All he'd needed was the invitation, because his mouth was on hers in an instant. Hard, firm lips pressed her mouth open, his tongue boldly taking what he wanted as she moaned and let him in. His arm wrapped around her waist and pulled her under him, his other hand behind her head to cushion her from the window. She reached up and wrapped her arms around his neck, pulling her body up to meet his, returning the kiss just as fiercely as him. Their heads turned for better access, their teeth clicked together at one point and neither backed off. They were two starving people, devouring each other.

His body weight was on her now, and she'd never been so angry at the concept of clothing before in her life. She wanted nothing between them. She grabbed at his T-shirt, tugging it up and shoving her hands beneath it so she could touch his skin. He growled into their kiss, which hadn't slowed one bit. Her nails dug into his back and he growled again, shifting so his thigh was between her legs, pressing against her until they were both rocking together.

Holy... She hadn't been dry-humped since college, and it had never done a thing for her. But now? With Sam? Her mind went white-hot with desire. That low glow she always had deep in her belly when she was around Sam blazed into an all-consuming fire. It didn't matter if it was smart or not—and it probably wasn't. She didn't care that they were in the open night air—that was actually part of the sexiness. She didn't care that the fiberglass deck beneath her was hard and unforgiving. She wanted to make love with Sam Knight right here and right the hell now.

She tugged at his shirt again, and with a curse he pulled away from the kiss and yanked it over his head, then tossed it to the side. Maybe in the water. *Who cares?* His hair was wild as he looked down at her. Her fingers must have done that, standing it on end. His eyes were slightly glazed and fully dark. She smiled proudly. She'd done *that*, too. One kiss had rocked him just as much as it had rocked her.

She'd known they had chemistry. She'd known they'd be good if they ever reached this point. But she'd never expected *this*. The desperation. The rush. The intensity. The way her brain became laser-focused, with no thoughts other than *how can I get physically closer to this man*?

He ground his thigh between her legs and she let out a

moan as her head fell back. He smiled… Was that *pride* she saw there? Was he feeling as powerful as she was?

"You like that, don't you, Lex?" The words had been ground through his clenched teeth, like he was holding himself back.

Did he really think she'd deny it?

"Hell yes, I like that. I want you." Her words came out on frantic breaths. "Naked. Now. Here."

He fell on her again, pulling her tight and plunging his tongue in her mouth. *Sweet baby Jesus.* This man knew how to kiss. She tried to return it, but the truth was her body was turning to jelly. She was nothing but sensation, every nerve ending sparking and pulsing. Sam lifted his head, then closed his eyes and shook it back and forth.

"Woman…" He blew out a long sigh, resting his forehead on hers. "What are we doing? This has *trouble* written all over it."

She put her hands on the sides of his head, tugging his hair until he lifted up again and met her gaze. She saw the doubts building, but she was not ready to call it quits.

"We are two very grown-up people who are single and horny and we are going to make—" She caught herself before saying the *L* word out loud. "We are going to have sex on the deck of this boat under the stars and it is going to be every bit as good as that kiss."

"And after that?"

"After that, we'll have all night to do it again and again until morning." There was no doubt in her mind that they'd want to. "And after *that*, who cares? We'll have had one incredible night. You *know* it will be incredible."

He nodded and smiled slowly. "I think that's a given. But—"

"No *buts*." She put her finger against his lips. "We're

both old enough and smart enough to know there's no fairy-tale ending ahead. All we're doing tonight is scratching an itch. Enjoying our chemistry without the need to get emotions involved. I'm not looking for a boyfriend, and I don't think you're in the market for a relationship."

Sam kissed a fingertip and moved her hand from his lips. "I suck at relationships."

"So there you have it…oh…" He'd pressed himself against her again. And this time it wasn't his thigh. He was hard as timber inside his shorts.

He dropped his head so that he was breathing his words right into her ear. "No emotions. No boyfriend-girlfriend messiness. Just us enjoying each other all night long." He was still moving against her, and he bit back another curse. She had the feeling that when he unleashed everything he was holding back, things were going to get very interesting. She turned her head, taking a nip of his ear and reveling in his full-body shudder.

"No emotions. No mess. Just very, *very* physical."

He took the opportunity to bite her ear now, holding the lobe in his teeth for a few seconds before releasing it and kissing her softly.

"I think we have a deal, Miss Bellamy."

Crazy. Stupid. Dangerous.

Yup. Sam knew this was all of those things. This was Lexi Bellamy. Usually a pain right in his behind. A woman who didn't like his hometown and didn't like *him* all that much.

She let out a soft moan of surrender beneath him, rolling her head and exposing her long, silky neck. He brushed her skin with his lips, and then nibbled her throat, right where her pulse fluttered. She gasped his name and that was it.

Future complications be damned—he was taking Lexi tonight and there wasn't a doubt in his mind that they were going to be spectacular together. He left a trail of kisses up her neck and across her jawline. She was quivering in his arms, eyes rolled back in ecstasy. And they were still fully clothed.

Yeah, this was going to be one hell of a night, alright.

He caught sight of her plastic cup, now on its side, with wine running along the deck. Without thinking, he reached out and ran his fingertips through the puddle. He traced it against her lips and watched her eyes snap open at the taste. His hand slid lower, brushing over her top, circling the rigid peaks of her breasts, then running down her stomach to the top of her shorts. She arched her back and gasped when his hand went inside her underwear, tracing her other lips with wine. He was obsessed with the idea of tasting her now. But one question needed to be answered.

"Lex, we've both had some wine. I don't want you to have any regrets. Are you sure…?"

She was still twisting and pressing against his hand inside her shorts, but her eyes were clear and serious when she answered.

"I'm not drunk, Sam. I appreciate you being honorable. Really—it's adorable and sexy and…decent. I promise I'm fully aware of what I'm proposing and I'm not going to change my mind."

He stopped. "Hey, you can change your mind at any point. I just want to be sure this…this idea…is being considered with a clear head."

"Do you want me to count backward from a hundred or something?" Sarcasm dripped from her voice. "I could get up and stand on one leg, but I'll be honest—I've never been the most balanced person and being on a boat might complicate things. Got a Breathalyzer handy? I've only had two glasses of wine, Sam, and one of them spilled. Trust me, I'm sober enough to go through with this." She started to giggle. "You can't be too terribly worried about it, since your hand is still in my pants."

He moved his fingers against her now, grinning when she gasped.

"You have a point," he said. "But there's not much room in there. Maybe those pants should come off—"

Her hands were unbuttoning her shorts before he could finish. He dipped his fingers in the spilled wine again, then touched them to the warm, wet spot between her legs. Without another thought, he slid down to do what he'd been dying to do—put his mouth where his fingers were. She tasted of wine and was slick with desire. He put her legs over his shoulders and it wasn't long at all until she cried out his name and gave a little squeal of release.

Lexi was spent, staring up to the sky with her lips softly parted, her chest rising and falling slowly. *Oh, hell no.* That wasn't the end. It was just the beginning. He wanted more of her. He wanted all of her.

He crawled up, helping her tug her shirt over her head. Her bra was simple cotton, with a bit of lace trim and a tiny pink bow in the center. She arched her back and reached back to unhook it.

When her breasts fell free of it, Sam felt like a teenager who'd never seen a woman's chest before. They weren't large, but they were beautiful. Perfect. He buried his face between them, holding them in his hands. As he toyed with them—pinching, nibbling, stroking—she moved beneath him, writhing and sighing with pleasure.

He wanted more.

She did, too. Her hands were pulling at his belt buckle,

working to remove his shorts. They pushed them off together, freeing him. And making him realize something was missing. Something important.

He ran one hand down her back, cupping her bottom. "This deck might be a little hard on your back for what I've got in mind for us. The bed will be more comfortable."

Her soft huff of laughter was deep and sexy. He wanted more of *that*, too.

"The deck won't be a problem if I'm not the one on the bottom."

He didn't think he could get any harder, until she put *that* picture in his mind. But the deck wasn't the only problem.

"I don't have condoms up here, babe. There are some in the cabin…"

She didn't hesitate, sitting up with a quick smile.

"Well, when you put it that way, I guess we'd better get down to the cabin."

They left the cushions on the deck, grabbing only their clothes, the cups and the wine bottle. She was laughing as she hurried in front of him.

"Why doesn't this feel weird, Sam? We should feel weird, right?" She glanced over her shoulder. "I mean, we're buck naked and carrying all this stuff. It's *weird*. But…it doesn't feel weird."

She was babbling. Was she nervous? She went into the salon and they dropped their things on the sectional. She turned for the stairs, but he took her hand and turned her toward him.

"Having second thoughts?" he asked. Her eyebrows leaped high on her forehead.

"Uh…no." She stepped closer. In the soft lantern light, he could see flecks of gold in her eyes as she studied him. "I was just saying it was weird that we're already okay with walking around naked with each other. I mean…look at us…" She gestured down, then looked up at him through long eyelashes.

"I'm looking. And, yeah, maybe it's weird, but this whole physical thing we have going on is weird. There's absolutely no reason for us to be attracted to each other." He pulled her closer. "This is the perfect situation. We're out in the middle of nowhere. No one will know."

She laughed up at him. "No one? Every single person back home asked me about the sleeping arrangements tonight. They all *want* this to happen for some reason."

"No. They want a *relationship* to happen for some reason. We're not doing that. We're just gonna rock this old boat for a few hours tonight, satisfy our curiosity and then move on with our lives when we get back to Winsome Cove."

Chapter Fifteen

Lexi rolled over in the dark and had no idea where she was. It wasn't her bed. Wasn't a room she recognized. She stretched and realized her body was achy. But in a heavy, warm, delicious way.

She blinked a few times, trying to adjust her eyes to the very faint light coming through an odd, horizontal window. The room was small. With lots of wood paneling. And it was *moving*—gently rocking. Her breath caught.

The *Katydid*. The fog cleared from her mind in an instant.

She started to turn, but a strong arm tightened around her waist, holding her in place. There was a grumble behind her, then silence.

Sam. They were spooning—her back to his front—and he was clinging to her as if he thought she might bolt. She might have thought about it if they weren't on a boat anchored in the ocean in the middle of the night. A shiver of fear ran over her.

Not fear of Sam. But fear of what this night might end up meaning for both of them. Fear of what could happen if the rest of the night went anything like the past few hours had.

She'd known they'd be good together, so that part didn't scare her—she'd had good sex before. She'd just never had sex like *that* before. And she had no idea what to do about it. Running was an attractive option. But that would mean they couldn't do it again, and she really, really wanted to make love with Sam again. And *again*.

It had started with their naked dash from the front deck to the salon. There'd been a slight pause while Sam verified one last time that they wanted the same thing—to satisfy their curiosity about what they could have together physically for just one night, and then forget it. Go back to their lives in the morning, no strings attached.

Once they'd both agreed, it had been off to the races. Scorching-hot kisses, hands flying over skin, a mad scramble down the four steps to the lower level without releasing each other.

Sam had basically tossed her onto the mattress, clamoring up after her like a starving man. It had only taken him a few seconds to grab and put on a condom, and then he was on her. Were there words? She didn't remember any. Just moans and gasps and sounds of absolute lust, as they came together and pounded their way to a swift and ecstatic release.

It was wild, hard and fast. And, oh, so satisfying. Not just the orgasmic release, but the way they were so in sync with each other. Equally desperate, and equally eager to please the other. As wild as it was, there was never a moment when she'd felt Sam wasn't focused completely on pleasing her. From the way his firm grip would turn tender at just the right moment, to the way his gaze stayed connected with hers. There'd been no need for words.

They laid together in the dark, sweat slicking their skin as they caught their breaths. And then…they'd done it all over again. The second time was slightly less wild and frantic, but it was no less intense. It hardly seemed possible, but it was even *better* the second time. The touches were softer.

The kisses more intimate. The positions more inventive, but still without awkwardness. He would guide her hips and she'd follow without question. She'd push his shoulder and he'd roll over immediately to give her a chance on top.

It was absolutely perfect. That's what was so frightening. How could they be expected to follow that performance? With each other, or with anyone else ever in their lives? How would they be able to see each other around town and *not* immediately drag each other to bed?

"I can feel your heart starting to race," Sam mumbled behind her. "What's going on inside your head?"

Blind panic is what's going on! She blew out a long breath and turned in his arms to face him in the darkness, staying in the circle of his embrace.

"I'm just..." She wasn't ready to dump all of her worries on him. "Wondering what time it is."

"No you weren't, but—" he reached up to the shelf by the head of the bed and tapped his phone screen "—it's one o'clock." He brushed her hair off her face, his fingers warm on her skin. Damn, she wanted him again. The glow of his phone screen must have been enough for him to read her thoughts, because he gave her a sly grin. "That means we have approximately five hours until daylight, and seven hours until we start looking for my cousin's arrival. What do you think we should do with all those hours?"

The screen went dark, and so did the room. Lexi nestled closer, with her head on his chest and his chin resting against her forehead. "What I *want* to do and what I *should* do are two different things."

"Ah...that explains what you were fretting about. You're trying to apply logic to what happened tonight. I'm not sure that will work." His hand cupped the back of her head, holding her gently, making her feel protected and safe. "Tonight is our one-time shot, remember? Have all the fun we can, then move on."

Was it possible that he hadn't felt the same mind-blowing experience that she had? Had this been *just sex* for him? Or worse—just *average* sex?

His hand slid to her chin, tilting her face toward his. "Hey." His voice was deep and tender. "I didn't mean to dismiss what we did as just a good time. It was a lot more than that. We were…epic together. Better than I'd dreamed, and my dreams were pretty great."

She couldn't help smiling. "You dreamed about us having sex?"

"Absolutely. Come on, you know there's been a buzz between us almost from the first time we saw each other. Sometimes I've fallen asleep cursing you, but…my dreams were about this. Lesser versions of this, of course, but my mind did its best to picture it."

"We're very good together," she agreed. "In bed, anyway."

"We were pretty good up on deck, too," he teased, reminding her of the way he'd ignited her with just his fingers. She nodded against him.

"This is nice." Like their naked dash below deck, they were surprisingly natural and relaxed with each other. His arm tightened briefly.

"It is." The boat rocked as a series of larger waves came into the bay. "The wake from some ship passing by the coastline. You still think you might like boating after all?"

Lexi huffed a soft laugh. "Like I said, I like it in a boat like this. The *Katydid* is very comfy. Your grandparents had very good taste." The casual comment was out before she could stop it. She didn't want to put a wet blanket on their night by mentioning his family. "Sorry. Forget I said that."

He hesitated, his body tensing ever so briefly against

hers. Then he sighed softly, his breath blowing across her hair in the darkness.

"It's okay. They loved this boat. They used to take it to Boston or Nantucket for little overnight getaways."

"You mean this isn't the first time *Katydid* has seen some action?"

Sam's laugh was quick and sharp. "Jesus. I didn't need *that* image in my head." He paused. "But I'm sure you're right. They were pretty frisky, and very much in love. Just like my parents."

"Tell me about them…" She wasn't sure how far to push. "I mean, if you want to."

The pause was much longer this time, and she thought he was going to shut down the conversation. Then his lips brushed the top of her head and he pressed a kiss there.

"The Knights have owned the marina, and most of Wharf Street, for a hundred years or more. Grandpa took over in the 1950s. He and Grandma were high-school sweethearts. She was the daughter of a lobsterman, so she knew boats and the ocean as well as most men did at the time. She was a feisty thing—five foot two, but every inch of her was pure sass. She didn't take crap from anyone."

Lexi was almost afraid to breathe, for fear of spoiling the moment. This was the most she'd heard him talk about the past. Sam continued.

"It was Grandma who'd suggested fixing up the Wharf Street businesses way back when. The real-estate market started to pop in the eighties, and she put three of the buildings up for sale. That's the money that bought the *Katydid*. This boat was going to be their retirement home. Grandpa had promised her they'd cruise up and down the coast, following the warm weather. She'd started making her packing lists, when…"

The silence made the room seem even smaller. Lexi knew if she spoke it would break the spell, so she waited.

"My parents had taken over the marina and the fishing boats by then." Sam skipped past the tragedy, and she was okay with that, as long as he kept talking. He *needed* to talk about this. He chuckled softly. "Dad leased the boats out to commercial crews because he'd never liked the hours of a fisherman. He blamed it on Mom, but he was never a morning guy."

"Why did he blame your mom?" Lexi couldn't stay silent any longer, and she hoped she hadn't spoiled things. But Sam seemed relaxed still.

"He said she didn't want him to be gone to sea for so many hours, but Mom always laughed when she heard that story. She said she might be a spoiled city girl, but she understood the concept of working and she was perfectly capable of running the marina when Dad was gone." Sam paused. "And she was, too. She had a different sort of strength from my grandmother, but her spine was solid steel when anyone pushed her. Including my father—they could fight as passionately as they…" He swallowed hard. "As passionately as they loved each other."

"How did they meet?"

"It was a total fluke. Mom grew up in San Francisco. Her parents were wealthy, and they came to the Cape for a family vacation while Mom was in college. She and Dad bumped into each other at the Salty Knight one evening… literally. She was with a cousin and turned around from the bar, making some gesture with her arm. Dad had been walking by with a tray holding glasses and a pitcher of beer…which Mom ended up wearing."

"Oh, no!" Lexi laughed.

"Yup. She and Dad got into an argument, but he eventually gave her a bar T-shirt to wear over her soaked dress, and he comped their drinks for the night. Then he walked her back to her motel and...they were married the week after she graduated college."

"That's quite a love story," Lexi said softly. She had to know. "What happened to them? I know it was a plane crash..."

And that was one question too many for Sam. He shook his head, then pushed Lexi back onto the mattress, sliding onto her.

"I can think of more interesting things to do than talk."

His mouth took hers, exploring until her body turned into jelly beneath him. She knew he'd started this to avoid answering her question, but she no longer cared. She reached up and wrapped her arms around his back, feeling the scratches she'd already given him, and digging in to add more. He cursed against her shoulder, his teeth grazing her skin as he settled his body between her legs.

They only had tonight.

And tonight was never going to be enough.

Sam woke up in the dark in an empty bed. He knew it before he even opened his eyes. Not only was he missing the physical heat of Lexi's body, but he also missed the electrical energy that warmed any space the two of them were in together. He opened his eyes and frowned, checking the time. Four o'clock. They'd done more sexing than sleeping so far, and he was very much okay with that. He could always catch up on sleep. When they only had one night together, they needed to use every moment wisely.

He listened, trying to determine where she was. The door to the head was open. The kitchen and the salon above it were quiet. Then he heard a soft movement directly above the cabin. She was up on the front deck, where tonight had started. He got up and pulled on a pair of swim trunks from the drawer beneath the bed.

It had been a wild night, that's for sure. Wild sex. Wild emotions. Wild expectations that had been obliterated by reality. He'd been so wiped out that she'd managed to get him talking about his family, and he didn't do that for anyone. But all Lexi had to do was render him weak-kneed with her body and whisper, "Tell me about them," and his mouth had just started running.

For some reason, his mind had been on his parents' and grandparents' early days—how they'd met, how their marriages started. How happy they'd all been, despite facing changing times. The words had poured out of him until she asked about the crash. No matter how mellow Lexi had made him, he still didn't want to go there. Not tonight.

Was it wrong of him to stop the conversation with a kiss? With more sex? Maybe, but she hadn't objected.

He hadn't lied when he confessed he'd dreamed of having Lexi in bed with him. Or when he said the dreams had nothing on what actually happened. They were good together. Like…crazy hot great together. He'd had some ambitious sex in his life—even wild sex. But with Lexi, it was completely different. Put them in the same room with clothes on, and it was all snark and snarl between them. But remove those clothes and it was a whole new ballgame.

She knew what he needed from her before *he* did. It meant no thinking was involved. The lovemaking had felt so freaking *pure*. He went up to the back deck, then walked along the side gunwales to find her. She was reclining where they'd been earlier, wearing nothing but one of his oldest, softest T-shirts. She had a thin blanket wrapped loosely around her shoulders. He handed her one of the bottles of water he'd grabbed on his way up here. She took it, but she wasn't smiling. Her expression was pensive.

"You okay?" he asked, staring down at her. He wasn't going to join her until he was sure she wanted him there.

She nodded. "I just needed some fresh air and chance to…think."

"You want me to go?"

She hesitated, then patted the spot beside her, inviting him to sit. "You don't need to go. Nothing's wrong. I'm just a little overwhelmed." He sat next to her and she smiled. The moonlight made everything look silver and soft. "Tonight was…a lot."

"A lot of sex? Yes, ma'am, it was." He wanted to lighten her mood, but her smile faded. "Hey…" He lifted her chin with his fingertips. "It was really good sex, babe. And that's what we agreed to, right? A night of great sex and then—"

"It's the 'and then' that's worrying me," she answered. "Tonight was more than some random one-night stand. For the rest of the summer, we're going to see each other regularly. We have mutual friends. Every time I see you, I'm going to be thinking…about tonight. We said nothing would change, but…"

He saw where she was going with this. "But everything *has* changed."

"Exactly. I mean, maybe daylight will bring us back to our senses, but right now, I don't see how we just go back to normal."

He pulled her close, kissing the top of her head when she rested it on his chest. She had a point. He'd never see Lexi the same way again. And daylight was coming—there was already a narrow sliver of pink along the horizon.

"Do you *want* to keep this going? Just the physical thing?" He liked the idea of her in his bed at home.

"That feels like a really bad idea." She wrapped her arms around his torso and snuggled in. He tucked the blanket around her. "You and I forming any kind of ongoing... *thing* is bound to get messy. And complicated. People will get invested."

"People don't need to know. This would just be us having a good time. Nothing more." As those last two words came out of his mouth, he felt the alarms going off in his head. After tonight, could it *really* be "nothing more"?

Would he be able to say goodbye, which was the natural end to any relationship he'd ever had? She raised her head to stare up at him. Her hair was wild from their lovemaking, and her lips were kiss swollen and full. And her eyes... He would happily drown in the depths of those eyes.

"So..." she began. "You think we should lie to our friends and families, then run around meeting in secret for hot sex and nothing more?" He watched her think about it. "Tempting, but still feels like a bad idea. I think we're better off keeping this to one very memorable night, then move on the best we can."

She was right, of course. Make a clean break before emotions got involved. Avoid making up stories. That was the smart way to go. He didn't like it, but it was smart. He leaned down to kiss her, closing his eyes at the velvet touch of her mouth on his.

"You're probably right," he whispered. "But if tonight is it, let's not waste any more time talking."

"Funny," she answered. "I was thinking the same thing. But remember what we said about this hard deck..."

"I remember. I believe you offered to be the one on top?" He pulled her up until she was straddling him. "There's a condom in my pocket. Don't get too carried away—it's *my* back against the deck now."

"So romantic," she teased.

"There's no romance involved." He said it more firmly than he intended, and softened his voice to clarify. "I mean…"

She put her fingers against his lips. "I get it. No romance. Just a good time."

She didn't seem to mind, but the words didn't sit well with him for some weird reason. That was their agreement. No emotions. And definitely no romance. No relationship at all. She tugged the T-shirt over her head, silencing his thoughts with the sight of her body bathed in moonlight.

One night only. One incredible night.

And nothing after. Nothing at all.

That was the deal.

Chapter Sixteen

"**Y**ou're telling me nothing happened between you and Sam out there on the ocean last night." Carm said it as a statement, but hidden in there was definitely a *seriously?* Lexi tried to focus on shaping crab cakes for the special at the restaurant tonight. The two women were in the kitchen at 200 Wharf.

"You've seen us together, Carm. Sam and I can barely stand each other." She stacked another crab cake on the pile, separating them with squares of parchment paper. She did her best not to think about the fact that she now knew every inch of Sam's body, from the tiny scar on the back of his shoulder, to the ornate anchor tattoo on the back of his right calf. She cleared her throat. *Focus!* "I told you what happened. The engines quit. It was late, so we dropped anchor. You've seen Sam's boat—there's plenty of room for two people to sleep without even being on the same *level*, much less the same bed."

Carm's eyebrows rose. "I never said anything about sharing a bed."

"Well…*good*. Because we didn't." Lexi didn't dare make eye contact with Carm—she was the *worst* liar. This was going to be even tougher than she'd thought.

By the time Devlin's lobster boat had arrived in the bay

to tow them home, she and Sam had christened the bed, the top deck *and* the sectional in the salon. They'd barely pulled their clothes on before Devlin called on the radio to say he was ten minutes away.

One night. No strings. That was the agreement.

Lexi finished the crab cakes and set the covered tray on a shelf inside the cooler. She was exhausted, and the restaurant wouldn't open for another two hours. Being towed was a slow process, and it was late morning before they'd arrived back to the marina. Devlin's dad and Joe Toscanio had been waiting on the docks to help pull the *Katydid* into the service boathouse. Sam figured he'd have to drain the fuel tanks and refill them with clean diesel.

Neither of the older men had said a word of innuendo while she was there, but she'd seen the sly smiles they'd shared between themselves. Sam had probably been grilled the same way she had—first by her mother, and now by Carm. You'd think no one understood the concept of two adults being able to sleep on a boat without having sex. That's not what had happened with her and Sam, but it *could* have. People didn't have to assume it was inevitable. She stepped out of the cooler and Carm was still talking.

"It's none of my business, of course, but if you two *did* feel any feelings out there, it would be understandable. Floating on the water under the stars on a warm, calm night like that. Back in the day, if Rick and I had been out there, that boat woulda' been a'rockin'!"

"Which makes sense, considering Rick was your *husband*," Lexi pointed out. "Sam and I are barely civil to each other on our best days. We managed not to kill each other last night, which seems pretty good for us."

They'd hardly slept all night, and they'd been very, *very*

busy. It was a wonder that kind of sex—frantic and intense—hadn't killed them both.

Carm stared hard at her, then shrugged. "I thought maybe I'd seen a little spark of something between you two, but I could have been wrong."

Lexi made sure the kitchen staff had things under control, then she and Carm went out into the dining area. She smiled at Carm when they got to the door. "There's nothing between Sam and me but annoyance."

Carm gave her one last suspicious look before heading out. That wasn't a lie. They'd agreed that last night was it. No sneaking around for hot sex now that they were home. So there *was* nothing between them now. This conversation with Carm just proved Lexi had been right when she'd said it would be a messy mistake to even try.

Thank God, Sam had agreed.

By the time the kitchen closed at nine o'clock that night, Lexi was dead on her feet. She couldn't *wait* to get home and crawl into bed for about twelve hours. But first, she had to put together her orders for the weekend—a job she normally did on Tuesdays, but she'd spent yesterday on a boat. With Sam.

She tossed her apron into a laundry bin along the back wall. Randy and Eric, her line chefs, would take care of cleanup. She peeked into the dining room. Only three tables still had diners, and they were finishing their desserts. That was the nice thing about weeknights—people tended to eat earlier and head home.

She finished up her orders and placed the ones she could online. She'd make calls on the rest of the orders in the morning. But first…*sleep*. She made sure the guys were okay closing up and grabbed her bag.

Then she heard a whoop of victory coming from the bar. Was that her *mother*? Mom hadn't worked tonight—she only worked Fridays and Saturdays. The waitresses walked over to get their own drink orders on the other nights, when it wasn't as busy. Lexi walked down the hall.

Fred and Mom were behind the bar, and they had an audience. Devlin and Shelly were watching, along with John and Steve—two of the regulars at the Salty Knight. It seemed Fred and Mom were having a drink-making competition of some sort.

"Ha!" Mom shouted. "I told you I could make a better Bloody Mary than you!"

"Lady, I've been making Bloody Marys at this bar for forty years and never heard a complaint." Fred was scowling. He gestured at Mom's drink. "Is that a *shrimp*? It's a drink, not a damn appetizer plate."

Mom put her hand on her hip. "Listen you, this is Cape Cod. You have a pirate on your sign. You should be putting shrimp and lobster in *everything*."

"Oh, really?" Fred mimicked her pose. "You want me to plop a shrimp in your Manhattan Friday night?"

"Okay…maybe not *everything*. Besides, the shrimp is just garnish. The difference in my Bloody Mary is the lemon and using real tomato juice and Worcestershire sauce instead of cheating like you do with the vegetable juice. And stop being so sensitive. I gave you credit last week for making a stellar Manhattan."

"That's high praise." Lexi stepped into the bar from the hallway. "This lady has had her share of Manhattans through the years." Her father used to expect a Manhattan ready for him when he got home from work in the evening. He and Mom would sit and drink them together in front of the fireplace in cold weather, or out by the pool in the summer. It was interesting that Mom was still drinking them. With Fred.

"Hi, sweetie!" Mom came from behind the bar to give her a hug. She was wearing her favorite torn jeans with a green sequined tank top. "How was business over there tonight?" She held Lexi at arm's length and frowned. "You look tired."

"I *am* tired, Mom. Long day after a long night."

"Long night? I thought you said you slept like a baby on Sam's boat?"

As if on cue, everyone turned to look at Lexi. *Dammit.* This was the problem with lying. It was hard to remember the stories you'd told.

"Well, I *slept*, but…you know… We didn't have power. It was hot. I've never slept on a boat before." She was grasping now. "And we had to be up early to be ready for Devlin. But I'm fine."

Devlin's eyebrows rose at that, but he didn't say anything. He hadn't been there *that* early.

Her mother put her hand to Lexi's forehead. "You don't look fine. I hope you're not coming down with something. You go straight to bed when you get home."

"That's the plan. See you in the morning." She gave her mom a quick kiss on the cheek, then waved to the group in the bar. Fred was glaring at her mom's cocktail, then reached for it to take a sip. She had a feeling the bartending battle wasn't over yet. "Good night, everyone. Don't drink too many of those Bloody Marys."

She headed out the door and across the street to the parking lot. Her mind was already envisioning her welcoming bed when she realized someone was standing near her car in the dark. No—someone was *leaning* on her car. And that someone was Sam Knight. And just like that, she wasn't tired anymore. Instead, every nerve in her body was on alert.

"What are you doing here?" She blurted out the words without thinking.

He chuckled. "Well, hello, to you, too. I just wanted to see how you were doing. It's, uh…been a weird couple of days."

And one very special night. But that was over. And Sam had never checked on her welfare before.

"This is breaking our deal," she pointed out. "This is *not* going back to normal. We're not…"

"I'm not stalking you, Lex. I walked down to get a drink and saw you heading out." He glanced around. "I thought meeting you at your car would be more discreet than talking on the sidewalk right outside the windows of the bar."

"Oh." She barely whispered the word. It was just a coincidence. Nothing special. That was good. That was what she wanted. The minute her nerves stood down, her exhaustion returned. She must have wavered, because Sam was suddenly much closer, holding her by the elbow.

"Hey, you're *not* okay." He looked around again. "Did you get any rest today?"

"Of course not," she snapped, pulling away from his grip. "I have a business to run. I've been on my feet since we got back to the marina. But I'm heading home to sleep right now."

"Give me your keys."

"Excuse me?"

"I'll drive you back to the Mermaid, then walk home."

Now it was her turn to look around, but Wharf Street was quiet. Sam knew what she was thinking.

"No one will see us if we go now. You're too tired to drive."

"It's not that far."

"That wasn't a *no*," he pointed out. "Give me your keys. I don't want to worry about you."

The longer they argued, the more chance that someone would see them standing close in a dark parking lot. That's the only reason she surrendered her keys to him and got in the passenger seat.

He slid behind the wheel and moved the seat back. "This feels like a toy car."

"Don't mock my Mini. It's perfect for the city." She rested her head back on the seat and closed her eyes. Sam started the car and pulled out of the lot. She'd wanted to fight his plan to drive, but now that she was sitting down, she was glad he'd taken the keys. She was already half-asleep. And… "I'm starving."

"What?" His voice was sharp. "You work in a restaurant. You didn't eat?"

"I grabbed a bite here and there, but I was afraid to sit and eat. I was afraid to sit and do anything—I wasn't sure I'd get back up again." She rolled her head to look at him. "I'll make something when I get home."

He muttered something under his breath that sounded a lot like "The hell you will." He made a sharp left turn.

Lexi sat up. "Where are you going?"

"My place." He looked over at her, reading her mind. "To *feed* you. Then I'll get you home."

"I'm a big girl. And I'm a *chef*, so I can feed myself."

"You've been a chef all day and didn't manage to do it, so now you're stuck with me. I grilled up a pork roast tonight—they usually last me a few days, so there's plenty for sandwiches." The car stopped. She recognized the big old house. This was probably a colossally bad idea after last night. But she was tired and hungry. She was also incredibly curious to see the inside of Sam's home.

Would it tell her more about who he was?

* * *

Sam had no idea what he was doing, ushering Lexi into his home. He *never* had people here, other than family and the closest of friends. People who knew what *not* to say or do. But good grief, the woman was dead on her feet with exhaustion because of him. He unlocked the back door and gestured for her to go ahead of him. At least he'd had the chance to catch a nap in the afternoon. Workaholic Lexi had gone straight to the restaurant. And now, she was standing in his kitchen, wide-eyed and starting to smile as she looked around.

"Who's your decorator—Betty Crocker? This looks straight out of the fifties. And this floor…" She turned on her heel to face him, her expression softening. "This was your grandmother's kitchen, wasn't it?"

He swallowed hard and nodded. Devlin constantly said the house was like a museum, and the kitchen was a prime example. The plain wood cupboards were painted bright white, with ornate black hardware. The counters were pale yellow Formica, with a mint-green backsplash. The floor was a classic black-and-white checkerboard pattern. Not the most masculine of kitchens, but he kept it clean and it was functional. He had many memories of Grandma and Mom cooking in here, laughing together. The wonderful aroma of rising bread or baking lasagna.

Which reminded him—he was supposed to be feeding Lexi. He gave a nod toward the dining room.

"Have a seat. I'll warm up a plate for you."

She walked through the doorway and started to chuckle in disbelief.

"Is this the original maple dining-room set, too? And pineapple wallpaper. I knew you didn't like change, but this…"

Sam started the microwave and didn't hear the rest. He'd heard it all before, anyway. He put the sandwich together and went into the dining room, but she wasn't there. He found her in the pine-paneled living room, staring at the family photos on the mantel. He should have let her feed her own damn self.

"This isn't the dining room," he pointed out.

She gave a quick glance over her shoulder. "This also isn't 1985. I can't figure it out. Your kitchen is from the fifties, the dining room is seventies, but this room looks more…nineties? The shiny brass fixtures and taupe walls are a giveaway."

Sam's jaw tightened. "My parents lived here, too. It's where I grew up. Mom and Grandma shared…" He caught himself before he opened even more memories. The more he shared, the more memories that swept through his mind. He wasn't sure he could bear it.

"That explains the different decades of decor. None of which are current." She looked at Sam, and her smile faded. "I'm sorry for wandering, but—" she looked back to the photos "—this place is fascinating to me. Are these your parents and grandparents standing with you? Looks like a graduation… College?"

Sam's teeth ground hard against each other. He didn't answer, but turned away and took her plate to the dining table, where it—and she—belonged. She took the hint and followed, but she wasn't done with him.

"What college did you graduate from? Looks like it was a happy day." She took a bite of the warm pork sandwich and moaned. "This is delicious. Thank you."

"You're welcome." He hoped the food would distract her from her questions.

"So…" She looked up from the plate. "College? Did you major in boat repair or…?"

"I majored in marine biology and minored in business at UNC Wilmington in North Carolina." Maybe the bare facts would satisfy her. But he forgot who he was talking to.

"Wow. Graduate school or…?"

"No." That had been the plan before everything changed. "Just a bachelor's degree. It comes in handy for lobstering and stuff. I do some charters for folks who want to see the sharks and seals, so at least I know what I'm talking about."

She considered that, then nodded. "Makes sense. You could be doing marine research now instead of…"

"Instead of wasting my life in Winsome Cove?" His temper rose. "You may not think much of this town, but it's been my family's home for—"

"For generations. I know. I just meant you…" She stopped, pressing her lips together and meeting his gaze. "Never mind. I'm sorry. I don't have much of a filter on a good day, and when I'm exhausted I have no filter at all. I'm prying where I shouldn't be."

She continued eating, finishing her sandwich in silence. He got what he wanted. She'd stopped asking questions. *Perfect.*

"I'd planned on doing more with it." Sam blinked at his own words. She'd let him off the hook, and he'd blurted out a response, anyway. "I wanted to be a research scientist, studying the effects of global warming on the fishing industry and how to deal with it."

"Why didn't you?" He'd poured her a glass of red wine, and she picked it up as she asked the question. He could have refused to answer. But this was Lexi. The woman who'd somehow wormed her way into his trust. Into his heart. The barriers he'd thrown up around that heart turned to dust under the power of her soft gaze.

"Because the day that graduation photo was taken was the day they all died, and it was my fault."

The wineglass shook in her hand and rattled on the table as she tried to set it down. Color drained from her face.

"That was the day of the plane crash?" Her voice shook. "God, Sam. Saying 'I'm sorry' feels inadequate, but… I really am so sorry. That must have been just awful."

"Yeah." He couldn't believe he was still talking. "I had no choice but to come back and run the marina."

She frowned. "Well, you had a choice. You could have sold it or hired someone to run it. I mean, I understand why you felt that way, but…" Her forehead furrowed. "Wait. Why do you think it was your fault?"

"Grandpa loved flying. He flew Grandma and my parents down to Wilmington with the idea that I'd fly back with them, since I'd sold my car down there. But my buddies had rented a beach house and I wanted to stay for an extra week to just kick back and have a good time." He stared straight ahead, not seeing Lexi or…anything, really. Just his memories, as crushing as they were. "I told them they could take my stuff, but I'd catch a ride home in a week with a friend from Rhode Island."

"But staying behind doesn't make the crash your fault, Sam. You would have been killed, too."

"They were flying home from my graduation. A trip they wouldn't have taken if it wasn't for me."

"That doesn't make it your—"

"It *does*, Lex. At least to me. There was a storm front that came up the coast, and they went inland to go around it, but it shifted. They wouldn't have faced that except for me."

"Sam, you were graduating from college. Of course they

wanted to be there, because they were proud of you. This is not—"

He shoved his chair back from the table and stood so quickly that the chair toppled over backward, smacking on the hardwood floor. Lexi flinched, and Sam stormed out of the dining room, desperate to be away from her pity and attempts at comfort. There was no comfort for him when it came to the crash. He refused to hear it. His life had crashed with them, even if he hadn't been on the plane.

And he *should* have been on the plane. He should have gone down with his family. Instead, they'd left him alone and broken. He rested his arms on the mantel, then dropped his head to avoid looking at that photo. His last day of innocence and joy.

Their last day, period.

Chapter Seventeen

Lexi stared at the fallen chair, wishing it could give her some answers. She had no idea what to do. What to say. The fact that Sam's family had died so terribly was tragic. The idea that he held himself responsible was incomprehensible. It was a burden far too heavy for most people to carry without breaking. She looked around the dining room. The realization hit her like a truck. Nothing in this house had changed since that day.

It was clear his parents and grandparents hadn't been big on change in general. Like the Sassy Mermaid, this house was stuck in the past. But there was a difference between not *wanting* to change things and not being *able* to change things. It felt like Sam was trapped here. Probably to punish himself for his survivor's guilt.

She was setting his chair upright when her phone buzzed in her pocket, making her jump. It was a text from Mom.

Your car's not here. Everything okay?

The only excuse she could think of was pretty feeble. She started typing.

Stopped at Shelly's for a drink. Don't wait up.

The answer came almost instantly.

Ok. Say hi to Sam for me.

She stared at the screen. How the hell did Mom know? She saw bubbles floating as Mom typed something more.

Shelly was still sitting at the bar when I left. And I'm not stupid.

Mom followed that text with a winking emoji. Lexi would have to have a talk about Mom about keeping her speculation private. But for now, there was a man in the next room with a gaping, raw wound from sixteen years ago. And she had to do something.

She walked in, and her heart sank when she saw him at the fireplace, his head on his arm, his shoulders slumped. He didn't move when she rested her hand on his back, but his breathing caught.

"Go home, Lex." His voice was flat.

"Not gonna happen." She continued to stroke his back, working her fingers into his taut muscles. She gripped his shoulders with both hands, giving a gentle tug. "Come sit with me."

"Seriously…go home. I am not going to be good company."

"Lucky for you, I'm not looking for good company. I'm looking to get off my feet and lean on someone." She tugged on him again. "Be my someone, Sam."

He didn't answer, but he straightened, turning to face her. The shattered look in his eyes nearly made her knees give way. He had been in this pain for far too long. They walked to the oversize upholstered armchair with a big ottoman in front of it. Sam sat and she immediately joined him, curling up at his side with his arm holding her close and her legs over his. She rested her head on his chest.

It wasn't like last night. The heat was missing, or at least tempered somewhat. The emotion between them wasn't desire. It was…affection. Comfort. Need, but not the sexual kind. Sam's fingers stroked her shoulder absently.

"Your mom's gonna be looking for you," he said softly.

"She already did. She told me to say hi."

"You told her you were with me?"

"She guessed that on her own. I told her not to wait up."

Sam crooked his head to look down at her. "Really?"

"You want me to leave?"

"No." She smiled at how quick his answer came. "You can stay. But I'm not in the mood for talking."

She snuggled into his embrace. "Oh, well. At least you make a great pillow."

She felt more than heard his short, soft laugh. His fingers continued tracing circles on her back as silence settled in. This house might be dated, but it was also cozy and comfortable. Maybe this house wasn't Sam's prison as much as it was his safe haven.

Her eyes fell closed at the same moment she felt his breathing slow under her cheek. He was connected to his family here. So many pieces fell into place. Everyone in town thought of him as easygoing Sam Knight. But he was so much deeper than that. So much more complicated.

And oddly enough, so much more desirable.

It wasn't unusual for Sam to wake up in the middle of the night in the living room easy chair. He'd never been great at sleeping through the night, and he often nodded off in the chair while reading or watching TV. But something was different. There was a warm, softly snoring body curled up around him.

He'd discovered Lexi snored last night on the boat. It wasn't loud or constant, but once in a while she snored so quietly that it was almost a purr. He liked it. He liked *her*, even when she poked and prodded at his darkest feelings.

He had to move—his foot was asleep. He shifted as carefully as he could, but Lexi's eyes swept open. She frowned for a second, then relaxed against him.

"I keep waking up in unfamiliar places." She yawned. "What time is it?"

He checked his phone. "Two o'clock."

"In the morning?"

He huffed. "Did you think you slept sixteen hours into the afternoon?"

"Ugh." Lexi stretched like a cat, then smiled up at him, finally starting to wake up for real. "I feel like I could *use* that much sleep. But four hours is a start. I should probably go…"

"You don't need to. But we should find someplace more comfortable than a chair. My bedroom's upstairs."

She stared. "That would break our agreement. One night only, remember?"

"One night only was referring to *sex*. We didn't make any rules about sleep."

"Fair enough." She sat up, giving him a mischievous grin. "What decade is the bedroom from?"

Her teasing was gentle enough, or maybe he was tired enough, that it didn't bother him. "Come see for yourself."

She followed him up the narrow staircase, and he could feel her curiosity growing as they reached the hallway. The hall had its original pine paneling, with a few pieces of his grandmother's paint-by-numbers paintings on the wall. Most were of sailing ships, but one was of a beach and the Nauset lighthouse. She'd been so excited to find a kit for a familiar landmark—she'd saved it as a surprise for Grandpa's birthday. Sam paused outside the bedroom door, staring at the painting as if he'd never seen it before. That sort of memory was usually accompanied with razor cuts of pain, but all he felt right now was a sense of peace.

Lexi's hand rested on the small of his back.

"Sam? Are you okay?"

He cleared his throat roughly.

"Yeah. I'm fine. Here's my room."

Sam suddenly realized this might be another bad idea. Maybe they should have stayed downstairs. He hit the light switch and she walked in. She stopped abruptly in the center of the room, turning in a slow circle to take it in.

It wasn't a big room. The dark blue walls made it seem smaller. He'd chosen that color back in high school.

Lexi stared at a framed poster promoting Old Harbor Days. Sam braced himself for her reaction—the poster was from 2003. It was the year he and his dad won first prize in the annual raft race. She turned to him, perplexed.

"Sam, is this your *childhood* bedroom?"

He straightened, looking around quickly. There weren't any toys or anything childlike in here. Well, except for a few model boats on a shelf by the window. And maybe the old beanbag chair in the corner. Other than that, this was a perfectly grown-up room.

"It's the room I grew up in, yeah." He shrugged. "I didn't see a point in changing it."

"Aren't the other rooms bigger?" She put up her hands. "Don't get me wrong, there's nothing…bad about this room. I'm just wondering why…" Her mouth snapped shut and she spread her hands wide. "You know what? Never mind.

It's a great room and the bed looks comfy. That's all that matters."

He saw the moment the truth dawned in her eyes. He hadn't moved into one of the two master suites in the house because they didn't belong to him. They'd belonged to his parents and grandparents, and it never felt right—or necessary—to take over one of them for himself. It had never bothered him before. But seeing Lexi come to that realization, even though she hadn't said anything, made him feel weird about it for the very first time.

Lexi pulled off her pale green top and stepped out of her black capris, then took a step toward the bed, reaching behind her back to unhook her cotton bra. Sam moved to unfasten it for her, his fingers brushing her soft skin. And just like that, the old fire was back between them. How could he have possibly thought they could lay together in his bed and just sleep? He'd never be able to keep his hands off of her. Even now, he couldn't resist leaning over and kissing her neck from behind her.

Her breath caught, but she didn't resist. Instead, her head tipped to the side to give him better access. He traced kisses and nibbles from her shoulder up to her ear. Her eyes were closed and she swayed in his arms.

"We had an agreement…" she whispered. Her voice caught as he nipped her earlobe, then ran his tongue across the tender skin behind it. She tasted salty from sweating in the restaurant kitchen. He could smell the aroma of her musky perfume beneath the salt, and the soft, fruity smell of her shampoo as he nuzzled his nose into her hair.

"I know what we agreed to," he said quietly. His hands pulled her back against him, so she could feel his hardness. She let out a soft moan, and he smiled against her skin. "But now that we know what he have together…is one night going to be enough for you? Because I'm thinking it's not gonna work for me." He hesitated. He didn't want to push her into anything. "But if that's all you want, I'll go sleep on the sofa. Because being in this bed with you and not being able to touch you is going to be more than I can handle."

She turned in his embrace, sliding her arms around his neck and pressing her near-naked body against his. Her sultry smile and hooded eyes told him her answer before her words did.

"Screw the rule. Come to bed with me, Sam. And not just for sleeping."

He didn't remember how they got his clothes off. One minute they were standing there, and the next they were in bed, skin to skin. They knew each other's bodies now, but that just made the lovemaking sweeter. Softer. More intimate. It was just as hot, if not more so, but in a deeper, more emotional sense. It was more than sex. It was *more,* period.

His worry from the night before was confirmed now—he'd never have enough of Lexi Bellamy. Somewhere in the back of his mind, he knew that was a problem. But he dismissed the thought and pulled her languid body closer, kissing her forehead and falling asleep in her embrace.

He woke a few hours later in the same exact position, in the same warm embrace. The only difference was the placement of one of her hands, which was on him and very busy at the moment. He let out a hiss of ecstasy and rolled his head back against the pillow as she worked him perfectly. He mumbled her name between clenched teeth, then yelled her name as she brought him to the peak and pushed him over, colors exploding behind his tightly closed eyes.

He lay there in silence, trying to get his heart beating a halfway normal rhythm again.

"Are you okay?" Lexi's voice was soft and amused.

"I'm not sure," he answered, being honest. "That's definitely my preferred way of waking up from now on, but I'm worried my heart might explode if it happens every day."

She laughed softly and cuddled against him. His arm folded her even closer, until her head was on his chest. "I'd hate to be responsible for that. Maybe we should avoid *every* morning. We could take turns—you take care of me, then I take care of you…"

"That would work." He took a deep breath, trying not to lose the glow of what she'd done to him. "It's your turn tomorrow."

Silence filled the room as they both realized they were talking about having tomorrows together. Lexi finally spoke.

"So we're not just making an exception to the one-night rule…we're trashing it completely?"

"Is that okay with you?" *Please say yes.*

She hesitated. "I think we need some new rules if we do this. I don't want people gossiping about us. I have a business to think about, you know?"

"People are already gossiping. Your mother knows you're with me tonight." He kissed the top of her head. "I'm not saying I'm against keeping things on the downlow, but it will be tough in a town like Winsome Cove."

"It's important to me, Sam. I've already had to deal with the fallout of one disastrous work relationship."

Anger rose at that reminder of her past. "I'm not involved with the restaurant, and I can stay away completely if you want. But you have to know I'd never do anything like what your ex did."

She didn't respond. Did she not believe him?

"Lex? I'm not that guy." Her continued silence annoyed him. "I'm sure as hell not some drug-dealing loser! How did you fall for a guy like that, anyway?"

He felt her body tighten. She was ticked off, too. "I didn't fall for a *drug-dealing loser*. And he wasn't a drug dealer. I don't think he even used." A pause. "My point is that he wasn't some knuckle-dragger when we met. Karl was charming and hardworking. It took a while for me to realize he'd stopped being very charming. Especially once my reputation as a chef started carrying more weight than his as a restaurant manager."

Not charming. Sam scowled into the semidarkness. A predawn light was filtering through the curtains.

"Did he—did he hurt you?"

She took a breath and held it so long that Sam wondered if she was breathing at all.

"No." She shuddered against him. "I mean…not like you're thinking."

"It's a yes-or-no question—did he hurt you?" He didn't mean to bark the question at her, but his temper was getting the best of him. She propped herself up on one elbow and looked straight into his eyes.

"What are you going to do if he did? Go beat him up?"

"Maybe." He'd never been the physical sort. Violence never solved anything. But if her ex had hit her, all bets were off as far as he was concerned.

She stared, her eyes going soft again.

"Well, good luck. He's in prison and will be for a while. He was working for some very bad men."

He reached up and moved her hair from her face, tucking it behind one ear. She was so beautiful like this, with her hair wild and her eyes soft and affectionate. Her lips were kiss-swollen and her smile… Her smile was powerful enough to make him want to do something else rather than talk, but he needed to know what happened.

"So he wasn't a drug dealer, but he *worked* for drug dealers?"

She sighed, then filled him in on more details of the story. How this Karl guy had swept her off her feet in Chicago when they met while working at the same restaurant. How he'd proposed on the shore of Lake Michigan on a beautiful summer day. How he kept changing jobs, hopping from restaurant to restaurant and insisting she follow, assuring Lexi they'd go further as a "package deal." Even Sam could tell that Lexi was becoming a star, and that jerk didn't want to leave the money train.

"But he was never satisfied," she explained. "We achieved what we'd wanted, then he saw some of our well-heeled customers and wanted *that* life."

"The criminal life?"

She chuckled. "The *rich* life. The criminal part was just the unfortunate shortcut he chose to get there. I ran the kitchen and he ran the front of the house, so I had no idea he'd made a deal to launder money through the restaurant. It never once occurred to me that he would do something so stupid." Her smile faded. "The day the federal agents showed up was the worst day of my life. They *handcuffed* me, Sam. I thought someone must be pranking me, but it was real. Not only that, but they ransacked their way through our apartment looking for...whatever. But they didn't find anything that tied me to Karl's scheme." She blinked a few times, as if trying to wash away the memory. "I was cleared eventually, but the media attention just...destroyed me. The restaurant was shut down. No one wanted to hire me because they thought I might bring those dangerous criminals to their places."

"But you were innocent."

"The arrest was front-page news. Me being cleared barely made a blip. I lost everything."

He brushed her cheek with his fingertips. "I'm sorry."

"So you understand why I don't want this little fling of ours to interfere with 200 Wharf?" Sam tensed, and she felt it. "What?"

He wasn't sure which was more irritating. Describing them as a *little fling* or worrying so much about a restaurant she wasn't going to be working at long-term. Which explained why it had to be a fling. He needed to remember she was leaving the Cape.

"I get it, but I don't know how practical that will be in a town like Winsome Cove. People pay attention here, and they talk." In one smooth move, he rolled Lexi onto her back so that he was the one looking down. "What exactly are we hiding? What are we doing here, Lex?"

Chapter Eighteen

That was a very good question. And Lexi didn't have an immediate answer. Two days ago, they barely tolerated each other. One day ago, they'd agreed to have one wild night of sex on the boat with no strings and no encores. And to-night…they were naked in his bed, rules be damned.

There was a soft morning glow outside the window. The window that was framed with nautical red-and-blue curtains. The window Sam had been waking up to his entire life.

"I still can't believe you sleep in your childhood room."

"A—that doesn't answer the question. And B—stop calling it my *childhood* room. It's just my room. There aren't any stuffed animals in here or anything."

"Sam, there's a poster on the wall and there are models on the shelves."

"The poster is framed. It's…vintage. And it means something to me."

She looked at the poster. It was from 2005. There was a stylized image of a commercial boat with a sunset behind it. Knowing this was his room as a boy made it feel like everything else in his life—the poster was there because it had always been there.

"Framing it doesn't make it art…"

His fingers touched her lips, silencing her. "I don't want

to talk about my room. I want you to answer the question at hand—what are we doing? Is this just sex? Are we exclusive? Are we friends with benefits? How often? How—"

"Okay, okay." She was going to have to deal with this. "I don't think we need to *name* it, but we're definitely not boyfriend-girlfriend. You and I are not sweethearts."

"Trust me—I know that."

He didn't need to be so emphatic.

"The idea of us being in a relationship sounds that bad to you, huh?"

"You're the one who just said—"

"Okay. Whatever. Let's define this thing." She looked up into his blue eyes—soft, gentle, curious. "I think 'friends with benefits' works best, even though it means we have to be actual friends."

He grinned. "I think we can do that."

"And it's temporary. No messy emotions required. I think we should be exclusive while we're together, though." The thought of Sam with another woman made her blood run cold. "We'll keep it casual. By the end of the summer, I hope to be winging off to a fresh start somewhere, so we have an end date."

He nodded, teasing her with an overly serious expression. "Temporary, which is the only way I do things, anyway. Exclusive friends with benefits. Casual. No emotions. And—" he winked at her "—top secret for as long as we can manage it. Anything else?"

"I think that covers it." She wondered about his comment on being temporary, but let it pass for now.

Sam glanced at the window. The sun was up. "I'm going to have to get up soon—some of the commercial boats have probably already left. I'm usually out there in case they need anything." He dropped his head and kissed her gently. "But I have a few minutes if you want to, you know, *benefit* each other."

They made love again, getting more and more familiar and comfortable. Sam grimaced when he left her in bed. "I hate leaving you here, but—"

"I get it." She stretched with a sigh. "You have a morning job. I have an evening one. Probably a good thing we're temporary." She sat up, wrapping the sheet around her. "But I cook a mean breakfast. Do you have eggs and meat handy?"

He pulled a T-shirt over his head. "There are eggs in the fridge. And cheese. And a package of precooked bacon." She wrinkled her nose and Sam stopped moving. "What? It's still bacon, and I don't have to fuss with it and make a mess of the stovetop."

"Remind me to show you how to cook bacon in the oven. Give me half an hour or so, then come back up to the house for breakfast."

Thirty minutes later, she was sliding the bacon-and-cheddar omelet from the skillet onto a plate when she heard the back door open. Perfect timing. She'd cut up the cooked bacon and pan-fried it like pancetta before adding it to the omelet.

She and Sam were so comfortable around each other that she hadn't bothered getting fully dressed. In fact, she wasn't wearing any of her clothes, but she was wearing a few of his. She'd tugged on a pair of dark blue boxer briefs and one of his T-shirts, which was so long that it covered the briefs.

Someone cleared his throat behind her and she turned from the sink with a big smile, eager for Sam to see her ensemble. There was just one problem. It wasn't Sam standing there. It was Devlin. The shock on his face rapidly slid into amusement. She glanced down at herself. Everything was covered, if barely. She wasn't showing any more skin that she would have if Devlin saw her in a bathing suit on the beach.

But she was in *Sam's* clothes. In Sam's kitchen. The speculative gleam in Devlin's eyes told her he knew exactly why she was there, so there was no sense pretending. But she was still nervous, and her words came out in a rush.

"Hi, Devlin. Would you like an omelet? I can whip one up for you in no time. In fact, take this one, and I'll make Sam a fresh one. There's toast on the dining-room table and the coffee's fresh."

Devlin leaned against the doorjamb and folded his arms on his chest.

"Good morning, Lexi. This is…quite the surprise."

"What, me cooking?"

"No, you cooking *here*. Wearing *that*."

The back door opened and closed behind him and footsteps rushed up behind Devlin, who never bothered to look back. Sam stopped right behind his cousin, his eyes heating at the sight of Lexi before he mouthed *sorry* at her. He clapped his hand on Devlin's back.

"Do you always just walk into people's houses unannounced and uninvited?"

Devlin still didn't look back at Sam, but his smile deepened. "I haven't knocked on the door to this house once in my entire life. And I'm glad, because this sight has made my day. I saw Lexi's car outside, but I figured she was down at the marina, not in your kitchen."

Sam scowled, then spun Devlin to face him. "You can put your eyeballs back in your head anytime now."

Devlin stepped back with a laugh. "Easy, Sam. I wasn't ogling your girl. I was just appreciating seeing *any* woman

standing here, cooking breakfast and offering *me* some."
He rushed to clarify. "Offering me *breakfast*." Devlin's
forehead furrowed. "Dude, I don't think I've ever seen you
jealous before."

Lexi poured more egg mixture into the skillet, and the siz-
zle got the men's attention. "Why don't you both chill. Devlin, take that omelet into the dining room for yourself. Sam,
this one will be done in two minutes, so wash your hands
and take a seat." She met Sam's gaze and shrugged. "You
were right when you said we wouldn't keep it quiet for long."

He watched Devlin pick up his plate and head into the
dining room, then looked at her, some of the tension easing
around his eyes. One corner of his mouth lifted. "I didn't
think it would be public *this* fast."

"Devlin can't keep a secret?" She slid Sam's omelet onto
his plate.

Devlin called out from the other room. "Yes, Devlin *can*
keep a secret, but this is…huge." She and Sam joined him
at the table. "Sam hasn't been in a relationship in…forever."

She and Sam answered in unison.

"It's not a relationship."

Devlin's eyebrows rose. "Girl, you're wearing his underwear."

Her cheeks warmed. "Still…what we're doing is casual.
No relationship. No commitments."

Sam chimed in. "No strings. Just…"

Devlin looked back and forth between them. "Just sex?"

"Well…" Sam cleared his throat.

That was the plan. She stared at her plate. They'd made
the rules together. They'd agreed on everything. But hearing Sam say it out loud to someone else was jarring. She
didn't like it one bit. She looked up and found Sam staring

at her. He looked like he'd swallowed half a lemon. Maybe he didn't like it, either.

But what was the alternative? To *have* a relationship? To be *serious*? Those two things didn't meld well with something that was temporary.

They locked eyes, then she blinked away. Devlin was watching them, chewing his omelet thoughtfully. A smile grew on his face.

"Oh, this is gonna be fun."

Chapter Nineteen

"So...you and Lexi, huh?" Carm laughed, nudging Devlin with her shoulder. "I saw that one coming."

Sam glared at his cousin. "You couldn't keep your mouth shut for more than one damn week?"

They were in the fish market on a Friday morning. He'd stopped by to pick up some fresh tuna steaks, figuring he'd grill them as a late lunch for him and Lexi before she went to the restaurant. Ironically, he'd discovered the chef really wasn't very good about feeding herself.

Carm laughed. "Oh, he couldn't keep the secret for one *day*, Sam. I knew almost as soon as he did." Her laughter faded. "But I *can* keep a secret, if that's what you really want. If you think it's smart."

He rubbed the back of his neck in agitation. "I don't know *what* I want, and I don't think any of this is smart. But..."

"But you can't quit her?" Devlin asked with a grin.

And wasn't that the truth? He *should* quit her, but he couldn't.

Not now. Not yet.

"Dev told me you guys are just casual," Carm said. "Sort of a no-strings deal? How does that work?"

Really, really well. As long as they didn't talk about it. She'd spent almost every night at his place. Other than a few teasing comments about sleeping in his childhood room, she hadn't said much about the house itself. He knew how she felt, and he had no intention of changing anything, so what was the point?

That was the nice thing about being casual and temporary. Those issues didn't get in the way. They shared some laughs. They'd had some great meals, although he was feeling a little inadequate in that area. And they'd been having some truly great sex.

"Carm, I think it's going really well," Devlin said. "Judging from that smile on his face."

"I'm not smiling."

Carm patted his arm. "You're glowing, babe. And I'm glad. I don't quite get how this is going to work out, but it's lovely to see you happy. I just don't want to see either of you end up being hurt."

He gave a quick shake of his head. "Impossible. We have an agreement."

"Oh, well, that sounds romantic." Carm folded her arms in disapproval.

"It's not supposed to sound romantic," Sam insisted. "Romance has nothing to do with it. We're having a good time while she's on the Cape, but we all know she's leaving at the end of the summer."

"So this is just a summer fling?" Devlin asked. "Like Danny and Sandy in *Grease*?"

"Exactly! Just a summer fling."

Carm wrapped up the tuna steaks, but held on to them when he reached to take them. Her smile was way too wide right now.

"You *do* remember Danny and Sandy fall in love in that movie, right?"

"Are you for real right now?" He pulled the steaks from

her hands. "I am *not* falling in love with some chef from the Midwest who has no intention of staying here. I'm not falling in love with *anyone*."

Sam watched Lexi sunning herself on the front deck of the *Katydid*. It was a Monday afternoon, and they were both on the front deck, chilling with their glasses of wine. It had been a couple of weeks since that first night on the boat, and this was their first overnight trip. They'd moored the boat at Martha's Vineyard for the night—he had a friend who owned a marina there. With Lexi's "weekends" being Monday and Tuesday, they missed the worst of the crowds. They still couldn't get dock space, but the weather was supposed to be nice, so a mooring would do. He'd brought a semi-inflatable dinghy for trips to shore. They'd get some rocking and rolling from the wakes of other boats, but Lexi had excellent sea legs.

Despite her initial worries about the dangers of boating, she'd become a natural on the water. They'd had to race home to the cove one day last week when a squall popped up, and she'd been sitting beside him up on the bridge, laughing as the spray from the waves kicked up as high as their seats. The wind and rain whipped her hair around her face, and it made her laugh even more.

He liked the sound of her laughter. It did something to him that he couldn't define. It…*changed* him in ways he didn't necessarily like, but that he didn't want to give up, either. Her laugh, her smile, her eyes, her touch—all of it made him a different man. Or at least, made him *want* to be a different man. To be a man worthy of her.

She removed her wide-brimmed cotton hat and slid her sunglasses down her nose to look at him over the rims.

"Why are you staring at me?"

"Because you're beautiful."

And I think I might be falling in love with you.

No, that couldn't happen. He chased the thought out of his head.

She took a sip of her wine. "Flattery will get you every-where. What time is dinner?"

"Our reservations are for five o'clock. That'll give us time to walk around after dinner. Don't forget, we'll have to take the dinghy to shore."

"You mean that kiddie boat you strapped on the back of *Katydid*? Are you going to row us in?"

He chuckled. "Uh…no. There's a small motor stowed in back for it. We won't win any races, but it'll get us where we want to go."

"Okay. I trust you, captain." She put her sunglasses back on and put her hat back in place.

Her words struck deep. He'd been waiting for a snarky reply…something about not getting her wet or not liking being moored instead of at the dock. But she was totally relaxed. Totally trusting him. His stomach soured. Should he tell her that was a mistake? He shook it off. *No.* They were temporary, and she knew that as well as he did.

It was easy to trust someone you knew would be out of your life by the end of the summer. That was probably why he thought he was falling for her, too. Easy to do when there are no long-term commitments. No need to overthink something that was specifically designed *not* to last. It was already August, so their time was winding down.

She turned and looked up at him. "You're staring again. I'm not *that* beautiful. What's on your mind?"

"I like how easy things are between us." He said it with-out much thought. And he knew why. "There's something to be said for the whole short-term friends-with-bennies thing."

He couldn't see her eyes behind her sunglasses, but he caught the way her mouth tightened just a little. Her voice was soft and calm. "How so?"

"There's no pressure to behave a certain way. No worries about building a relationship, you know? We're really good together, and I think a big reason for that is we're not trying to impress each other. The physical chemistry has been there from the start, and we're just…letting it play out."

She didn't answer right away. "That's a very practical way of looking at it."

"Right?" He was glad she saw his point. "We approached this whole thing maturely, and look how well it's worked out. Okay, it hasn't been that long, but still… Not investing our entire beings into it keeps things lighter. Easier."

Lexi turned her head so he could no longer see her face under the hat's brim, taking another sip of her wine.

"You don't feel invested?"

There was something in her tone that gave him pause.

"Well…yes, but I'm invested in what we agreed to. Committed, but only for the summer." He thought of Devlin's words. "A summer fling."

"A summer fling…" she began.

"Exactly. Neither of us has to worry about changing to make the other one happy." He draped his arm around her shoulder and pulled her closer to his side. "I wasn't sure we could do the whole no-emotions thing, but we're making it work, and having a good time, too." Usually, Lexi melted into him when they were this close. Instead, she seemed to be holding back. "Lex? You okay?"

She set her hat on the deck, then took a long breath and let it out slowly, relaxing into him as she did.

"I'm fine. And you're right—we're doing exactly what we agreed to do. We're all about the chemistry, and chemistry is physical. None of those messy emotions. We're keeping it…easy."

She looked up at him, and he removed her sunglasses himself so he could see into her eyes and gauge her thoughts. She smiled, and he relaxed. Whatever weird vibe he'd picked up from her was gone. All that was left was a trace of sorrow that flickered in her gaze before disappearing so quickly that he wasn't sure he'd seen it. Her hand patted his chest.

"I should go shower and change. We can either head into town early, or you could join me in the—"

He didn't even let her finish the sentence. He got up and grabbed their wineglasses, dumping the contents overboard while she giggled behind him. He turned and extended a hand to her.

"Just so we're clear, we are *not* going into town early."

"Just to be clear," she replied, "that's the answer I was hoping for."

She hurried ahead of him, giving her fanny a little wiggle for his benefit in her bright yellow bikini. Yes, what they had was easy. A realization sobered him.

What *wasn't* going to be easy was seeing it come to an end.

"You and Sam aren't fooling anyone, you know."

Lexi spun to face Fred as the regulars in the Salty Knight all chuckled quietly at their barstools or tables. It was just after noontime, and she'd stopped over to give Fred last night's liquor receipts. She'd come into the restaurant early today to give an interview to some food blogger from Boston.

"What do you mean?" She did her best to sound perplexed by his comment, but Fred just snorted.

"Just because Sam avoids the restaurant doesn't mean your little affair isn't public knowledge." Her heart fell. Had Devlin shared the news with more than just Carm?

"How...?"

He snorted, counting off on his fingers as he talked. "Joe Toscanio saw you two gettin' off the back of Sam's boat last week, and you were carrying an overnight bag. Then John *he-yah* saw you coming out of Sam's house one morning a couple weeks ago, all cozy with each other. And—" he leaned over the bar dramatically "—*I* saw you two kissing out on the overlook at the Sassy Mermaid yesterday."

Lexi groaned. Sam had warned her that kissing in the open like that would be risking their secret, but the moment was just too perfect to resist. The sun was warm, there was a soft breeze off the water, and everything just seemed to be glowing as they'd stood on the deck and looked out over the beach. They'd just come from a late-morning cruise on the *Katydid*, and Lexi was so completely, blissfully happy. It felt like her life was coming together at last, and her usual anxiety had vanished. Sam had done that for her. He'd erased her worries and opened up a future she never would have contemplated a year ago. A future here. With him.

She'd moved closer, until he'd finally slid his arm around her and gave her his warning about being in public. Her response, after glancing back at the quiet motel to be sure no one was around, had been to stand on her tiptoes, close her eyes and wait.

He hadn't hesitated to oblige, pulling her in tight and kissing her hard and long. When he'd released her, he'd given her his crooked grin.

"You know I'll never turn you away, babe. Maybe it's time we stopped caring about what anyone knows or doesn't know." She'd paused for just a moment, and some of the light in his eyes dimmed. "You're still worried about the restaurant? Why? Everyone knows you're leaving."

It was a topic he was quick to bring up, almost on a daily basis. They'd agreed from the start that their relationship had an end date. But Sam mentioned it constantly. Was he mad about it? Was he reminding her? Or reminding himself?

But…what would he say if she *didn't* leave?

"Yep…" Fred was still talking. "Right out there in the wide open, where everyone on the beach or at the motel could see. No effort to hide at all." He straightened and started wiping down the bar with a towel. "I don't know why you bother. No one cares if you two are boinking each other."

Lexi gave a startled laugh. "Boinking? Really, Fred?"

John and Steve laughed at their corner table, and her face heated. Fred didn't seem to notice. Or care.

"Well, you *are*, aren't cha?"

"Are *what*, Dad?"

Devlin had just walked in, and Sam was right behind him. *Uh-oh*. Sam's gaze caught hers. He must have sensed her discomfort because he frowned at Fred. The old man didn't look uncomfortable at all. He was enjoying this, and his chest puffed a little as he answered Devlin.

"I was just telling Lexi that her and Sam aren't kidding anyone. We all know they've got a thing going on."

"He said you guys are *boinking*!" Steve called out from the corner. John was laughing. Devlin and Sam were *not*. Sam's frown turned into a scowl.

"What business is it of yours?"

Fred threw his hands up. "It's none of our damn business at all. I was just trying to say that no one cares, so pretending it ain't happening is stupid."

"He's right," Lexi sighed. Sam and Devlin both looked

surprised, and she nodded at them. "We didn't want everyone getting invested in us being together, but they're already invested. Pretending we're not—" she glanced at Fred "—*boinking* is just a waste of energy." She walked to Sam and took his hand, pressing close to his front and staring up into his bemused blue eyes. "Our secret is out, babe."

A slow, sexy smile spread on his face and he put one arm around her waist before looking up at their audience. "Okay, you old horn dogs, you got us. We're together. But not...*together* together. It's nothing serious."

Lexi took a sharp breath, feeling those three words like daggers. *It's nothing serious.* It was sure as hell becoming something serious to her. But that wasn't the deal, was it? The deal was nothing more than friends with benefits.

"Hey." Sam's voice was low, just for her to hear. "You okay?"

"Absolutely," she lied. "Feels good to stop hiding, right?" She forced a smile.

He studied her eyes before answering. "Right. Want to grab lunch together to celebrate? Sal's Seafood up on Main is open."

She wrinkled her nose. "I'm not in the mood for fried everything, and that's the last thing your stomach needs." He'd told her about his heartburn issues and the foods he tried to avoid. He'd been rubbing his chest more often lately—a telltale sign his heartburn was flaring up. And heartburn was often triggered by stress. "Come on over to the kitchen. I've got enough cooked lobster for a couple of lobster rolls."

Ting! Ting! Ting! Devlin was tapping a spoon against a glass, the way they do at weddings when they want the couple to kiss.

Sam's eyes narrowed dangerously. "What are you? Twelve?"

Steve and John did the same with the beer glasses on their table. Lexi couldn't help laughing.

"Shall we give them what they want?"

Without another word, Sam dipped her backward and kissed her as everyone hooted and made catcalls. His smile when he stood her back up made her pulse race. There was something deep there, as if he was letting himself feel actual joy instead of talking himself out of it. They ignored the applause and headed down the hallway to the restaurant, hand in hand.

Chapter Twenty

"Oh, honey, I'm so glad you and Sam stopped sneaking around before Old Harbor Days." Her mother was carrying a box of plastic utensils out of the restaurant, and she set them down on the folding table on the sidewalk in front of 200 Wharf. "You'll be able to enjoy the fun together."

Lexi plugged an extension cord into the steamer she'd just carried out. In an hour, she'd be serving walk-about shrimp skewers to the Old Harbor Days crowds. She and her mother had worked for hours last night cooking the marinated skewers. She'd reheat them in the steamer, then drizzle them with a citrus balsamic glaze and wrap each skewer with brown paper so the customers could walk and eat.

"I'm not sure how much time I'll have for fun, Mom. If we can entice people down to Wharf Street, I have a feeling we'll be busy all day."

Wharf Street had never looked so good—at least not since she'd arrived. She looked up the hill toward Main Street. Devlin and Sam had power-washed the fronts of all the buildings this week. Even if the paint was still faded and chipped, everything was clean, including the windows and sidewalks. Carm had bought brightly colored potted flowers and set them in front of each storefront, vacant or not. A banner hung across the road near the top, inviting people to see the Original *Old Harbor* of Old Harbor Days.

They'd all agreed to donate a portion of their sales to a fund to beautify their street as well as giving a portion to the children's charity the festival supported. Would they make a profit today? Maybe not, but hopefully they'd gain a lot of new business from people who hadn't known Wharf Street existed.

Carm was selling individual steamed clams at her sidewalk table in front of the market. Devlin's real-estate office had set up a table of brochures and flyers about what made Winsome Cove special, including one featuring the Sassy Mermaid Motor Lodge. He was also selling raffle tickets for a chance to win one of three Wharf Street prizes: a $300 fresh seafood order from Carm, a $200 gift certificate for 200 Wharf or two free cocktails from the Salty Knight.

Fred Knight had immediately declared he had no interest in "pandering" to tourists. If they wanted to find his bar, they would. If they didn't, he didn't give a damn. Everyone agreed it might be for the best if Fred stayed indoors and behind the bar. In other words—as far away from the festival crowd as possible. So Sam volunteered to man the Salty Knight table. He'd be selling virgin Bloody Mary's, using Phyllis's winning recipe, minus the booze.

"I'm sure you two will figure out a way to get some time together," Mom said. "And even if you don't, you'll be working side by side all day. And now that you're a couple, you can just grab the man and kiss him whenever you want to."

Lexi spread out some mini menus she'd had printed as flyers for the restaurant, fanning them out on the table. "We're not really a couple, Mom."

"Then what are we?"

Sam's question made her spin around. He was standing at the bar's table, his arms folding on his chest, staring at her.

"Yeah, sweetie," Mom said, jumping in. "What *are* you two exactly?"

"I...well... We're *together*. But, you know..." Why was she struggling with this? "We're casual. You said so last week in Martha's Vineyard, Sam. I think of *couples* as being serious, and we're...not. Right?"

Sam looked like he'd been ready to agree until she added that last one-word question. He froze at that, as if he might have the same doubts she did about how casual they really were.

Sam stared at Lexi, not sure what she was saying. They were not a couple. They were just casual. But then she'd added that little question mark at the end. Was she looking for him to agree to the casual deal they'd made, or was she feeling the same way he was—that there could be something *more* with them?

"Sam?" Lexi stepped closer, probably wondering why he'd suddenly been struck mute. He gave himself a mental shake and put on his best good-guy-Sam smile.

"Right. Casual. Temporary. Nothing serious happening here, Phyllis. I promise."

If only his heart had gotten the message.

Lexi watched him for a moment, then nodded in acceptance. "Exactly. But Mom's right about one thing."

"Yeah?" Sam asked. "What's that?"

"We can kiss anytime we want."

She pressed against him. He cupped her face in his hands and kissed her gently, teasing her lips with his until she was trembling. That's when he pressed in and kissed deep, holding her up with his arm around her waist. When he released her from the kiss, he had to hold on to her for a moment until she regained her balance.

"Are you going to do this show on the hour or on the half hour today?" Shelly Berinson was giving them a slow clap. "Because I definitely want to catch that action again."

Shelly was standing with Genevieve and Amy from the T-shirt shop on Main Street. Amy was taller, and she had her arm draped over her wife's shoulder.

"Yes! We need more of that, please," Genevieve said, her Jamaican accent deeper than usual as she laughed. "Perhaps we should print flyers with the schedule—I'm sure that would bring more people to Wharf Street today, no?"

Her wife nudged her in the ribs. "Stop. You're embarrassing them."

Genevieve just laughed harder. "I know this Knight boy pretty well, my dear, and he doesn't embarrass easily. Look at him! He's proud of himself. He has a beautiful woman to love."

Sam felt Lexi tense at that last word. He did, too. It was the first time it had been spoken out loud near them. *Love.* Definitely not part of the deal. As if sensing his and Lexi's discomfort, Phyllis jumped in.

"These two are special people, alright, but they're just having some summer fun." She pulled a couple of plastic cups from the stack and set them on the table. "Are you ladies ready for some Bloody Mary mocktails?"

And just like that, the moment was broken. Sam went to work making drinks, and Lexi went back to the restaurant's table to begin serving shrimp skewers. Phyllis bounced back and forth between the tables, running the cash boxes and just generally charming anyone who came by.

Surprisingly, a lot of people did stop by. He'd been worried that Wharf Street would get ignored during the festival. They hadn't participated in years—usually, people parked on the lot on Wharf, then scurried up to where the action was. But this year, they caught their attention. Main Street was such a crush of people that Wharf Street was like a little oasis from the chaos.

He watched Lexi working her table, and realized she'd been making friends here this summer. She knew a lot of people by name—both locals and seasonal residents. She chatted with them about their pets or their kids or their summer homes. She was wearing a green Salty Knight ball cap, her hair pulled through the back in a ponytail. Her white top and black capris—her kitchen uniform— were covered with a dark green 200 Wharf apron. She looked like she belonged. For someone who'd arrived on Cape Cod a few months ago with plans to leave as soon as possible, she was making connections in Winsome Cove. It was almost enough to make him wonder if she might stay after all.

But that line of thinking was foolish. She was a city gal all the way. She'd never wanted to run a small restaurant in some little New England tourist town. She'd made that very clear, right from the start. Besides, he knew better than to think people ever stayed in his life. One way or another, people always moved on. His chest went hollow. That's why he didn't get attached.

Lexi's head fell back as she laughed loudly over something Loretta Toscanio was saying. The sound made his heart skip a beat. She caught him looking at her and playfully blew him a kiss. Without thinking, he reached up and pretended to catch it. He'd seen his parents do it a hundred times. It was a silly, intimate thing that people in love might do.

Luckily, he'd decided a long time ago to protect himself

by never falling in love. Loving and losing a woman like Lexi would break him beyond repair. Love hurt too much.

A small voice in his head whispered *too late!*

Chapter Twenty-One

Lexi's body was groaning as they started putting everything away. She was used to being on her feet and on the run, but to do that on a sidewalk in the hot August sun for hours added a whole new level to it. And this hadn't been cooking, which was her comfort zone. This had been hours of socializing and talking and laughing with the people of Winsome Cove. And with total strangers. It was…a lot. But it was over now, or at least *her* portion was over. The crowds had left downtown to head to the small waterfront park near the marina to watch fireworks.

Having Sam working at the very next table had been a nice distraction. In his snug Salty Knight T-shirt and his cargo shorts hanging low on his hips, he'd been a distraction for most of the women that came to the bottom of Wharf Street. He wore sleek wrap-around sunglasses most of the day, but once the shade hit their side of the sidewalk, he'd flipped them so they were resting on the back of his head. It was a low-key look that was high-key sexy.

They'd enjoyed their ability to be openly affectionate, but it seemed every time they tried to grab a kiss, someone was around to razz them about it. It made no sense—half the town had been encouraging them to have a relationship, and now that they were, they were catching grief about it. It was good-natured grief, but still. She wasn't used to being the center of attention like that. She was more of a blend-into-the-crowd kind of person.

That was one of the advantages of city life. People didn't pay that much attention to what anyone else was doing. Walk down a Chicago sidewalk during rush hour and you'd be hard pressed to make legitimate eye contact with one other person. But in Winsome Cove? Sure, there was plenty of Cape Cod saltiness and fierce New England independence, but people here connected with each other. Sometimes they bonded over complaining, like Fred and his cronies at the bar. Sometimes they bonded over their love of the Cape or the sea or their gardens.

Lexi was finding connections with a lot of Winsome Cove natives. Shelly and she had lunch together often. Carm would stop by the restaurant near closing time to chat about business and fill Lexi in on the local gossip. Genevieve and Amy from the souvenir shop had invited her to join the local business-owners association.

"Here, let me get that." Sam took the now-empty steamer from her arms. "Open the door, babe."

They got the steamer to the kitchen and she removed the liner to let it soak in the commercial sink. The restaurant had been closed for the day. She'd been too busy outside, and she wanted to give the workers a chance to enjoy the festival. She'd sold out of shrimp an hour ago, so she had a feeling they'd ended up turning a profit. Sam helped her fold up the table and set it inside. They put the cash boxes in the safe behind the bar for the night, and started walking toward the marina when the first volley of fireworks went off.

They stopped on the sidewalk where there was a break in the trees, so they could see the fireworks clearly. People were out on their porches or standing near Sam and Lexi, oohing and ahhing with every beautiful burst of light in the sky. There was Brenda Sims with her newborn son. She and her husband had been in the restaurant several times, and he'd picked up two chicken dinners the week after the baby was born. Over there was Lennie Carlisle, a lobsterman who kept his boat at Sam's marina. Lexi always thought Lennie was gruff and grumpy, but there he was, with his little granddaughter sitting up on his shoulders, and he was acting as excited as she was at all the noise and lights.

Connections. Lexi blinked. She'd allowed herself to connect to this town. To its people. And they'd all connected to her, too. It wasn't the hustle and bustle of a city, but there was an energy pulsing here in Winsome Cove all the same. It was the energy born of history and community.

Lexi spotted her mother in the crowd. Phyllis Bellamy was beaming as she walked around hugging everyone. She'd changed into skintight red shorts and a blue-and-white striped top with a plunging neckline. Her hair was swept back and up, with enough gel and hairspray to hold it like that, as if an ocean wave had been captured.

She didn't think she'd ever seen her mother looking this happy. The motel was doing better business every week, and was fully booked for the festival. Mom had invested a lot of her own money from the house sale, but Lexi had a feeling that investment would be repaid by next summer and then some. Phyllis let out a loud laugh and slapped some guy's back. She was in her element here. She looked more than happy. She looked fulfilled.

"I love this." Lexi blurted out the three words. Sam was standing behind her, with his chin resting on top of her head and his arms around her waist.

"Love what? The fireworks? Yeah, they're good this year."

"No. I mean…yes, the fireworks are good. But I meant…" A toddler hurried by them, with short, beaded braids, with her laughing father on her heels. Lexi felt something begin to settle inside of her. She had a sense of contentment that had been lacking in her until now. "I mean I love *all* of it. I love this place. I love the people."

He kissed the top of her head as a massive green firework filled the sky.

"Are you saying little old Winsome Cove won you over, city girl?" There was a series of loud booms and more fireworks began filling the sky as the finale began. "Have you fallen in love with this dodgy old town of mine?" The blasts were loud enough that she could feel them in her chest. Or maybe that was something else she was feeling. Another round screamed into the sky before exploding.

"I've fallen in love with *you*, Sam."

She didn't say it very loud, and she had no way of knowing if he'd heard it or not. Or what his reaction was, with her back to him. The fireworks display built to its final crescendo, and silence fell over the cove. People around them began to applaud the show. Car horns blew, and boat horns blared on the water. Bluish smoke wafted past them, smelling like sulfur. It wasn't until people began heading into their houses and cars that Sam slowly turned her to face him.

The instant their eyes met, she knew he'd heard her. His eyes were wide with alarm.

"Don't say that."

Have you ever seen blazing hot steel dipped into a cooling tank? The way the water boils and steams, but the steel goes gray and hard?

That's how Lexi's heart felt.

"Not saying it out loud doesn't make it less true, Sam."

The sidewalks had emptied quickly, and they were alone in the dark. "I'm in love with you."

He looked like she'd just stabbed him in the chest. Then anger overtook him. He stepped back.

"I said *don't*. I mean it. We're not going there. We agreed—"

"I know what we agreed to, but you know that we've gone way beyond any deal we made." She tried to touch his arm, but he pulled back sharply, like a wary dog. "Sam... I'm not saying you have to feel the same way." Although she'd hoped he would. "I'm just telling you how I feel. I'm in love with you." She said it as gently as possible, but she could see the impact the words made on him. He stood there, staring straight at the ground. His fingers were pressed against the center of his chest—not rubbing, but just pushing there as if trying to stop pain. She didn't want her love to hurt him. "Sam..."

He took a deep breath, raising his head but staring at some distant point over her shoulder. "You're smarter than that, Lexi. Why love someone you're going to leave? It's a waste of emotion, and it ruins what we have."

"It doesn't have to ruin anything. I'm not demanding anything from you. And I don't have to say it again. I just thought you deserved to know how I felt." She stepped forward quickly, before he could react, and took his hands. "And it won't be wasted if I stay in Winsome Cove."

He shook his head. "You're not staying."

"I might. I told you, I've started to love this damn little town. I love working at 200 Wharf. I'm creating something special there, and—"

"The first offer you get from some fancy city restaurant will make you realize this was just a stopping place. That *I* was just a stopping place. We're great together, but you know I don't want anything long-term. There's no room for that in my life, and it wouldn't work. It would…" He struggled for words. "It would hurt us both in the end."

They were both silent. She took her hand off his arm and stepped back, stung and angry.

"Heaven forbid."

His forehead wrinkled. "What?"

"Heaven forbid you take a chance at happiness, Sam."

"Now you sound like everyone else in my life," he said. "For one thing, my life is just fine. I *am* happy. And trust me, once you've had your heart burned as bad as mine has been, you wouldn't want to put your hand back on the same hot stove."

She put her hands on her hips, not sure she was hearing this right. "Excuse me? The last guy I said 'I love you' to almost got me sent to *prison*. I've been burned, pal, but I'm still standing here, willing to take the chance with you. I'm not afraid."

That wasn't true. She *was* scared. Especially now that he'd not only *not* said the words back to her, but had also rejected them completely. That's when she realized she'd just nailed the problem. She may be scared, but Sam was terrified. Borderline phobic. This was panic she was seeing. That's why he was snarling like he'd been cornered. She needed to back off a bit. He needed time.

She stepped forward again, looping her arm through his and forcing the tension out of her voice. "We're both tired and emotional right now. Let's go back to the house and get some sleep." He didn't argue, falling into step next to her. "Sam, if you don't want to talk about the *L* word right now, that's okay. But I'm not kidding when I say I'm staying. What we have doesn't *need* to be temporary."

It might even be *forever* if he could let himself love her.

* * *

Sam woke up alone in his bed the next morning. He was surprised that he'd slept at all. The conversation last night had spiked his adrenaline to the point where he'd paced around the marina for an hour after he and Lexi got to the house. She'd left him to it, going up to bed, knowing he needed time to regroup.

She said she *loved* him. That was the worst thing she could have possibly said to him. Love never ended well. His entire life proved it was true.

And she claimed to be *staying*. How did she go from hating how provincial Winsome Cove was to wanting to live here forever? With him?

No. There was no way that could be true. She'd leave as soon as she had the chance. She was just panicking because she hadn't had a job offer yet.

"Hey, Smoke, how are you, kitty cat?" Lexi's soft voice came from the hallway. Smoke answered with a low meow right outside the door. "No, you let your daddy sleep—he's tired this morning."

Sam scrubbed his hands down his face. How had he become a cat daddy? He was about to call out that it was okay to let Smoke into the room when he heard a soft scramble in the hall.

"Wait, Smoke. No, you can't go in there. Oh…"

A door opened, but it wasn't the one to his room. He sat up abruptly. If it wasn't his door, then… He jumped out of bed and hurried to the hall. It was empty, but there was sunlight shining through an open door. His parents' suite. He walked slowly to the doorway.

The walls were papered with wide stripes of yellow and cream, with tiny blue flowers running up the center of the cream stripes. Blue drapes hung at the three windows in the room, with deep swags at the top of them. Mom had been so proud of those things. The sculpted wall-to-wall carpet was blue, too. Smoke was up on the four-poster bed. Lexi was standing in the middle of the room. She'd clearly been awake for a while, because she was fully dressed and had a mug of coffee in her hand. She turned to face him.

"I'll admit I've peeked into these two rooms before," she said. "But I've never walked in. This is a beautiful room. A little dated, maybe, but beautiful." She walked to the window. "And what a great view of the cove. Why don't you use—"

"You know why I don't."

"It's not like you're incapable of walking in here. You're here now, and the room is spotless, so you've been here before."

Sam looked around, feeling the weight of his entire life pressing down on him. "Every corner of this room holds a memory. Every inch. Every piece of furniture. It's..." He sighed. "It's too much for me, Lex. Come on."

Lexi picked up Smoke from the bed and followed Sam out to the hall. "I'm sorry. The door was ajar and Smoke went in, so I..."

"I must not have latched it after I vacuumed. It's not your fault. I just..."

She let Smoke jump to the floor. "Sam, you can't live your life like this. You really should talk to someone."

She's right. He shook off the traitorous thought. This was all he'd known.

"I've lived it this way for sixteen years."

Lexi rolled her eyes. "And how's that working out for you?" Her expression softened. "I'm sorry. I know you're doing the best you can. And I promised not to push you about it, but..." She bit her lip. "Okay, I'm stopping now.

I've got blueberry-pancake batter ready for the griddle if you're hungry."

She was stopping for now, but he knew she'd circle back around to it again, because that's the kind of woman she was. She was determined. She cared. She loved him.

Breakfast was quiet. There was a heaviness in the room that hadn't been there before. It had been the same last night. They'd made love before falling into an exhausted sleep, but there was a shadow—almost a presence. Something was between them, or trying to be. It had arrived the moment Lexi had declared her love and suggested she might stay in Winsome Cove.

They cleaned up the kitchen, and Lexi explained she had to go help her mom that morning with rooms because the motel was full.

"So business is good?" Sam took the damp towel from her hands.

"Yes, we're getting great reviews, and we're already getting more bookings for the next few months." Lexi always talked fast and bubbly when she was anxious. "We've heard autumn on Cape Cod is still considered in season?"

"I guess you could say that. Kids are back in school so families aren't renting during the week, but we get a lot of adults who like the slightly quieter vibe in September and October. And the weekends stay busy pretty much through the holidays these days."

Lexi nodded solemnly as if he'd just imparted some great wisdom on her. They were trying too hard to be normal with each other. They were in the center of the kitchen now, facing each other. Talking about nothing, to keep from talking about everything.

"Well," Sam said. "I've got stuff to do, too."

More awkward silence.

"Okay. I'd better get going." Lexi reached for her bag sitting on the end of the kitchen counter. She tried to give him a soft kiss on the cheek, but Sam turned his head and caught the kiss with his mouth.

She sighed into him, wrapping her arms around his waist. He held her close and the kiss grew deep and passionate. In the back of his mind, he wondered if this was what their goodbye kiss would feel like when she left him. Because she would. Everyone did.

She stepped back, her eyes dark with emotion. "You're already pushing me away."

"What? I just kissed you. How is that…?" He did his best to deny it.

She studied him, and a slow smile grew on her face as her chin raised. *Uh-oh.* That was the smile of a woman who wanted something, and wouldn't stop until she had it.

"You'll see, Sam. I'm staying, and you're going to see that we can be more than casual. More than temporary. I meant what I said last night." She slid her bag over her shoulder, bent over to scratch Smoke's head, then walked away. She didn't look back. "You'll see!"

He stood there a long time, wondering what it would be like if she really did stay. Wondering what forever with Lexi might be like. She'd want to live here. Hell, she was practically living here now. But if things got official, she'd expect it to be her home as well as his. And that meant things would change. He frowned, fighting the voices fighting so hard to be heard. The voices of ghosts.

It's time, Sam…

Chapter Twenty-Two

One week after the festival, Lexi was still trying to get her and Sam back to a more normal place. Her declaration of love had raised a wall inside of him that she couldn't move.

It wasn't like they were fighting. In fact, to anyone observing from the outside, nothing had changed. He met her after the restaurant closed, and they spent nearly every night together at his place. Sometimes she'd sleep at the Sassy Mermaid just to spend time with Mom and to give Sam the space he seemed to need occasionally.

They'd made love just as much as usual. There was nothing wrong with *that* part of their relationship. But their conversations were more careful and cautious. She was trying not to scare him off with talk of love, although her love had only grown since the night she'd proclaimed it out loud. Sam seemed to be constantly on guard in case she said it again.

It was frustrating for her not to talk about it. They certainly couldn't go on for long pretending it wasn't an issue. But she could wait a little longer. She figured if she could convince him she was really staying here in Winsome Cove, then maybe he'd start believing she was really in love with him, too. One step at a time.

She'd made her usual Monday-morning trek to her produce supplier in Barnstable, checking to see what would be available this week so she could tweak her menu to feature the freshest items.

She stopped at a cranberry bog owned by Bonnie Becker. It wasn't a planned stop, but she saw Bonnie hosing down one of her tractors in the driveway, so she'd pulled in and rolled down her window. The two women met last month at a business-owners seminar in Falmouth, and they'd become friendly. Bonnie was a fourth-generation cranberry grower, and she'd shared a lot of information with Lexi, and given her a tour of the bog operations.

"Lexi Bellamy!" Bonnie turned off the power washer. "What brings you to the bog? I would have thought you'd be basking in your success today."

She didn't understand the reference, but it had been a good weekend at the restaurant, and maybe Bonnie had heard.

"No rest for the weary, Bonnie." She nodded to the water-filled bogs behind the house. "We still thinking mid-September for harvest?"

Bonnie wiped her brow. She was in dirty overalls tucked into rubber farm boots, with a tattered T-shirt and a wide-brimmed canvas hat that had seen better days. She wasn't much older than Lexi, but she looked and talked like an old-time Cape Cod native. "*Ay-yah*, just a couple more weeks. It's lookin' like a good harvest this year, so I hope you have a lot of fancy recipes in mind."

Cranberries weren't something she used often, but she'd figured it would be expected on the Cape. She wanted to create more than muffins with them, and wanted to serve them with something other than turkey. She'd already been working on some ideas.

"Don't worry, I've got plans for those berries! I just

stopped to say hi, but I've gotta run. Have a good day, Bonnie!"

Bonnie chuckled. "You, too. Don't let all that fame go to your head!"

Lexi pulled back onto the road, wondering what her friend meant by that. She drove through Winsome Cove, and several of the locals waved enthusiastically as she drove by. Shelly saw her and made a bowing motion, rolling her hands with a gesture as if honoring royalty. Lexi waved back, having no idea what was happening with people today. She parked her car at the motel and grabbed her canvas shopping bags. She'd picked up some fresh produce for Mom.

"There she is!" Mom looked up from the desk with a bright smile when Lexi walked into the office. "I can't wait to tell the gals back in Des Moines that I'm the mother of a cover girl."

Was there something in the water today?

"Okay, Mom, what have I missed? What are you talking about?" She set her bags on a nearby chair.

Her mother jumped up, holding a glossy magazine. "Oh, my God, do you really not know? You haven't seen it?"

She threw up her hands. "Haven't seen *what*?"

"This!" Mom thrust the magazine at Lexi.

She turned it over and stared at…herself. She was on the cover of the quarterly issue of the Boston newspaper's New England dining magazine. Lexi Bellamy. On the cover. She remembered being interviewed a few weeks ago, and the writer had taken photos of her in and outside of the restaurant. She had no idea she'd end up on the cover.

The photo was of her standing in the kitchen, holding a plate of lobster Chambertin. She'd put on her whitest top and apron, and had laughingly put a tall chef's hat on her head. Her expression was proud, but also...contented. Calm. There was no stress in her eyes. Her smile didn't hold her usual cynicism.

The night before the interview and photo shoot, she and Sam had taken the *Katydid* for a sunset cruise. Then they'd come back to the marina, but they hadn't made it up to the house until dawn. They'd stayed right on the boat, making love until they'd fallen asleep, exhausted.

That explained the *Mona Lisa* smile on her face in the photo. It had nothing to do with the restaurant, and everything to do with falling in love with Sam Knight.

But now, looking at the magazine cover, all she could think was *what will Sam think*? He was already convinced she was leaving, no matter what she said. This kind of coverage for the restaurant—for *her*—would just add fuel to the fire. He'd say she was *too big* for Winsome Cove. That the restaurant headhunters would make her an offer she couldn't refuse. All the same nonsense he'd been saying ever since she'd said she wanted to stay.

"Alexa?" Mom touched her arm, her voice low. "What's wrong, sweetie?"

Lexi blinked at the tears that sprang to her eyes. "Nothing, Mom. It's a great cover."

"Yes, it is," her mother agreed. "So why do you look like someone kicked your dog?"

"I don't have a dog."

"Then why do you still look like someone kicked it?"

"Mom..."

Her mother turned Lexi to face her. "This is what you wanted, right? To get the food world's attention? To get out of Winsome Cove and get a great job offer from New York or DC? To run a high-end restaurant in a big city?" She tapped the magazine. "Read the article! It's nothing but glowing praise for the food at 200 Wharf and your 'unique approach' to capitalizing on locally sourced foods. Carm said it's already online, so people from all over the country will see it. This is nothing but good news—for the restaurant *and* for you." Mom reached up and wiped Lexi's cheek. "So why are you crying? And don't even try telling me those are happy tears."

Lexi sat in one of the new turquoise chairs in the lobby, and Mom sat next to her, waiting patiently for her to speak.

"What if…?" Lexi began. "What if I *don't* want those things anymore?"

Her mother sat back in her chair. "You don't want to have that dream restaurant on Fifth Avenue?"

"No."

"Or that beachfront bistro in Miami?"

"Nope."

"Or the fancy place in DC, where all the power brokers come to dine?"

"No, Mom. I don't need that anymore."

Her mother was silent for a moment.

"Baby, you never *needed* any of it. But you sure *wanted* it pretty bad. Does this change of heart have to do with a handsome marina owner?"

Lexi let out a long sigh, staring at the floor.

"It did. Now? I don't know."

"Explain."

"We had a bit of a…disagreement, after Old Harbor Days. He doesn't believe I could change my mind and stay." He especially didn't believe she'd stay for *him*.

"I see." Mom paused. "I guess that makes sense."

"What? You *agree* with him?"

"I didn't say that. I said it made sense. As in, it makes

sense that Sam would feel that way. Everyone he's loved has left him, one way or the other."

"He's never said he loves me. In fact, he *refuses* to say it." She had a feeling he was holding back his feelings, refusing to feel them. Just like he did with his grief.

"But you know he does, right?"

She wanted to believe that, but she'd been burned before. Just blindly trusting anyone's love, even Sam's, wasn't something that would come easily for her.

"Is it really love if the person can't even say it out loud?"

Mom took Lexi's hands in hers and squeezed them tight until Lexi looked up and met her gaze.

"Oh, sweetheart, it's not the sound of that one word that makes it real. It's the emotion. It's how he treats you. How he makes you feel. It's forever…" Mom's voice trailed off as she realized the corner she'd talked herself into.

Lexi tipped her head. "Says you, the divorceé."

"Just because my love story didn't work out doesn't mean yours won't," her mother answered. "Millions of people fall in love forever. None of us know what the future holds, but we put our faith in love. It's worth the risk."

Lexi thought about that. "I'm willing to take that chance. But Sam… He doesn't believe in forever."

"You understand why, don't you?"

"Of course!" Lexi flopped back in her chair. "But that doesn't change anything. If he doesn't believe in forever, what chance do we have?"

Mom stood and walked to the windows, staring out at the bright blue sky, filled with puffy marshmallow clouds. The ocean was a silvery blue, and rolling with large waves. She nodded at the water, her hands in her pockets.

"The fishermen will have a rough ride out there today, but at least it's warm."

Lexi had just asked how to resolve the biggest problem she'd ever faced, and her mother was discussing the weather. *Perfect.*

"Mom?"

"Yes, dear?" Her mom was still staring out the window.

"I'm asking for your help here."

Mom chewed her lower lip, not answering. Lexi had a feeling she had a lot to say, but wasn't letting herself say it. Finally, she gestured for Lexi to join her. Lexi groaned, but she did what was asked. Her mother slid her arm around Lexi's waist.

"Do you remember that day, not long after we arrived here, when we watched the seals and saw the mama and her baby?" Lexi nodded, and her mother continued. "I told you then that the ocean was always full of sharks, remember? But it's also full of yummy fish to eat and other seals to love."

Lexi couldn't help laughing. "I don't recall you saying anything about seals looking for food *or* love that day."

Mom chuckled. "That's because it wasn't the lesson you needed to hear that day. We were talking about you needing to push past fear, and that still applies today."

"Wait…we're talking about *Sam* pushing past fear, not me."

"Are you sure about that?" Mom gave her a quick hug, then walked away, effectively ending the conversation.

Of *course*, Lexi was sure. This issue wasn't about *her* being afraid. She wasn't afraid of anything.

Except losing Sam.

Sam had woken up unsettled that morning. He didn't like waking up alone anymore, and that realization pissed him off. He'd spent his entire adult life perfectly fine with being alone, awake or asleep. One summer of sleeping with Lexi had ruined that. But once a week or so, she stayed at the motel to help her mom. He didn't like those mornings one bit.

And then he discovered he was out of coffee. This morning just kept getting better. He tugged on a T-shirt and walked into town, finding the coffee he needed at Jerry's Java House on Main Street. Jerry, short and wiry, with a mop of chemically enhanced cherry-red hair, looked up in surprise when Sam burst into the coffee shop. He hadn't intended to open the door with quite that much force, and the bell above it rang out.

"Well, I'm used to people desperate for a caffeine fix, but it's been a while since I've seen *you* come charging in here, Sam. Having one of those mornings, huh?"

"Sorry, Jerry. I didn't have a great night's sleep, and I woke up with no coffee in the house. Can I get a medium roast with three sugars?"

"Sure thing." Jerry turned to grab a mug. "Would you like a muffin or scone with that? Cliff made muffins this morning with blueberries he picked himself yesterday, and they are to die for. I can warm one up for you."

"Sounds good." He took the mug Jerry slid across the counter, and dropped a few bills near the cash register before taking one of the small café tables near the window. Jerry's husband, Cliff, didn't bake a lot of fancy pastries, but what he *did* bake was hearty and delicious. A minute later, Jerry brought a giant muffin on a plate, sliced in half and shimmering with melting butter. "Whoa. This will take care of breakfast *and* lunch."

Jerry laughed as he turned to take care of a couple who'd just walked in, sending them off with coffee and a box of muffins, along with a map and recommendations for which trails to walk at the national seashore. Jerry prided himself on being an ambassador for their stretch of Cape Cod. When they'd left, he walked back to Sam's table. So much for a quiet breakfast. Jerry was obviously eager for conversation—he was practically bouncing with news of some sort. That was another thing he took pride in—knowing *all* of the local gossip.

"So…" He helped himself to the other seat at Sam's table. "I'm guessing this will be a big week for the restaurant, eh?"

Sam frowned. Was it some special anniversary already? Was there something going on that Lexi hadn't mentioned? Jerry was still talking. "That magazine article will probably bring *all* the Boston folks to check out 200 Wharf this weekend. They'll want to be part of the in crowd so they can say they've sampled chef Lexi's menu. She'll be fighting off job offers from Boston proper, I'm sure."

Sam gave up. "What article?"

"Oh, my God, she didn't tell you?" Jerry turned toward the back of the café, then cupped his hand to his mouth and shouted, "Cliffie! Bring that dining magazine out here! Sam hasn't seen it yet!" He turned back to him. "That restaurant is going to put Winsome Cove on the map as a destination, Sam. It's bound to bring new business for the rest of the places in town. Maybe we'll become a foodie mecca." He laughed. "I won't complain if business picks up, that's for sure. The tourists tend to stick to the national chains, but if they think this town is full of the quote-unquote 'hidden gems' like 200 Wharf, they might check us out more often."

Sam appreciated Jerry's enthusiasm, but he still had no idea what the guy was talking about. Cliff hurried out from the small kitchen in back, holding a glossy magazine.

Cliff and Jerry were opposites in appearance who somehow complemented each other perfectly. Cliff was tall and broad-shouldered, with short, spiky pewter hair. He was dressed in jeans and a black T-shirt. Jerry was slight, with his flaming red hair and rainbow-patterned shirt. He was in constant motion, like a colorful hummingbird, where Cliff was more thoughtful and soft-spoken.

Jerry grabbed the magazine and slapped it onto the table in front of Sam. His chest went tight and hot when he saw Lexi staring back at him from the kitchen of 200 Wharf.

"It's the *dining* issue," Jerry said, flipping it open to a two-page spread on Lexi and the restaurant. "And our little town landed on the *cover*! The editors gave Lexi five stars and a load of free publicity. They predict she's destined for great things." He pointed to a paragraph near the end of the article. "Instead of saying the world is her oyster, they said the world is her *lobster*. Get it? So clever!"

He scanned the article, his heart dropping at the words that jumped out at him.

…a Midwest chef with a surprising gift for seafood…

…brilliant use of locally-sourced ingredients…

…should be in a Michelin-rated venue somewhere…

…get to this tiny restaurant before someone snaps her up…

Jerry was right. Lexie *hadn't* told him anything about this. It was easy to see why. What he didn't understand was why she got so angry when he told her basically all of the things the article said—she was too good, too big, too ambitious to stay in Winsome Cove. She'd made it clear from the start that the restaurant was just a stepping stone for her. And he'd been *okay* with that.

So why had she muddied the waters with all her talk of staying? He closed the magazine and stared at her image, with her soft, proud smile. Maybe she'd just wanted to soften the blow somehow…to give him hope before dashing it. He wanted to believe her intentions were good, but he couldn't help feeling the result was cruel. Despite all his denials and doubts, she had given him a tiny glimpse of what life *could* be. And all the while, she'd known this was coming. She'd done the interview. Done a damn photo shoot. He flipped the magazine over so the cover was hidden. This was the review that would erase what happened in Chicago. This was her launch into the restaurant world's stratosphere.

This was her, getting ready to leave.

Proving him right.

Nothing lasted forever.

Chapter Twenty-Three

Lexi had been looking for Sam for an hour before she noticed the *Katydid* wasn't in her slip at the marina. He'd taken the boat out alone. A chill rippled down her spine. This was not a good sign. Especially after coming from the coffee shop, where Jerry and Cliff said Sam hadn't reacted well to the magazine article that morning. In fact, he'd hardly said a word and slammed the thing facedown—*her* face down—on the table before abruptly leaving.

She walked back toward her car, then stopped. Sooner or later, he was going to bring that boat back. She needed to be here when he did. She grabbed her water bottle from the car and sat on the bench in front of the office, trying not to worry about how rough the ocean was today with a brisk wind blowing.

Devlin's lobster boat was tied up at the dock, but she wasn't sure if he'd been out and back, or if today was one of his off days. He'd said his real-estate business was taking up more and more of his time…and paying better. Sam had suggested Devlin check with one of the oceanography schools near Woods Hole to see if they might want to lease the *Suzie-Q* to use for research.

At the time, Lexi had suggested Sam do the same thing with the *Katydid*, but he'd brushed her off, saying a lobster boat, with its open back, would be more functional for catching, tagging and releasing the great white sharks roaming the Cape waters. She leaned back against the office building, with its weathered cedar-shake siding. There were two cats sunning themselves near the building, on the side away from the wind. Smoke strolled up to join them, then saw Lexi and decided her lap would be even warmer. She stroked his head and waited.

She understood what Sam was saying, but with his degree and his practical knowledge of the area, it seemed he'd make a good member of any research team. If not on his boat, then on Devlin's. She closed her eyes. Here she was trying to plan his future, when he didn't even believe she wanted to be a part of it. And that magazine article probably hadn't helped.

The rumble of diesel engines made her sit up. The *Katydid* was working her way through the harbor. Lexi went down to the dock to catch the lines. Sam didn't seem surprised to see her. He didn't seem thrilled, either. But he did toss the lines to her before turning away to shut down the engines and lock up the boat. She wasn't sure if she should go aboard, since she hadn't been invited and things were… tense between them. So she waited on the dock until Sam locked the cabin door and hopped off the boat.

He looked at her for a moment before sliding his arm around her shoulders and heading toward shore. It wasn't exactly an embrace, but it wasn't a rejection, either. He was guiding her more than hugging her. She went along without saying anything until they reached the parking lot, where he stopped, dropping his hand from her shoulder.

"Are you sending me home?" she asked. She understood if he needed some time.

"I don't know." He scrubbed the back of his neck. "Maybe this is the best time to…stop."

"Stop?" Her heart jumped in panic. "Stop *us*? For good? Just like that?"

He headed toward the house and she hurried to follow, catching the door before he close it on her. He didn't get to make this decision then walk away.

Sam paused, then went inside with her on his heels. He turned when they got to the kitchen. "Look, we always knew you were leaving. You made that clear when we started. It was part of the deal—"

"Forget that stupid deal!" She braced her hands on her hips, hoping he couldn't see her hands were shaking. "Deals change. We've changed. We also agreed to keep emotions out of it, and *both* of us broke that rule. Don't try to deny it."

Sam chewed the inside of his cheek, his jaw working from side to side as he stared at the floor. Oh, yeah—there were a lot of emotions inside him right now. He'd just never admit it. His gaze lifted to meet hers.

"Here's what I don't understand. Why tell me you were staying when you obviously aren't? You did that interview. Posed for pictures. You knew that article was coming."

"No. I sat down with a food writer a few weeks ago and she snapped a couple pictures. None of that is unusual." She lifted her hands and dropped them. "I've done half a dozen of these interviews since we opened. They need photos for their blogs or whatever. She mentioned the magazine, but I had no idea it would be a cover story. In *Boston*."

He didn't seem convinced. His face was still hard as stone.

"Sam, I meant it when I said I was staying. This doesn't change anything."

He shook his head sharply. "That sounds nice, but it's

not true. Uncle Fred told Devlin the bar phone's been ringing off the hook with people who are trying to get in touch with you or someone at the restaurant. Devlin said the online reservation app shows the place already fully booked for the next three weeks."

"And how is that a bad thing? The restaurant is successful!"

"Your plan all along was to get the restaurant doing well, get some positive press and go." He gave her a hard look. "Mission accomplished. Even if you think you want to hang around, I'd be a fool to think it would last. Eventually an offer will come along that's too good to say no to, and you'll be gone."

Anger flooded her veins. Why wouldn't he believe her?

"I've been turning down offers for the past month, Sam. Good ones. Two in Boston, one in Albany, and one in Baltimore." His eyes widened a bit in surprise and she pressed forward. "The kinds of offers I was dreaming of when I got to Winsome Cove. Hell, I got three more calls this afternoon while I was waiting for you." She checked them off on her fingers. "New York, DC and Atlanta. I turned them all down." She moved to him and took his hand. "Don't you get it? I'm *staying*. I *love* you. I broke all of our rules, and I don't care."

Sam's face was gray, with blotches of red on his cheeks. Anger? Panic? Both?

"I think you should go." His voice was hard and flat. "I'll drop off your things at your mom's."

Realization dawned on her. "You're so convinced you're going to lose me that you're willing to throw me away."

"I don't do relationships. I've never lied to you about that, Lex."

"Fine. If that's true, then tell me you don't love me." She

folded her arms on her chest—mainly because her hands were shaking, and she was also holding on to herself tightly. It felt entirely possible that she was about to crumble into little pieces.

"I… I don't."

"Don't what?"

"You know. We agreed not to."

"Tell me you didn't break the agreement. Tell me you don't want more. Tell me you didn't fall for me as hard as I fell for you. Say it out loud, Sam."

Silence made the air thick and tangled between them.

"I don't love you." His voice was twisted and tight, as if he'd spat the words through broken glass. He met her eyes, and his were shuttered and cold. "I want you to go, like you promised."

So many thoughts ran through her mind at once that she wasn't sure how to process them all. But one stood out. She straightened, fighting off the grief and panic rising in her.

"You're a terrible liar. And a coward."

The lines around his eyes tightened briefly, like he was absorbing a blow.

He nodded slowly. "All the more reason for you to leave."

"Oh, no. You don't get to take the high road here, Sam Knight." Her words shook with anger. "If you want to stay in this prison you've built for yourself, alone and afraid, that's your choice. If you want to lie to yourself as some sort of punishment for whatever it is you think you deserve out of life, that's your choice. If you want to hide from a shot at happiness, go for it. But you don't get to choose for *me*."

His forehead furrowed into deep grooves. "What are you saying?"

"I'm saying I'm staying." She stepped forward, shaking a finger in his face. "I'm saying I'll be in Winsome Cove

every day, doing my job, hanging out with my friends…
who happen to be *your* friends, too." She gave a huff of hu-
morless laughter. "You're stuck with me in your life, Sam.
You'll see me all the time. Hell, I might even buy a boat,
just so I can dock it here and make you look at it. Look at
me, living my life. Just so you'll know exactly what you
gave up."

His face hardened again. "You don't think I know what
I'm giving up? What you said before was true—I'd rather
throw it away now than lose you in the end. Why wait?
You'll leave. Everyone leaves." His voice was rising with
every sentence, like a volcano getting ready to blow. "Look
around, Lexi! It's an empty house. An empty life. I've accepted it."

"Bull."

"Excuse me?"

She stormed into the living room, but he only followed
as far as the doorway. "You haven't accepted this—you've
chosen it." She gestured around. "You've suffered unimagi-
nable pain, Sam. I get it. But you made the choice to wal-
low in it. Which is weird, because while you keep every
relic of the past around you, you refuse to actually face
the past. You try to pretend your grandparents and parents
didn't exist, while enshrining them at the same time. It's
like some weird self-flagellation technique, like mental tor-
ture that you'd rather cling to than deal with the loss and
move on with your life."

She stopped for breath, realizing she was on a rant, but
knowing she was right. His eyes shone with raw pain, and
his posture was stiff and resistant. Her shoulders dropped
in defeat. Love shouldn't be this hard, or hurt this much.
She headed toward the doorway, but he didn't move. She
stopped in front of him.

"I'm leaving. Not to go to some new job somewhere. I'm staying in Winsome Cove. But I'm leaving this house, and I'm leaving you."

"Of course, you are." His words were smug, but his voice cracked.

"Yes, Sam. You can tell yourself you were right. That everyone leaves. You win. But your family didn't *choose* to leave you. It was an accident. You need to talk a professional who can get you through this…" She gestured around them again. "Because it's more than I can fix. You're not honoring your family by living like this. From everything I've heard about them, they'd be horrified that you've done this to yourself. They wanted you to be happy then, and they'd want you to be happy now. They'd want you to have the same sort of love story that they all did. They loved you, and so do I. That won't change." She pushed past him and didn't look back. "But I deserve a man who isn't afraid to love me. If you ever become that man, let me know."

"I don't get it," Devlin said, sitting on the plaid sofa in Sam's living room. Shelly was sitting with him. They'd shown up at his door with beer and food like they were on a mercy mission. "How did you two break up over such a simple misunderstanding? She told you she didn't know about the cover story. She told you she's staying on Cape Cod. She told you she loves you. And you just…let her walk?"

Shelly took a long swig of her beer. "I think it's more like he pushed her out the door, right, Sam?"

It had been five days since Lexi had walked out. A long, infuriating, stressful five days. Days where he couldn't sleep, couldn't eat and sometimes felt like he couldn't breathe. He'd spent most of his nonworking hours pacing through the old house, looking at every little thing as if he'd never seen it before. Grandpa's favorite fishing reel, sitting on a shelf. Mom's basket of knitting yarn still sitting next to the hearth. Grandma's dishes, now chipped and worn, in a kitchen thirty years overdue for a remodel. Dad's German steins on the fireplace mantel. The wall-to-wall carpeting with worn areas between the furniture that hadn't been moved in sixteen years.

Your family would be horrified by this...

"Shelly, she literally said to me 'I'm leaving you.'" And he hadn't stopped her. Hadn't said a word as she strolled right out of his life, taking his heart with her.

"And what was said *before* that?" Devlin reached for another cookie from the box on the coffee table.

Sam really didn't want to have this conversation. He'd been avoiding everyone all week. News had spread fast about he and Lexi not being together, and he couldn't stand all the sad looks people gave him. From what he could tell, Lexi wasn't talking about it, either. She'd been busy at 200 Wharf, and when she wasn't there, she was laying low at the Sassy Mermaid with her mom. He swallowed hard.

"She told me she deserved a better man than me, and she's right."

Shelly nodded. "That's fair. What else did she tell you?"

"She said I need professional help."

Both Devlin and Shelly choked on that, coughing and sputtering. Devlin got his voice back first. "She looked you in the eye and said that?"

"Yeah. Can you believe it?"

"Yes," Shelly said. "I can. Because she's right."

"What? I'm fine."

"Bull." Devlin echoed Lexi's response. "You're a long, long way from fine. And now you're pushing away your shot at having an actual life." Devlin looked at Shelly. "This is our fault as much as it is his. We've all enabled him ever since the accident." He turned to Sam. "We humored you and waited, thinking you'd snap out of it on your own. But you're stuck, and if the chance of having a woman like Lexi in your life can't motivate you to break free of all this—" he looked around the room "—then, yeah, you need to talk to an expert."

Chapter Twenty-Four

Sam went to the Salty Knight the next afternoon. It was a Tuesday, so Lexi probably wouldn't be around. He wasn't ready to see her yet. Just because he had an inkling she was right about everything, that didn't mean he'd know what to say. He'd already made enough mistakes.

Fred was alone behind the bar.

"Hey, Uncle Fred." Sam slid onto a barstool.

His uncle looked at him under bushy eyebrows. "Hey yourself. Is this a beer afternoon or a whiskey one?"

"Definitely whiskey."

Fred slid a glass down the bar toward him, then carried the bottle of whiskey over and plunked it on the bar in front of Sam, who smiled in spite of himself.

"Do I look like I need a whole bottle?"

"You look like you need a kick right in the ass, but a bottle is a good start."

Sam rolled his eyes. Everyone in town was invested in what was happening with him and Lexi. "Have some mercy on me, Fred. I came here for a drink, not a lecture."

Fred shrugged. "Good thing I've never given a damn what my customers want. Go ahead, drink it up and have your one-man pity party."

Sam blew out a long breath, counting to ten in his mind.

His uncle was pushing him on purpose, and Sam didn't feel like playing along. He drained his first shot, then filled it up again. As long as he was here, he may as well drink. He was pouring his third before Fred walked back down to his end of the bar.

"My son said something to me this morning that's had me thinkin'."

He was afraid to ask, but knew he had to.

"And what was that?"

"Dev says we've all coddled you to the point where we're responsible for the sorry state you're in."

Devlin and his big mouth. "I'm trying to imagine a time where you coddled *anyone*, Uncle Fred."

The old guy stood straighter. "I coddled Devlin's mother when she got sick."

Sam bit his lip. He'd walked right into that one. "You took good care of Aunt Lois. And you've been good to me, Fred."

"Except you ain't sick," his uncle answered. "But we've all been tiptoeing around you for...well, since the wreck. And that's been what—fifteen years?"

"It was sixteen in May. Can we *not* do this?" Sam begged. "I've spent way too much time lately thinking about that."

"Well, good for you. From what I hear, it's about time you started thinking about it instead of whatever you're doing. Dev said you live in a time machine."

Sam's mouth twitched. "I think he said time *capsule*, Fred. There's nothing wrong with the house. I'm fine."

He'd been saying that a lot lately.

"I hear Lexi Bellamy doesn't think so. Not on either count—your house or you." Fred rested his forearms on the bar and leaned in, his voice low and uncharacteristically solemn. "You need to move on, son. What you're doing isn't healthy. And what you're doing with Lexi is just plain dumb. That woman loves you."

Sam thought for a moment, not sure if he was ready to yell or cry. His self-control had gone to hell this week, so either one was a serious option.

"Don't do this, Fred. I mean it. I just came for a drink."

And because the walls of his home were closing in on him.

"Like I said," Fred answered, "I don't much care. It's time for you to hear some hard truths."

Sam slapped a couple of bills on the bar and stood. "I gotta go. Thanks for the booze."

He was almost to the door when his uncle spoke.

"You're not the only one who lost his parents that day, you know."

Sam's heart dropped, leaving his chest hollow and empty. He turned to face the bar.

"I know that, Fred. I'm sorry. I'm so sor—" His voice broke and he took a little hiccup of breath.

"Dammit, boy." Fred came out from behind the bar. "You don't need to apologize. There was a storm that my dad thought he could beat. You know how he was—stubborn and always in a hurry to get somewhere. He wouldn't have wanted to set the plane down and wait, so he pushed on."

"It wasn't his fault." The investigators had ruled it a weather-related accident—a sudden wind shear—with no pilot error.

"It wasn't *your* fault, either."

A shudder went through Sam at Fred's soft-spoken words, ahead of a tidal wave of emotion. He began to shake, and Fred led him to a corner table away from the windows.

"Have we ever talked about this?" Fred asked. He grabbed the bottle of whiskey and two glasses from the bar and joined Sam.

"I'm sure we haven't." Sam knew he never would have allowed it. He would have changed subjects, made a joke, left the room. Whatever it took to keep from talking.

"Well, I'll be damned," Fred grumbled. "Devlin was right. We all let it slide. For way too long."

Sam was shocked to feel hot tears on his cheeks. He hadn't cried since the day they buried his family. He scrubbed his face with his hands and took a ragged breath.

"Lexi said they'd all be horrified at how I've been living."

"Smart woman. She's right." Fred sat back in his chair and took a sip of whiskey. "Your grandparents and your parents loved their lives here. But it's not like they never left. Hell, your grandparents were planning on leaving Winsome Cove every winter after they retired, to live on the *Katydid*. You're not doing them any favors by living in fear. By God!" Fred slapped the table. "That's the *last* thing they'd want. My dad—your grandfather—didn't know what fear was. He served in the navy for four years, and told stories about his aircraft carrier being in waves so big the bow went under water."

Sam smiled softly. "I remember hearing the stories."

"Now your *dad*…" Fred waited until Sam looked across the table at him. "Well, Bill was more like you—even-keeled and quiet. I was like your grandfather, quick to fly off the handle, but Bill… I swear you could take a two-by-four to the guy and he'd shrug it off and assume you were having a bad day."

"That's how I remember him."

"Yeah? How often?"

"How often what?"

"How often do you really remember him?"

Sam sighed. "I get your point." He was hanging on to the fragments of their lives, instead of remembering the people.

Silence fell in the bar. The after-work crowd, such it was, would be arriving soon. Sam started to push back from the table, but his uncle had more to say.

"There's only one time I saw your dad ready to kill a man." Shocked, Sam settled back into his chair to listen. "He and your mom were newlyweds. She had a minor fender bender here in town, no big deal. The other guy missed the stop sign and she couldn't avoid hitting him, but no one was hurt. He was some hotshot from Duxbury, and he got out of his convertible and started screaming at your mom. He was a big guy, and she tried to calm him down and give him her information, but he kept yelling that he was suing her. They attracted a crowd, and someone called Bill." Fred chuckled. "Let me tell you something, your dad showed up and was ready to lay that guy out right there. Bill was half the man's size, but he grabbed him by the shirt, cussed him ten ways from Sunday and shoved him back against his fancy sports car, and had a little chat. By the time he was finished, that guy was apologizing to your mom and offering to pay *her* damages!" Fred stared at Sam. "My point is that your dad would have done battle with Goliath to protect your mom. He loved her so much he would have done *anything* for her. I have never seen two people who said 'I love you' as often as they did, and they meant it every single time."

Sam frowned. He remembered how lovey-dovey his parents were, how they held hands all the time and blew kisses and things that, as a teenager, he thought were cringe-worthy. But he wasn't sure what his uncle was trying to tell him. Fred saw his confusion.

"The point is your parents would hate to see you turning down a chance to be in love with someone. They'd especially hate it if you're avoiding it because of *them*. That's just…backward thinking, Sam. You're spitting on everything they taught you about love."

Lexi sat on the observation deck and watched the peach-colored moon rise over the ocean. She'd tugged the big Adirondack chair close enough to the edge that she could rest her feet up on the wooden railing. Maybe she'd try sleeping out here tonight.

Labor Day weekend had come and gone. The weather had been glorious, and the motel had been packed. Mom had grilled hamburgers and sausages by the pool, and they'd sat and laughed with their guests, and what seemed like half the town, until after sunset. Well, everyone else had laughed. Lexi spent most of her time staring out over the ocean, wondering for the hundredth time if she was doing the right thing by staying.

She loved the restaurant, and business had been booming ever since that cover story. Her employees were talented and energetic, and it was reaching the point where she didn't feel she had to be there every single minute to supervise.

She loved Winsome Cove. She'd started looking at rentals with Devlin. If she was staying, she needed her own place. And she still felt staying was the right thing. There was a connection here that tugged at something deep in her soul. She belonged here.

The only problem? Lexi also loved Sam Knight. And he couldn't love her back. Wouldn't even try. She shifted, trying to get comfortable. She'd brought a soft quilt with her, and she tugged it around her now to keep herself warm as the ocean breeze cooled. Rest had been elusive since she'd walked out of Sam's house.

Whenever she did fall asleep, she dreamed of him, alone in that grief-shrouded house, pretending everything was fine. She loved him so much it hurt. The thing was, she didn't believe that love *should* hurt. But God, she missed him. She worried about him. She thought of him every minute—while cooking, while talking with friends, while alone in her bed, aching for him. She'd only seen him from a distance since she'd walked out. On the sidewalk in town, or working in his yard while she was running. They hadn't spoken a word to each other, carefully avoiding each other's eyes.

Every time, it was like a knife in her heart. She wanted to run to him. To try to fix the brokenness inside of him. To make him happy and hopeful again. But he had to do some of that work himself. If he didn't even want to try, she'd only frustrate herself. He'd be miserable because she wanted him to change, and she'd be miserable because she just wanted him *whole*.

For now, she'd love him from a distance and hope he'd find his own way. Her eyes fell closed to the sound of seals gathering on the rocks below the cliff, chuffing to each other as they settled into sleep.

A hand brushed her arm, and she heard a familiar voice speaking her name. Sam had returned to her dreams. She smiled in her sleep.

"You're back."

"Yes, love, I'm back." His voice was so clear in this dream. So real.

"Every night you're here in my dreams…"

A soft laugh. "Yes, and every night you're in mine, Lex. It's the only thing that kept me going. You're the only reason for me to still be breathing."

Lexi frowned. He didn't usually talk this much in her

dreams. She turned her head and inhaled. She could even *smell* him tonight. Sweat, salt water, Sam. Someone moved in the chair. Her eyes swept open. He was here. Holding her against him, smiling down at her.

"Sam?" She tried to sit up, but he held her.

"Don't go. Let me say something first."

She thought about walking away, and knew she couldn't do that again. Not without hearing him out. She settled back, but tried to keep some distance between them. She needed to keep her wits about her, and she couldn't do that if she let herself melt into him the way she wanted to.

"I'm sorry for waking you." He rested his head back against the chair. "I'll admit I'm jealous you can sleep at all—I don't think I have since you left. But at least now I know you dream of me."

"I do." She was afraid to let down her guard and be disappointed again. "Why are you here, Sam? It's late."

"I'm here to apologize. For…everything. I've been a fool, Lexi, and I lost you because of it. I'm hoping you'll give me a chance."

"A chance at what?"

"A chance to love you the way you deserve to be loved."

The stars above them spun across the sky like a whirlwind, shining brighter and sparkling just for her. Did he just say he *loved* her?

"Come to my place tomorrow."

She sat up, looking down on him. "What?"

"Come to the house in the morning. I'll make my famous waffles."

She grinned in spite of her confusion. "You mean the frozen waffles you cook in the toaster?"

"Those are the ones. But I do have real maple syrup for them. And that Irish butter you love so much." His smile faded. "Please say yes, Lexi. All I'm asking for is breakfast." He paused. "And a chance."

"Why can't you talk now?"

"Me being here right now was unplanned. I was walking because I couldn't sleep and ended up at the Mermaid. Phyllis was cleaning up the picnic area, and she pointed me this way. When I saw you sleeping in the moonlight... Well, I had to lay here and hold you."

He sat up now, one hand cupping her face. "But moonlight isn't where I want to talk. Moonlight is where I want to make love to you, Lex, and I can't let that happen yet. I need to show you something first. Come to the house for breakfast."

"For toaster waffles."

He grunted. "I'll make those waffles worth your while." He kissed her, then kissed away the tears that sprang from her eyes. She didn't understand what was happening, but she could tell something had changed in him. She was happy. And also terrified of what this all meant. What could he possibly need to show her?

He pulled back and rested his forehead against hers, looking straight into her eyes.

"I love you, Alexa Bellamy."

Chapter Twenty-Five

Smoke the cat greeted Lexi at the back door, meowing and crisscrossing between her ankles as if to say *where have you been*? She found Sam in the kitchen. But it wasn't the kitchen she'd walked out of a few weeks ago.

The cupboards had been painted a soft, mossy green. The colonial black hardware had been replaced with brushed metal pulls and hidden hinges. The appliances were all new, in gleaming stainless steel. The floor hadn't changed, but the countertops were shiny white granite. Even the light was new—the fluorescent tubes were gone, replaced with a contemporary fixture.

"Um…" Lexi looked around. "Where am I?"

He laughed as he walked over to her. "You're in the right house, I promise." He gave her a quick kiss, then turned her around. "Check out the living room while I toast up breakfast for us."

She walked through the doorway and had the same out-of-body experience as she'd had in the kitchen. The walls were painted a soft white. The carpeting was gone. The hardwood floors had obviously been hidden under the carpeting before, and they needed polishing, but they were beautiful narrow boards of maple. There was a large Oriental rug, and all new furniture. It was casual and overstuffed—the type of furniture two people would love to curl up in together. The fireplace bricks had been painted a deep nautical blue. Resting on the mantel was the long, blueish-green painting that had been hanging in the restaurant. The watercolor of a man standing alone on a dock. She remembered Sam noticing it the first time he saw it in the restaurant.

He walked up behind her. "It reminds me so much of my dad. I called in a ton of favors. Shelly busted her rear getting all this done for me, but the furniture and rug are only on loan. I want you to pick out what you'd like for us."

Us?

"This is what you wanted to show me. But...why?"

He turned her to face him, cupping her face in his hands. "I want us to build our own home here. Our own life. Our own memories. You told me to let you know when I'd become the man you deserved. A man who wasn't afraid to love you." He leaned close. "I haven't had time to get there yet, but damn, girl. I'm trying. And I'll keep trying to be the man you deserve every day of my life if you'll let me." He paused, then one corner of his mouth lifted. "Just to be clear, I know for sure I love you. I don't have to work on *that* part. But it still scares me. It...terrifies me. All of this does." He glanced at the newly painted fireplace. "But you're worth it to me. You're worth the effort. Not that loving you is an effort—"

"Oh, my God, stop talking!" Lexi laughed, her heart light and warm. "Don't talk yourself into a hole you can't dig out of." She kissed him softly. "And loving me *might* be an effort at times. All I care is that you're trying. That's all either of us can do." She kissed him again. "Just love each other, and we'll figure out the rest."

"Losing you made me feel like I'd lost a part of me—

the most important part of me. I don't ever want to feel like that again. I don't ever want you out of my life. I will love you so much…"

She kissed him, then sniffed. "Is something burning?"

He pulled away with a curse and hurried into the kitchen. She followed, laughing as he pulled thin, charred waffles from the smoking toaster. He tossed them into the sink. "I've got more—"

"Forget the waffles, Sam." She slid her arms around his waist. "I've got a better idea for starting our day."

"I like the way you think, Miss Bellamy."

Before she could react, he turned and pressed her against the wall, kissing her hard and deep. This was the man she knew—the man who set her soul and body on fire. The man who made her laugh. The man who made her melt. She was in the process of untucking her shirt from her shorts when he pulled away from her.

"I forgot something."

She didn't look up. "Well, hurry it up, buster. I'm taking you upstairs."

"Oh, yeah. I forgot *two* somethings." He waited for her to look at him. "I haven't had time to do any work on the upstairs, but I want you to choose a room and we'll make it ours." He grinned. "On one condition."

"What's that?"

"The poster comes with us."

Lexi laughed. He'd told her the story of him and his dad winning some home-built-raft race at the fair that year. "I think I can live with that, but…are you sure? About the room, I mean. Are you ready?" This seemed like a lot of big steps for him. She didn't want him to push himself too far.

He hesitated. "I'm working on it. With my new therapist."

"You… You have a therapist?"

"That's the other thing I forgot to tell you. It was an online meeting, a video-call thing. But...yeah."

"And?" This move—asking for help—was much more meaningful than redecorating the house. This meant his desire to change was more than surface deep. Her heart swelled with pride for him. And hope for their future together.

He shifted his feet. "It was just one meeting, so I'm not exactly cured or anything. But it was a start. She seemed like a nice enough woman. I made another appointment."

"Oh, Sam. All of this—" she gestured around the room "—is big, but it's for me more than you. And I appreciate everything you've done here and what you're saying to me. But talking to a therapist is...huge. Because it's for *you*." She put her hand flat on his chest, feeling his heart beating strong and steady. "I'm so proud of you."

They stood like that for a moment, bathed in emotion.

"Lex..." Sam's voice broke. "I'll do anything for you. Just promise me..."

She knew what he needed to hear. And she knew he might need to hear her say it for a while yet.

"I'm not leaving, Sam. Not ever. I promise to stay. However long that happens to be here on earth, and then for eternity, wherever we end up after this. I'm yours."

"And I'm yours. I'll never stop loving you, Lex. Never."

They kissed, but there was no scorching flame of desire to it. Instead, it held the lingering warm glow of burning embers. The kind of heat that would last far longer than any bright flame.

The kind of love that would last forever.

* * * * *

HARLEQUIN
Reader Service

Enjoyed your book?

Try the perfect subscription for Romance readers and get more great books like this delivered right to your door.

See why over 10+ million readers have tried Harlequin Reader Service.

Start with a Free Welcome Collection with free books and a gift—valued over $20.

Choose any series in print or ebook.
See website for details and order today:

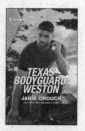

TryReaderService.com/subscriptions